DESTRUCTION ALONG THE NILE

An opportunity arises for Israel to gain an unlikely ally in its
war against Palestinian terrorists.

BOOK EIGHT OF THE GEOPOLITICAL TECHNO-THRILLER SERIES

ANDREW B. LOUIS

This is a work of fiction. All characters, organizations, and events portrayed in this novel are either products of the author's imagination or are used fictitiously.

For information regarding permission, please write to:
info@barringerpublishing.com
Barringer Publishing, Naples, Florida
www.barringerpublishing.com

Cover, graphics, and layout by Linda S. Duider
Cape Coral, Florida

ISBN: 978-1-954396-75-3
Library of Congress Cataloging-in-Publication Data
Destruction Along the Nile / Andrew B. Louis

Printed in U.S.A.

DEDICATION

To all victims of terrorism.

OTHER BOOKS BY THE AUTHOR

Other novels by Andrew B. Louis include:

 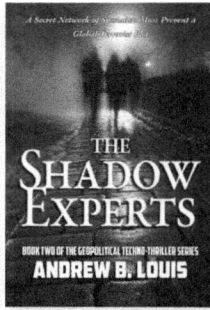  

Operation Kovesh, The Shadow Experts, Below the Surface, The Crypto Trap, Escaping the Bear, Glitter and Smoke, Trouble in the China Sea, The Improbable Collector, Seven Miracles to Save the World, A Crooked Few and *Tough Choices* available at Amazon.com.

www.AndrewBLouis.com

ACKNOWLEDGMENTS

Though all the writing and errors are solely my own doing, a number of people contributed to the creation of the text. I would like to thank the numerous friends and family members who were kind enough to comment on various drafts and led me to make material changes for the better, as usual, my dear friend Jeff, my wife, and especially her first-year college roommate and ever since dearest friend, Cyndy.

SYNOPSIS

Mossad, the national intelligence agency of the State of Israel, also known as the Institute for Intelligence and Special Operations, came across a surprising piece of news. Somehow, the Afghanistan-based Taliban had reportedly struck an alliance with the Muslim Brotherhood, an extremist Islamist organization based in Egypt. With a first bombing having proven successful, *Mossad*, working through The Shadow Experts, the group founded by Countess Renate, warned the *Mukhabarat*, the Egyptian Secret Service Agency, as soon as it heard of the second of what might be an impending series of terrorist actions aimed at destroying vestiges of Pharaonic Egypt. While the *Mukhabarat* was able to prevent that bombing, *Mossad* developed a series of retaliatory steps aimed at punishing those terrorist agents while keeping Israel below the radar.

Mossad's forceful operations, first in the Horn of Africa and afterwards at several of Iran's main oil and gas production facilities, were designed to cause significant disruption in Iran and meant to encourage the country to reconsider a foreign policy based on proxy-terrorism. Various Israeli teams worked together to pull off the attacks which required the use of new and original weapon systems. The story would have had a successful conclusion but for the discovery that local *Mossad* contacts in Egypt were not all they appeared to be.

Disclaimer: All the parties to this story are fictitious and if there was some resemblance with individuals or institutions, it would be purely coincidental.

PROLOGUE

2011 & 2023
CAIRO, EGYPT

2011

Suddenly, three words resonated throughout all offices of the Israeli Embassy in Giza, located across the Nile from Cairo. They came from the Embassy's Head of Security, Elihu Massler:

"Evacuate the building."

■ ■ ■ ■ ■

In fairness, one should note that very few people within the Embassy, on the top two floors of the building, and more broadly in the apartments or offices within the rest of the building, were surprised when they heard Elihu Massler's announcement. Trouble had been brewing in Cairo for several days. In fact, everything had started with the incident in the south of Israel. It really had followed a two-step sequence. First, after the attempt of the Palestinian Authority to gain membership in the United Nations as a fully sovereign state had failed, sporadic rocket attacks from Hamas-controlled Gaza on Israel and retaliatory Israeli air raids started to occur more frequently. Second, more recently, on August 18, 2011, a small group of Palestinian militants crossed from the Sinai Peninsula into southern Israel; the attack killed eight Israelis, near Eilat, an Israeli resort town at the top of the Gulf of Aqaba, one of the two northward extensions of the Red Sea. Predictably, Israel launched a punitive airstrike in the Gaza strip; it killed six Palestinians, including the leader of the Popular Resistance Committee. Unfortunately, the retaliatory strike reportedly also killed three Egyptian soldiers. This was more than enough to inflame local passions in Cairo and elsewhere in Egypt.

Though Egypt was the first Arab country to make peace with Israel in 1979 and is still one of only two to have formal reciprocal representation with Israel at this time, relations between Egypt and Israel had never really been warm. The truth be told, they tended to be frosty most of the time. This illustrates the usual dichotomy between what pragmatic governments may feel they have to do and what the general population desires and, in fact, attempts, to do. Governments often tend to appreciate that there are "certain things that must be overlooked or left unsaid" so that diplomatic relations can remain unscathed and ongoing cooperation maintained. On the other hand, the general sentiment within the population does not practice anywhere near the same restraints; extremists within the political spectrum have long known that passions can be inflamed with ease. For instance, one does not need to go too far back in history to observe the importance of propaganda, which always involves projecting one's own version of the truth to gain popular support, often with disastrous consequences.

■ ■ ■ ■ ■

In Egypt, historical and religious circumstances have driven the country's population to be supportive of Palestinians—fellow Arabs and Muslims. Admittedly, the creation of the State of Israel by definition in the geographical area where Jews originally lived—and in fact prospered as a religion way before Christians first and seven centuries later Muslims came to exist—was going to lead to people being inevitably displaced. They had to move away from land which they and their ancestors had occupied for centuries. An interesting thesis could be written on the topic of who really was the occupier in the area where the state of Israel is located. The Balfour Declaration on November 2, 1917, offered its support for the proposition that there should be a national home for the Jewish people and that it should be in Palestine. Yet, for centuries prior to then, Jews and Arabs had co-existed in that same territory, though at least three different diasporas, defined as situations when people were forced to leave their traditional homeland, affected Jews through history, leading them viewed as a "diasporan people." The first diaspora took place with the conquests of the eighth to the sixth century B.C.E. The Israelites were forcibly exiled first to Assyria and then to Babylon. The second was the Roman-triggered expulsion of Jews from their traditional land because of the Jewish Revolt of 70 C.E. and the subsequent *Bar Kokhba* revolt which resulted in the destruction of the Second Temple. The third, which continued at least until the establishment of the state of Israel in 1948, started in the Middle Ages as Jews moved into Europe, Spain (Sephardic Jews), and later into the Christian areas of the Rhineland (Ashkenazi Jews).

Unfortunately, as is often the case when politicians try to impose a solution, the United Nations may not have anticipated what the creation of a state where Jews could live in peace after the horrible shock of the Holocaust might bring about as they "returned" to a land their ancestors had fled for the prior twenty centuries. What was unquestionably meant as a good deed, to alleviate the collective guilt triggered by the Holocaust, turned out to be a plague for others, namely for Arabs who had hitherto lived in pre-1948 Palestine.

Israel's response to the original border incident provoked anger in Egypt, which had been ruled by the Freedom and Justice Party since the elections of April 30, 2011. That party was launched by the Muslim Brotherhood, an Islamic group which was perceived to be the most powerful and the best structured political movement in Egypt at the time. It was known for its unique ability to organize and mobilize its followers; this probably reflected its practice of using religious themes to achieve goals, many of which were at least as political as religious, if not more so. The incident and what followed illustrated the complicated situation between two countries whose governments would have liked to have better relations, and yet could not because of popular sentiment. A cynic would observe that fifteen years later, the environment had not really changed much, with some Arab governments unofficially willing to entertain direct relationships with Israel and yet unable to do so because of what was often referred to as "Arab street."

Back in 2011, the Israeli Embassy occupied the top two floors, the 20th and the 21st, of an apartment building on the Nile Corniche, an avenue overlooking the Nile and Cairo beyond to the east. The building, located in a highly desirable area, sat amidst other apartment or office buildings, luxury hotels or even other diplomatic missions. In fact, many would call that area of Giza "Embassy Row," as it had more embassies than any other Cairo neighborhood. All the Israeli Embassy's west-facing windows overlooked Charles de Gaulle Street, an avenue parallel to the Nile Corniche, in Giza, better known to the local population as *Al-Jizah*. More precisely, those windows overlooked the major interchange as Charles de Gaulle Street passes under Nahdet Misr Street.

▮ ▮ ▮ ▮ ▮

Nahdet Misr Street, translated into "Egypt's Renaissance," is named after the "art deco-style" polished granite statue representing a woman and a sphinx, a pair which is said to summarize the essence of the country at a glance. The two figures stand tall in the boulevard in the middle of Nahdet Misr Street, looking almost due east toward Cairo University Bridge which spans across the Nile, the demarcation line between Cairo and Giza. Across and beyond Charles de Gaulle Street, the embassy's west-facing offices offer an unimpeded view of the full 28 acres of the Orman Botanical Garden. One of the most famous plant and flower gardens in Egypt, the Botanical Garden dates back to 1875. Khedive Ismail Pasha established it as a part of the Palace of the Khedive. To the left of the garden, across Nahdet Misr Street, another, even larger, open space houses the Giza Zoo, which is often described as having the greatest variety of animals and plants on its 80-acre site. Beyond that wonderful greenery, further west one could see the vast campus of Cairo University.

I I ■ I I

Late on Friday September 9, 2011, right after the end of the evening prayers at the Mosque, the protests which had started with the incident involving the border skirmish near Eilat turned more violent. It does not stretch one's imagination to assume that the proximity of Cairo university may have helped provide attendance to the large demonstrations which were all aimed at the Israeli Embassy; students often do not hesitate joining protests, whether they do or do not appreciate the actual issue. Earlier, before protests turned into near riots, the Egyptian government had already erected a solid barricade in front of the building, with the goal of protecting the embassy and its personnel. When matters deteriorated further, the ambassador himself was taken back to his residence in the Maadi district of Cairo for his own safety. It quickly became clear to all diplomats and employees of the embassy that the situation was critical: evacuation orders were likely to be a part of the next safety announcement. They knew that it would not take something drastic to occur, with bloodshed and its inevitable consequences.

The measures taken by the Egyptian government were eventually to demonstrate both their usefulness and their limitations. Violence reached a peak when the demonstrators rammed down the Egyptian government's barricade. Informed of that news, the ambassador gave by phone his last instructions to the Head of Embassy Security. He asked the six security officers to move as many sensitive documents as possible to the safe room and to lock themselves in it, after having ordered the evacuation of the embassy. The safe room had everything the security team needed, including breathing equipment, water, food, even toiletries, to allow them to survive for at least a couple of days.

All other staff and their families, as well as any remaining resident of the apartments found on the lower floors were escorted out of the building by Egyptian police officers. The embassy personnel and what family members were still in Egypt were taken to the airport, where they were met by the ambassador and flown out of Egypt. The sole diplomat who was not on the plane bound for Tel Aviv was the deputy ambassador who remained in the country under the protection of the U.S. Embassy.

Egyptian commandos eventually rescued the six security personnel, but not before they had spent 13 hours in their reinforced hiding place. The rioters had ransacked the whole building—and thus not only the top two floors—and thrown lots of paper from the embassy's windows. Yet, Israel was also confident that crucial documents had been protected and were therefore safe. In particular, the security personnel were able to provide total assurances that no information on local informers or contacts could have been uncovered. The head of *Mossad* in Cairo at the time had indeed taken all these documents himself and moved them into a safe place, even before the ambassador left the building.

■ ■ ■ ■ ■

2023

Benjamin Kaplan's day had started quietly. He had taken the short drive from his home in the near vicinity and was now sitting at his desk in the new embassy which had been constructed on the grounds of the official ambassador's residence in Maadi, a leafy residential area of Cairo. A purpose-built edifice, the offices were both quite functional and very well protected. On the other hand, there was no real view to the outside aside from the outline of several homes amid a literal forest of tall palm trees. Every building was a low-rise edifice, and the embassy was no exception. People might have felt they lived in a tropical garden but gone were the grand vistas of the prior embassy. Ben had already had the time to read all the official material which was prepared for him by his assistant and delivered either in paper format or, more frequently, electronically to his laptop computer. He was taken away from his thoughts when his cell phone, which he had placed on the right-hand side of his desk, rang. He picked it up and heard:

"Sayyid Kaplan, I must see you . . ."

Ben immediately recognized the voice of Ayman Al-Khafaji, one of a small group of informers on whom he relied. Though Benjamin was listed as a respectable Vice Consul in the directory of the embassy, he was the senior *Mossad* officer in Egypt. As such, he was always seeking any information which could be useful to the leaders of the agency in Tel Aviv and had painstakingly built a network, supplementing the work of his predecessors. No informer knew the identity of any of his other sources. No one knew Ben's official role, as he always introduced himself as a diplomat who was trying to learn as much as he could on whatever was happening in Egypt.

"Ayman. What a pleasure. Haven't spoken to you in a while. What's up?"

"Can't talk on the phone too long. I need to see you."

"Where are you?"

"Near the Pyramid of Djoser."

Ben knew that the Djoser Pyramid was about 20 miles from Maadi, where the embassy was located. He quickly figured that it would have taken Ayman no more than an hour to get there as he knew he resided in Cairo as well. He could not resist asking:

"What are you doing there?"

Ayman was not surprised or even taken aback by the question. Quite matter-of-factly, he answered:

"Don't have the time to say much. Yet, in short, yesterday evening I received a call from an informer who said he needed to see me urgently. He's always been quite dependable. So, I just jumped in my car and arrived at dusk last night."

"Do I know of this informer?"

Ayman hesitated as he replied:

"Not sure, Sayyid Ben. I may have mentioned his code name a few times, but you've never met him."

"Do you know anything more about his real identity beyond his code name?"

Ayman sounded almost offended:

"No. No, Sayyid. By the way, he does not know me by the name which you know either. On the other hand, I have checked him out and he seemed sufficiently reliable for me to maintain a relationship with him. Oh, come to think of it, I should add that I know he is mostly employed as a tourist guide."

He paused for a second and added:

"Back to why I called you. I've just learned from this informer something which could be very serious."

"And you can't say anything on the phone?"

"No. I don't want to take any risk. I can only mention a couple of words to you: Taliban and Brotherhood."

Benjamin thought for a second. Ayman's sudden care with respect to phone safety was not standard, for him at least. Ben was still not sure why he needed to endure an hour's traffic for something which could be relatively unimportant. Though his brains were telling him to watch out for anything that could be a trap, he still heard himself reply:

"Not sure I understand, but the juxtaposition of these two words cannot mean anything good. Hey, Djoser is less than 20 miles away. I can be there in an hour or so, depending on the traffic naturally. Is that, OK?"

"Sure."

"Where should we meet?"

"Let's meet at the colonnaded entrance, at the southeast corner of the pyramid complex, on the eastern wall. I'll be alone. And please, be careful. Not a word to anyone. Make sure you look like a tourist."

Ben could only offer the traditional Arabic greeting signifying, "Go in peace:"

"*Ma'a essalama.*"

■ ■ ■ ■

Though many Egyptian people might identify the Sphinx as their most important archeological symbol, most foreigners would probably pick the pyramids as the monument which most exemplify the country and its distant pharaonic past. In fact, when asked about sphinxes, most foreigners would typically only think of the "Great Sphinx," the limestone statue of the mythical animal with a head of a human and the body of a lion, located on the Giza Plateau, on the west bank of the Nile, near the famous three great pyramids. Most foreigners would thus ignore other sites, such as the famous "Avenue of Sphinxes," a nearly one-and-a-half-mile avenue on the east bank of Luxor. It connects the Karnak temple in the north to the Luxor temple in the south and is lined with more than 1,050 sphinx statues!

And this does not count the Sphinx bearing the head of Pharaoh Hatshepsut or the alabaster Sphinx of Memphis.

Admittedly, it is quite likely that when foreigners think of pyramids as uniquely Egyptian monuments, few of them think of any other than the three lined-up great pyramids of Keops, Khafre, and Menkaura on the Giza Plateau, next to the Great Sphinx. Most probably ignore that Egypt boasts a total of 118 such pyramids and that the oldest of them was built in Djoser in the 27th century before Christ. It is often called the Step Pyramid of Djoser.

■ ■ ■ ■ ■

Ben took advantage of the quiet thinking time, which his ride to Djoser provided him. There was no need for him to concentrate on driving as he had the luxury of being driven in the air-conditioned comfort of an official embassy car. Similarly, he did not feel inclined to look at the potentially interesting places he might have seen along the road. He had been in Egypt for nearly four years, and he knew the sites.

His thoughts wandered to the period in Egyptian history when the Muslim Brotherhood was in control of government levers, after the 2011 revolution that overthrew Hosni Mubarak. Initially, in the first couple of years after the revolution, tension prevailed between the religious Brotherhood and the secular military—the two strongest political forces in the country at the time. It was thought that the Brotherhood had at the outset made a deal with the military, though both sides vehemently denied that such was the case. Yet, the silence of the Brotherhood and other Islamists when the military which ruled Egypt then was taking a hard line against non-religiously affiliated revolutionaries made it seem as if there had to be at least partial tacit agreement.

As Ben was musing on the brief period when the Brotherhood ruled Egypt, he was thinking of the parallel which could be drawn between the Muslim Brotherhood in Egypt and the Taliban when they were in power in Afghanistan. Just as had been the case for the Taliban in Afghanistan, the Muslim Brotherhood, led by hardliners, had managed to alienate its revolutionary and democratic partners and to scare away a good part of society, particularly women and Christians. Eventually, a showdown between the military and the Brotherhood was inevitable and a former high-level official in the Brotherhood was elected president.

Though it would be interesting to continue to review the life and subsequent demise of the Muslim Brotherhood regime, it is not directly relevant to the issue which confronted Ben on this ride. One thing was clear to him: during its short rule, along with other extremists, the Muslim Brotherhood had sought to destroy the pharaonic sites which they viewed as idolatrous, in another example of wanting to eliminate anything which might distract from Islam. They reportedly considered, for instance, covering the great pyramids of Giza with sand. Thankfully for lovers of archaeology, such crazy initiatives turned out to be one of the factors which led the Egyptian people to revolt against the Muslim Brotherhood, even though it was the first democratic government in their country's history. The pyramids and the sphinx stood unscathed.

To the surprise of Meir, his driver, Ben could not resist saying out loud:

"Damn it, that's what he must mean when he talks of the Brotherhood and the Taliban."

Suddenly, the parallel which he had drawn between the Taliban and the Muslim Brotherhood became alive and took on an additional dimension. What the Muslim Brotherhood had thought of doing in Egypt while in power was like what the Islamic fundamentalist Taliban regime did in Afghanistan in March 2001. There, they blew up the two Buddha statues in Bamiyan, Salsal and Shamama, after declaring them to be unislamic. Optimistically, Ben did note that covering the pyramids with sand would have inflicted less permanent damage on Giza's treasures than blowing up the Bamiyan Buddha statues with explosives. Yet, Ben's imagination ran wild for a few minutes as he contemplated the enormous and diverse wealth of archaeological treasures located in Egypt, principally along the Nile. What if this was what Ayman had learned?

He calmed himself, remembering his *Krav Magra* training, focusing then on its mental rather than grappling dimension: *there is no point getting all excited based on speculation*. In fact, he recalled an important principle which he had then learned from his Master:

"Never allow yourself to speculate beyond the first degree. You are allowed to have worries; that's human. You may analyze the situation; your life may depend on it. But you must never take any analysis of a worry to the second degree or further. When you do that, you assume that your worry has come to pass, and you begin to imagine second- and third-degree consequences."

He remembered that he had asked his Master to explain the maxim and never forgot the reply:

"You must never allow a worry to become a reality in your mind unless it turns out to be one as a result of a factual observation. Until it is proven to be, treat a worry as what it is: just a worry which is only one of a number of possible outcomes of a question in your mind."

CHAPTER.01

CAIRO AND DJOSER, EGYPT

As he arrived near the front entrance to the vast mortuary complex in Djoser, Ben, who had already visited the site early in his tenure in the country, could still not help but be stunned, as he had been on an earlier occasion. The pyramid and the complex were built by Imhotep, high priest to the god, Ra, and vizier, sage, architect, astrologer, and chief minister to King Djoser, the pharaoh. Ra, besides being the god of the sun, was also considered the king of all the deities and the father of all creation. Imhotep was someone quite special and one of a few commoners to be acknowledged by the Egyptian people after his death as having divine status.

Though Ben did recall that the complex was quite large, the size hit him again as it rose from the sandy landscape in and around the Saqqara necropolis, near the ruins of Memphis. The mid-afternoon sun helped elongate shadows, exaggerating the difference between elements with relief and those that were flat on the ground. Measuring close to 500 yards from north to south and a good 250 yards from east to west, the scale of the complex was striking: the perimeter wall allegedly was a full mile in length and stood 35 feet high! Though he probably did not think of it at the time, Ben was probably feeling the effects of the brilliant sun shining on light colored sand and buildings. The contrast was powerful and, had he looked with more attention, he might have seen the heat haze which arose as hot air reverberating from the already hot ground mixed with cooler air above. As the air density increased, light traveling through it bent, leading to certain distortions which voyagers in the area had come to describe as mirages.

Majestically erected in the middle of the vast rectangle, the Djoser Step Pyramid stood slightly more than 200 feet tall, on an almost square base measuring 358 by 397 feet. Clad in polished limestone like many others, the real distinguishing trait of the monument when contrasted to all other pyramids was that rather than having a steady slope from top to bottom to its four sides, it comprised six steps, each defining a gradually diminishing surface area, ending with a point at its very top. The story does not say whether it was built with steps rather than uniform slopes, because Egyptian architects did not yet know how to erect what we have come to view as "normal" pyramids, or because it was the choice of its architect around 2780 BC.

The whole complex is comprised of the enclosure walls, the great trench, a colonnaded entrance, and several other structures including multiple other tombs. Under the pyramid itself, one found a labyrinth of tunneled chambers and galleries which, guides say, totaled nearly four miles. This was where the king and his family members were buried and where food for their afterlife was stored.

After he had passed the ticket office of Saqqara, right opposite the ruins of King Unas' Valley Temple, Ben's driver, Meir, followed the Djoser Pyramid Road, which described a one-mile-long loop covering three of the four sides of a rectangle of pure desert, where one might only occasionally see Bedouins, men of the desert, riding a donkey or a lonely, dried-up tree or bush. Meir parked the car in the lot reserved for visitors, letting Ben walk the last couple hundred feet to the entrance of the walled pyramid complex and of the colonnade where he was due to meet Ayman. A well-trodden path took him straight there and Ben did not have to look far to see his contact. He immediately picked up Ayman: he was seeking relief from the strong sun in the shadow of the first passageway, a narrow corridor cut into the walls of the enclosure. Smiling, Ben greeted him:

"Hello, Ayman. You seemed quite shaken this morning."

"I was. Frankly, Sayyid Ben, I still am. In fact, I am more shaken now than this morning."

Knowing his friend quite well, Ben decided to avoid the rabbit hole offered to him. He did not ask why Ayman would be more shaken now than when he talked to Ben in the early morning. He just asked:

"So, tell me what is it that you could not say on the telephone?"

Ben was surprised when he heard Ayman's reply:

"Better yet. I don't need to tell you now. Let me show you."

With a much tenser and less charming voice, Ben said:

"Just a minute, my friend. Not so fast."

Ayman could not believe the sudden change of behavior he noticed in Ben, particularly when he started to feel the business end of the barrel of a gun poking his left thigh through Ben's pant pocket. Ayman could only ask:

"Wait. What's wrong? I don't understand."

■ ■ ■ ■ ■

While riding to the necropolis and reflecting on the situation, Ben had drawn a sketch of what he knew and did not know. He always liked to start addressing any issue with what he called his "knowledge inventory." He had learned over the years that this allowed him to come more quickly to a semi-solid preliminary conclusion. In the current circumstances, Ben noted that he had known Ayman for at least three years and had so far had no reason to doubt his loyalty. On the other hand, the mystery surrounding the present development was abnormal. In fact, it was totally out of character. That told him that he needed to be more careful than usual, remembering the old lesson his mentor taught him, "It is always dangerous to get lulled into complacency by the routine. It's equally dangerous not to notice an out-of-character behavior; in fact, that could constitute the ultimate danger."

Ben had agreed to drive to the Saqqara Plateau to meet Ayman because the two words which Ayman had dropped made him fear that there was a real issue which he ought to investigate. Anything which internationalized the latent conflict driven by the Muslim Brotherhood was a major development, and one which could have an impact on Israel's security. Since the Brotherhood had been banned, it had gone underground, periodically sowing trouble; however, it had remained truly domestic operating solely within Egypt. Any intrusion by any foreign organization with terrorist roots into the domestic affairs of an Egyptian group could be the signal that serious unrest was about to happen. Additionally, Ben was fully aware that although the world officially only comprised three "superpowers," Iran, among a couple of other countries, was determined to get into the club. However, since it had neither the economic nor the military strength required to gain that status, it had chosen to be a terrorist sponsor, standing behind and supporting any and all organizations that fought the status quo, particularly if they had an Islamic bent to their underpinning ideology.

That was what led Ben to conclude that he had to follow up on the tip. Yet, he also knew quite well that he should do it with his eyes wide open. In fact, he went as far as asking himself: *did I make a glorious error hiring Ayman as an informer? Could he be a double agent?*

He knew that Ayman had once been involved with the Muslim Brotherhood, though Ayman had told him that he had dropped out after a few years when the Brotherhood had been banned by the Egyptian government. Ben did not know what name Ayman was using then. Yet, Ayman assured Ben that the name he was giving him was only known to him alone. That and other details had come out as Ben's junior colleague, Eli Goldberg, was putting Ayman through all the checks needed to verify his bona fide. As an organization, *Mossad* is indeed quite careful, as are all secret services, before accepting an informer and sharing with him or her the secrets they need to operate.

When Ayman was being checked out, he had outlined for Ben's benefit the five levels which one must pass through in order to become a real "brother," as members of the Muslim Brotherhood call themselves. A candidate starts as a follower (*muhib*) during which he is closely monitored by the captain (*naqib*) of the family (*usra*) to which he is assigned. Once vetted, the candidate becomes a supporter (*muayyad*) during which period he is a non-voting member of the family focused on studying the *Quran* and the teachings of Hasan Al Banna, the founder of the Brotherhood. The individual then graduates to become officially affiliated (*mubtasib*), the first step to full membership when he starts making a financial contribution, in effect paying a tithe. After another couple of years, the candidate reaches the penultimate stage, being called an organizer (*muntazim*), at which point he may be entrusted with minor leadership roles, though he has not yet reached the ultimate stage. Ultimately, the individual becomes a working brother (*ach'amal*), a full member of the Brotherhood.

The structure of the process and the length it took to become a full member of the Brotherhood was why it had seemed able to resist many, though probably not all, forms of penetration by security services. Yet, at the same time, Ben was convinced that someone like Ayman who had been through a part of the process but allegedly left without ever even becoming a *muayyad* had to have become somewhat of a marked man. Or had he managed to disappear into the woodwork, simply because he was not senior yet and there were people who like him abandoned the movement?

Ben had taken his time with the help of Eli before trusting Ayman and believing that the tidbits he was providing were not mere disinformation. His last insight had been quite valuable in that it allowed Ben to protect someone on the staff of the embassy who somehow had been uncovered as a junior member of *Mossad*. While that individual's tour of duty in Egypt was suddenly cut short, everyone was delighted that he was able to return home to his family alive and well. Agents that are uncovered are often killed; their bodies delivered to a side door of the embassy just so that everyone understands the point. Ayman had also pointed to an Egyptian junior embassy driver who, he claimed, was a member of the Brotherhood. The driver had been quickly invited to look for another job and the embassy had been able to avoid an alleged spy remaining in its employ.

Yet, in the car, Ben's trained mind started building a case suggesting that Ayman might be a double agent. At that point, it was a simple case of survival for Ben, and he could not reject any hypothesis. If he had in fact become a target for Ayman, Ben posited that Ayman's two most recent successes might have been a calculated minimal loss he had to give away to serve his other master and deliver a much bigger fish. That was when Ben decided to take Ayman for a ride when he got to the Djoser Pyramid to make sure he understood fully what the current situation was and to decide whether the risk was worth it.

■ ■ ■ ■ ■

As he was gently but firmly pushing Ayman to walk in the direction of the road to the immediate east of the complex and the parking lot beyond and to the right, Ben said:

"I sure hope I'm wrong. But I cannot take the risk of walking into the complex without knowing more. I've got to test you're for real, my friend!"

He paused for a second. Though Ayman could not see what he was doing, Ben reached into his right pant pocket and pressed a button on what looked like a tiny remote-control device. Ayman could not know that people of Ben's rank, and who had a driver, a *Katsa*—a *Mossad* agent—all had such a device. It allowed him to summon his driver from afar without needing to have an actual phone conversation. Here, Ben simply meant to ask Meir for the car to be turned around and ready to leave the lot. Ben and Ayman arrived at the entrance of the parking lot at the same time as Meir's car got there. Ayman hesitated but then felt he had no choice but to get into the vehicle through the right rear door that Ben opened for him. Ben asked him to slide across the back seat. He then sat down next to him. Meir had already started the car rolling forward before the rear door was fully closed.

Speaking to the driver in Hebrew, Ben instructed him to take them to a spot behind Maia Tomb—Bubasteion, less than a half mile away on the Pyramid of Djoser Road. The area Ben had chosen was still desertic, as were most of the surroundings. Ben was confident that there would be minimal risk of any distraction. He was counting on the fact that the tomb was less well-known as a tourist attraction than the nearby step pyramid. However, his own view was that *Maia,* who was the wet nurse of Pharaoh Tutankhamun in the 14th century BC, and her tomb deserved a visit. Meir retraced his steps on the Djoser Pyramid Road but did not turn right at the first opportunity; it would have taken him back to the ticket office. Rather, he drove on for another 500 feet, turned right, and followed that road for nearly a quarter mile until he found the small parking lot reserved for the tomb's visitors.

Ben told Ayman that they would not get out of the car, whose doors were kept locked by Meir. He argued, persuasively as it turned out, that this allowed them to keep enjoying the Mercedes Benz's welcome air-conditioning. He immediately asked Ayman to explain why he needed to see him and why they had to meet near the Djoser Pyramid. Ayman tried to resist for a short while, but it quickly became obvious to him that he really had no choice. He then explained that he had received a call from an acquaintance several days earlier. He conceded that the individual was a middle-of-the-road member of the Muslim Brotherhood. Ben immediately interrupted:

"What's a 'middle-of-the-road' member of the Brotherhood? Never heard of that?"

Ayman made a sign with his hand suggesting that Ben should not lose his patience. He reminded him that the Brotherhood was banned in 2013, adding:

"As you know, that's when I left."

Ben nodded; he had no choice but to be patient and listen to the rest of Ayman's story but was already dreading Ayman's tendency to take the long way around, asking himself: *why doesn't he just come out with what he knew?* Ayman started his story with the observation that the group, the Muslim Brotherhood, re-formed with an official purpose focused on religion rather than politics. That was why his friend stayed in, or more precisely went back in after having briefly left. However, observers note that the Brotherhood's official position against violence has been tarnished by a number of exceptions that were somehow tolerated, including acts which most everyone would qualify as violent. Ayman added that there was a split within the Brotherhood with one part becoming more militant and the other remaining committed to its religious foundation, adding:

"The militant branch did not want to break up in full because they felt they enjoyed slight cover through the more religious branch. As a purely military and violent organization, they would have been hounded into oblivion."

Returning to his story, Ayman said that Gamal Al-Sahid, his contact, was a part of the group that honestly believed that violence should be avoided, and the focus remain on Islam. As such, he had found a friendly ear in Ayman who devoutly practiced Islam. Though, as firmly instructed by Ben and Eli that he never discuss his relationship with Benjamin Kaplan, he had come to the view that Gamal could be a useful contact.

■ ■ ■ ■ ■

Ayman told Ben that the prior evening he had received a phone call from Gamal Al-Sahid, adding:

"Remember, he knows me as Ammon, rather than Ayman."

Ayman proceeded to relate to Ben as much of the telephone call as he could remember. He started going through the dialog as he remembered it:

"Ammon, I must talk to you."

"Can we do it now?"

"Not really. Could you come to the Saqqara necropolis?"

"Sure could, but why?"

"I'm told something big is going to happen, and I need to talk to you before it does."

Though Ayman said it took him additional questions before he agreed to join his friend, he still quickly set out to drive to the necropolis. Once he had arrived, he booked himself at the Sakkara Inn, a cheap hotel near the Sacred Animal necropolis, as he had agreed earlier with his informer. He said that Gamal was waiting for him as soon as he approached the front desk to check himself in. He saw him sitting in the modest lobby on one of the two high-back rattan chairs with pamphlets and magazines loosely set on the rattan coffee table in front of the chairs.

After Ayman walked to greet him, Gamal hardly gave him the time to drop his light overnight luggage in his room. Rather, he immediately suggested a short walk in the vicinity. Ostensibly, Ayman thought that Gamal was looking for more seclusion and privacy than usual. He surely did not want to be overheard. Ayman said that Gamal told him that he had heard of a troubling development within the Muslim Brotherhood, or rather an extremist sub-group within it:

"I hear that they are receiving help from the Taliban . . ."

"The Taliban? From Afghanistan?"

"Correct."

"Why would they do that?"

Gamal explained that these hardliners had rekindled views they held in the early part of the 21st century, feeling that Islam was being corrupted by tourism in general and by a sort of fascination with the old archaeological treasures. Ayman, aka Ammon, said he interrupted:

"They want to destroy these treasures?"

"That's what I heard. But the difference this time is that they want to destroy them rather than simply hide them. Remember, back in 2012, they simply wanted to cover the Great Pyramids with sand."

"They want to use explosives now?"

"Yep! Again, that's what I heard."

Ayman said he did not ask his next question immediately as he was playing what he had just heard in his mind. Yet, he said that he next inquired:

"You said on the phone that something was going to happen here. Is that related to the news?"

"Yes. My friend, the one who told me of the Taliban connection, also said that they would be placing a bomb at the Djoser Pyramid tomorrow."

"And?"

"Isn't that enough?"

Ayman replied:

"It depends on what you want to do. I can't do anything to stop it?"

"Can't you talk to someone and get them to intervene?"

Ayman said he looked directly into Gamal's eyes and asked:

"Who do you think I am?"

Ayman said that Gamal replied that he did not know for sure, though he said he remembered that his friend Ammon had told him he had connections with certain influential journalists in Cairo. Ayman added that, looking straight into his eyes, Gamal had asked:

"Can you make sure that people hear about this? Can you do that without pointing to me?"

"I sure can. I'll make a couple of calls. But I can't do anything now. I've got to wait until tomorrow."

"What if the bomb has already exploded?"

"I hope I can reach someone early in the morning. But, at the very least, even if after the fact, I can suggest that the press should investigate."

CHAPTER.02

Back near Maia's tomb, Ben asked Ayman:

"And you believed him?"

Ben's tone of voice was definitely not amused, and Ayman understood that the question had to have an answer. He mumbled:

"What could be wrong, Sayyid Ben?"

"Come on, Ayman. By the way, I'm glad to hear that he knows you by a different name. One question though: Is either of them your real name?"

"No, Sayyid Ben. That's how I protect myself. I'm pretty sure that the chap I know as Gamal is not called Gamal either."

Ben whistled and simply said:

"Well, I'd love to know how you keep that straight. But I guess it's no different than code names in most secret services as I have been told."

Ben paused, noticing Ayman did not notice the reference to secret services, which he now thought was surely not necessary, and returned to his earlier flow:

"Ayman, I'm not a fool and neither are you. You have told me how hard it is to get vetted in the Brotherhood. You want me to believe that you, first, and your friend Gamal, second, managed somehow to get out of the group, while keeping contacts within and still stay under the radar?"

Ayman could not fail to notice the emphasis which Ben had placed on "and" in the question he had just asked. His voice rose a few decibels as he protested:

"Sayyid Ben, we've been over that as far as I am concerned. Your associate, Eli, and you, too, asked millions of questions as to how I had managed to escape the Brotherhood. I assumed you believed me. Why is this coming up again?"

He paused but did not allow Ben the time to reply, though he did notice a discreet nod. He just continued:

"And by the way, Gamal is not my friend. He's an informer of mine. I may use the word friend from time to time, but that's in our Egyptian culture. He is not a friend as you understand it in English; I've never been to his home, and he's never been to mine. Anyway, back to the Brotherhood, you know my position. I left when the group was banned. You know that I still sympathize with the religious aims of the Brotherhood, but it would have been too hard for me to get back in. That's why I am staying out. What's wrong with that?"

Ben nodded again and came close to a full apology, arguing that safety was always paramount in his mind. He conceded that he might have overreacted when he doubted Ayman's word, but quickly shifted the focus on Gamal, adding:

"I'd never heard of him, correct?"

"Correct. As I said earlier, I may have indirectly mentioned him once or twice, but you would have had no reason to notice it. Never talked to you about him, because I have never mentioned to you the name of any of my contacts."

He paused to check that Ben was on board and continued:

"Now, his situation in the Brotherhood is different than mine. He tells me he is still officially a part of the non-violent, mostly religious branch. He is known as such. To me, that means that they respect his views, probably because he does not oppose the other tendency head on. Yet, I can't believe he would be involved with the plot. Makes no sense."

Ben remained poker-faced, effectively waiting for Ayman to say more. Ayman, on his end, was a bit confused as he wasn't really sure what more he could say. After a few, long, silent seconds, he spoke again:

"You're right, Sayyid Ben. I understand your question. Here, there are two people you did not know. Gamal and his contact. I believe we can trust Gamal though I agree we still need to remain very, very careful. For instance, he has no idea that you exist and does not know my real name. Between you and me, you're the one to whom I refer as the journalist in Cairo."

With a smile, Ben quipped:

"Me, a journalist. Is it a promotion?"

Ayman did not seem to note Ben's cynical comment and kept going:

"So, I'm not going to assume he is a traitor. The real issue I was wrestling with myself has to do with Gamal's friend. Frankly, I wasn't sure; in fact, I'm still not sure. Gamal refused to say anything on the phone. And I understood that. Yet, a lot was riding on the fellow being genuine. Still, I agreed to come to Djoser to see Gamal, because the clues he dropped to get me here sounded too important to ignore. And he didn't tell me who his contact was."

"I see this, my friend."

Ayman smiled for the first time upon hearing Ben using the term "my friend" in a way he interpreted to be sincere. Ben did not notice the connection and asked further:

"But why in the world did you ask me to come here? Why did you believe your friend?"

For the first time, Ayman smiled broadly. He simply said:

"Because it sounded so plausible. Gamal was quite convincing. Anyway, in the end, it doesn't matter."

He paused for effect and almost immediately added:

"That's water under the bridge."

He stopped to see Ben's reaction and immediately noticed Ben raising his eyebrows. Ayman had certainly caught Ben's interest. So, somehow satisfied with his "performance," he added:

"Because what they told me would happen did happen. Early this afternoon in fact. Not more than a couple of hours ago."

Ben was stunned. That really did change things. He simply said:

"Wait a tick. I don't follow. What happened early this afternoon?"

Matter-of-factly, Ayman simply replied:

"A bomb went off."

"A bomb? Where? Can't see anything from here?"

"I know. It went off in a chapel at the periphery of the pyramid complex near the southwest end of the enclosure wall. No trace of it from outside the wall. You must get into the complex to see it."

"The place must be crawling with police and the like now. How about journalists? Do you want to be seen with me?"

Simultaneously, Ben was thinking but did not say it: *Do I want to be seen with you?* Ayman could easily see where Ben was leading and simply said:

"Oh. Not to worry. The journalists have mostly come and gone. The police did not allow them to stay there. The government does not want anyone to draw any link between this and any form of terrorism, particularly if there is a whiff of foreign influence."

He paused for a few seconds and added:

"There wasn't much to see really. The police are still there though, but they have re-opened the complex to visitors."

Seeing Ben raise his eyebrows, he paused again and concluded:

"Except for the area where the bomb went off, obviously."

Ben could only reply:

"Surprising, no?"

"Well, up to a point. For a start, I would guess that the police are trying to play it totally 'cool.' They don't want anyone to worry or, worse, to panic. We need tourists, Sayyid Ben. Without these revenues the country would be in a mess; people would starve."

He paused briefly and then took the conversation in a different direction:

"The government is not so concerned because the damage, though real, is still small. It's in a limited area near the enclosure wall, as I said a minute ago, in a chapel adjoining the tomb or some junior official, nowhere near the tomb of the Pharaoh. So, the area is still cordoned off. But the rest is still visible plus, quite frankly, hardly anyone ever visits that secondary part of the complex. Nothing much to see in the best of times. It's never even been totally restored."

Ben spent a good 60 seconds reflecting on Ayman's comments and then said:

"Objectively, I'm not sure that really changes anything about whether I should go in with you or not. You make some sense, but you'll have to concede there are plenty of loose ends. But at this point I don't have much choice. I'll take my chances, Ayman, but please understand. I believe I should continue to trust you, but I must be careful, very careful. You'd do the same thing in my place."

"Understood. But look at it from my vantage point. What could I have done differently?"

Ben simply nodded, though Ayman was still a bit surprised when he heard the end of Ben's statement:

"Yet, I'm not sure you needed me here. It could have waited until you came back to Cairo. A few photos would have done it. Anyway, you must know that I have a gun in my pocket. Plus, my gun has a silencer, and it will remain trained on you. I will not hesitate to shoot if anything seems unusual to me. Being a Vice Consul has its advantages when you figure diplomatic immunity into the picture."

"You don't need to worry, Sayyid Ben. I'm here to show you the proof that something happened. You're not in danger."

Only partially satisfied by Ayman's latest affirmation, Ben agreed to proceed with the initial plan but with an important change. Turning to his driver:

"Meir, can you get me the suitcase that's in the trunk, please?"

Meir came back with a small suitcase and handed it to Ben, who immediately opened it. Ayman was surprised at the variety of the items he saw, though Ben did not take the time to explain anything to him. He saw Ben grab a fake beard and mustache whose color was quite close to the dark brown of his hair. He placed it on his face and then took a wide-brimmed soft hat from the suitcase and donned it. The final element of the transformation was a pair of sunglasses, which Ayman did not know would allow him to film and record what he was seeing.

Meir drove them back where he had picked them up and parked the Mercedes Benz. They got out of the car, but not before Ben had told the driver, still in Hebrew, to watch very carefully and to be ready to pick him up and drive away if he pressed on the remote control a short and then a long signal. Once out of the car and despite his sunglasses, Ben immediately felt the eerie brightness one often encountered in desertic areas. Everything was in a light, sandy color, with a deep blue sky overhead. That light, which at times seemed to burn through everything, exaggerated areas of shadows, providing a sharp contrast between what seemed like just black and white, or rather dark and light.

Ben followed Ayman back to the colonnade entrance and walked into the first passageway which really was hardly more than a narrow corridor. They then reached the second passageway, oriented east-west as well. It was a wider corridor flanked by 40 limestone columns, each nearly 20 feet tall, though quite a few of them were missing their upper elements. Fashioned to resemble reeds, the columns were arranged in pairs and formed 24 alcoves. Returning for a short while to his official profession as a tour guide, Ayman told Ben that Egyptologists believed these alcoves had held statues of the king and of selected dignitaries, though he conceded that there was no hard evidence to back up this assertion. What light was available was filtering through windows cut into the walls near the ceiling, offering a sharp contrast between the partial shade where the men were and the bright blue sky they saw out of these openings. Emerging from the colonnade through its west wall's open door, they found themselves in the south court, not more than a couple hundred feet from the base of the step pyramid to their right. Ben could not help but note that the place was just as bright inside the walls. Sand or light-colored limestone was everywhere, and the afternoon sun combined to produce a glare which sunglasses attenuated only to some extent. Even with the beige, wide-brimmed safari hat he was wearing and sunglasses, Ben had to squint to be able to see anything, all the more so as he was emerging from a corridor with limited light.

Rather than turning right and walking toward the pyramid, Ayman took Ben to their left, in the direction of the south tomb and chapel, which backed onto the enclosure wall and occupied the southwest corner of the complex. Initially, all that Ben could see were small mounds of sand with openings near ground level that were delineated with a few large stones. He understood that these holes corresponded to underground galleries which he knew he would surely not visit today. As Ayman pointed out the site of the blast, Ben could see on its front left a dozen narrow steps which would normally lead to the platform one-story above ground level, from which one would normally access the tomb through a staircase diving down into the structure. Next to that staircase, one would see a rectangular opening revealing the chapel one floor below. Ben thought: *it's probably somehow connected to the galleries I've just imagined.* The small building had been cordoned off by police and sadly showed definite signs of explosion damage to its front façade, though the fact that the ground in front of it was sandy and uneven anyway served to diminish the perception of real damage. To the right of the steps Ayman had initially pointed to, Ben could see from a bit closer the tell-tale signs of the explosion: a portion of the wall had been partially blown out, allowing one to see a cavity inside. As the cavity was lit up by the sun through a hole in its ceiling, Ben could see that the damage had been noticeable but seemed to affect various walls. Further, as the inside of the building had not been renovated, there really was not much to be damaged within it. Yet, the straight internal staircase that allowed one to get down into the chapel and the tomb had been partially destroyed, leaving a gaping hole near the floor where the first six or seven steps would have been. Though he might have liked to conduct a more detailed inspection and taken the opportunity to shoot a few more surreptitious pictures, Ben followed Ayman as they were being shooed away by a policeman watching over the complex since the explosion.

Ben noted with a visible dose of cynicism:

"I hate to tell you, my friend, but I'm not sure I understand why whoever did that actually carried it out. Why did he bother? This is not the kind of action that makes a big statement: minor damage to a peripheral structure."

He paused as if to check his logic and then surprised Ayman with his next question:

"Did the bomber or bombers leave any sort of pamphlet?"

"No."

"Has anyone taken credit?"

"Nope."

"So, even if it is meant to serve as a warning, nobody knows what they're being warned against? Or by whom?"

Ayman reluctantly had to reply:

"Afraid so."

"Does that make any sense?"

Ayman could not help feeling that something was indeed amiss. He was in fact starting to ask himself whether Gamal's tip had really been worth the trip. Had he himself overreacted? Why would terrorists conduct a bombing without taking credit or telling the world why they were doing it? Why would they choose to place the bomb in an area where little damage could be noted, but where no damage would accrue to the main monument? Something seemed not to compute.

He started thinking aloud, sharing his ruminations with Ben:

"I agree with you, Sayyid Ben. There are really only two scenarios I can think of. Either the bomb was meant as a warning and, if that is the case, it makes no sense not to have taken credit for it."

Ben interrupted:

"Unless the terrorists are waiting for their announcement."

"Agreed, but why not be ready to do it immediately? Anyway, the other scenario is that the bomber suddenly had doubts. But how improbable is it that terrorists who picked the man or men who would drop the bomb would precisely choose someone who was beginning to hesitate about the cause?"

Ayman tried to elaborate on each scenario a bit further. He initially turned to the first one, which made no sense, as he had suggested earlier, unless someone was about to claim credit shortly. Digging further, he also imagined that the someone involved elected to make a physical statement that was sufficiently weak so that no real irreversible damage occurred. Ben recognized that Ayman was still at a loss as the logic simply did not stand up to even cursory scrutiny. He asked him:

"Why would anyone take that route?"

Ayman offered an interesting reply:

"The Brotherhood is banned, Sayyid Ben. Maybe they wanted to draw attention to themselves, to prove they could act as they wished while still avoiding too dramatic a provocation so that the government would not attack them too directly."

"I can see that, but that speaks of weakness, not of strength. The only circumstances that would make your logic work for me is if this were but a test."

"A test?"

"Yep, a test to see how the authorities react. You know that they are very sensitive to the kind of proxy-terrorism sponsored by Iran, just as Russia used to practice years ago: manipulate local discontent, finance and arm it, but always keep a position that allows you to deny any connection or even knowledge."

Realizing that this discussion could last a long time without getting them any closer to any resolution, Ben asked Ayman to turn to the second scenario. Noting that it was much more convoluted, Ayman explained:

"What if the individual who placed the bomb suddenly realized the consequences of what he was about to do? What if he had wanted to try to avoid destroying Egypt's historic heritage and yet as someone who had been a part of the group who agreed to take the action could not officially object so late in the game? He might then have decided to place the bomb in a different place than originally intended."

Ayman paused and then immediately added:

"A big problem with the scenario is that his bosses would eventually find out, wouldn't they?"

Playing devil's advocate, Ben produced an explanation:

"Sure, but he could come up with an excuse. For instance, what if he had seen guards at a time when they were not supposed to patrol the place? He might have felt he needed to place the bomb quickly to get far enough away himself. So, he dropped it in the chapel, going down the internal staircase and escaped as quickly as he could. Remember, the chapel is far closer to the entrance than the back of the pyramid."

Ben paused for a few more seconds and asked:

"Isn't that believable?"

"Sure is, though the group would likely not be happy."

"Can see that. By the way, Ayman, on a mission like this, would he have been accompanied by someone or would it be normal for him to be alone?"

"Don't know, Sayyid. Depends upon how senior he is. If he is senior enough, there wouldn't be any need for someone to be with him."

"But the more senior the fellow the less reasonable it would be for him not to carry out the decision that he had been part of—correct?"

Ayman sighed but did not respond to Ben's question. Ben parked that thought away in his mind, kept silent for a few more seconds, and then decided that he was not going to clear up any uncertainty now. Somehow, somewhere, he would like to meet Gamal to make up his own mind, but he immediately realized how imprudent this would be for his safety. So, at that point, he elected to behave as if he were trusting Ayman and his informer, Gamal, though he would surely ask Ayman a couple of difficult additional questions.

But first, he had to get Ayman to feel more at ease to make sure he could surprise him when the tougher questions came. So, he smiled and replied that whatever it was that was done, it seemed it had worked. There was damage; the government was aware of it and would investigate; so, they had been successful. His demeanor led Ayman to relax so that he was not ready for the next question delivered with a slower speech pattern and a very serious tone of voice:

"Ayman, I hate to tell you this. But something here is quite fishy. Let me try and help you through my logic. First, as I told you in the parking lot, I find it more than an odd coincidence that three individuals . . ."

"Three?"

"Yes, Ayman, you, your informer, Gamal, and his friend."

Seeing Ayman nod, though his facial expression surely did not convey real agreement, Ben continued:

"Three individuals, all sympathetic to the Islamic cause, somehow know one another, if not directly at least indirectly."

"Sorry, Sayyid Ben. I don't think 'know' is the right word. I think you must say 'are connected.' We are connected to one another. I certainly don't think I know Gamal's informer."

Ben conceded the point and continued with his logic:

"OK. One of them, the one you don't know yourself, is sufficiently trusted by the members of the group to be charged with placing the bomb. What does he do? He places the bomb in a place so that the damage is minimum. Do you follow so far?"

"I do, but I don't see where you're going. We've already established that it could be due to circumstances beyond his control."

"Wait a minute. I was the one who made up that excuse. Are there really guards that do rounds?"

"Oh yes, Sayyid. Given the time when the explosion took place, this might have coincided with their midday round, before they have lunch and rest a bit afterwards when the sun is at its highest . . ."

Ben had to concede the point, yet he added:

"Let me still finish; you'll see. How likely is it that the group of which Gamal's friend is a member would have failed to pick up that the fellow did not agree with all their policies?"

"Don't know. But, in Egypt today, I'm not surprised. You know, you surely would not let your feelings be known. You say too much, and you're simply killed. No trial, no defense; just a bullet and done!"

CHAPTER.03

DJOSER, EGYPT; AND TEL AVIV, ISRAEL

Still inside the Djoser pyramid complex, Ben decided to change tack. He asked Ayman:

"Tell me more about these two people."

Seeing that Ayman appeared to hesitate and seeking to clear out any confusion, Ben added:

"You know, Gamal and his friend. By the way, what's the friend's name?"

"I don't know his real name. Gamal referred to him as Mohamed Al-Shenawi."

Somehow, Ben's gambit seemed to work as Ayman opened up. He repeated what he had said earlier:

"I'm strongly tempted to believe Gamal."

Ayman continued, arguing that Gamal had been collaborating with him for a while. However, he conceded he could not say the same about Gamal's friend, Mohamed. Ben interrupted:

"Ever heard of him before yesterday?"

"No. But that doesn't mean a lot. In this business, you don't share the identity of your contacts. At best, you might mention their jobs or their connection to whatever you're discussing; you'd do that to establish their credibility. For all I know, he may have given me tips that came from Mohamed before. Back to my main point though. You don't use real names; you use code names. Question of personal safety; you understand?"

Ben nodded and asked:

"Forget about Gamal for a while and let's focus on Mohamed. By the way, why did Gamal give you his name? Isn't that strange given what you just said?"

"Excellent question. I hadn't thought of that. Let me think. I think it must have been the first time he ever did."

"So, why?"

"Well. I'm trying to make sense of it now . . . Maybe, he was flustered by my initial reaction . . . And let the name slip . . ."

"Flustered?"

"Yes, Sayyid Ben. Initially, I wasn't ready to travel to Djoser without a good reason. So, I pushed Gamal to give me increased details."

"So that's when he told you? Lack of self-control?"

"No, he did not reveal who his contact was then."

"So, when did he do it?"

"Still not sure. Wait a minute. It's coming back to me. He told me about Mohamed when I met him, and we were near the pyramid. It was then that he told me the whole story."

Ben's patience was being tested. He knew very well that he could not afford to lose his calm, yet Ayman's rationale was increasingly fishy. Ben said:

"Hold it right here, my friend. I'm totally confused."

Ayman looked as if he was going to interrupt, but Ben motioned with his hand that he was not through, adding:

"First, you think Gamal was flustered by your questions. Believable but surprising; you were not doing anything you shouldn't have done. Second, you tell me that Gamal told you about Mohamed after you had arrived. You were in Djoser; why would he still be flustered? Third, even if he were worried about some deadline then, after you had arrived in Djoser, why would the fellow's name make any difference to you then? Isn't it a code name? Something doesn't add up my friend."

"Maybe. But to me, at least, it makes the exchange less official, more like a tête-à-tête between acquaintances. In truth, it came out in the flow of his conversation. I was asking him why the fellow would be doing what he was talking of doing. That's when Gamal told me that he felt that Mohamed simply cracked when the threat was directed at treasures which he feels are a part of our country's history. The cat was out of the bag then."

Ayman paused and then asked:

"What do you think this means, Sayyid Ben?" Ben shook his head and simply said:

"I really don't know. I can't dismiss the thought that something doesn't compute. I don't know what though. I need to do more thinking. Let's regroup later, in Cairo."

With that, he left Ayman there and walked out of the Djoser site. A hundred yards away, he could see Meir and the car, ready to pick him up. Suddenly, he had a frightening thought: . . . *and what if this is not what it seems*?

I I ■ I I

"David, do you have a few minutes for me?"

Mark Levi, the man asking the question, was one of the closest associates of Colonel David Heller, the head of *Mossad's* Disruption Group. The group, probably the most secretive within an already very secretive organization, was in charge of activities which many would consider illegal. However, these activities still needed to be conducted in the interest of the state of Israel. They were thus considered within the spirit of Israel's Constitution: they included assassination of foreign leaders, sabotage of certain installations of which Israel did not approve, internet warfare and the like. His group did not appear on any organization chart—that anyone could procure. He reported directly to General Simon Rabinowitz, the overall head of *Mossad*.

"Sure, come on in. Make yourself comfortable on the sofa while I finish this email."

■ ■ ■ ■ ■

Mark had risen steadily through the ranks though probably faster than most would have expected. A jovial younger man in his late thirties, he had been involved in a number of missions, several of which proved to be critical to the safety of Israel. His rapid promotions were the direct result of his unusual abilities to see a situation, appreciate it, imagine the various possible outcomes, pick the best, and execute it. It was not that he had never made a mistake. More than once, he had found himself coming up short in his analyses; yet, he had been unusually quick at learning from his experiences. David Heller would readily say that one of Mark's strongest qualities was his ability to recognize a mistake and correct it. Rather than digging in and burying himself deeper and deeper when in error, he had made the famous quip his personal motto: "if in a hole, immediately stop digging."

■ ■ ■ ■ ■

Today, Mark was, as was his trademark, wearing well-tailored khaki pants with an open-neck white shirt which showed to anyone who would wish to look that he did not seem to carry much fat if any. He was of athletic build, though just short of six feet tall. He followed a rigorous regimen of exercise to make sure that he was always in tip-top shape. He would readily concede that he needed the exercise as his wife, Minoo, herself at one point a *Mossad* agent, was an exceptional cook. He had to find a way to eliminate the unnecessary but still delicious calories which she had prepared for him and their two sons, Cyrus and Simon.

"So, what's up?"

Mark smiled and told David that he had just had a very unusual encrypted videocall with "our man in Cairo."

"Benjamin Kaplan?"

"Himself."

"What was so unusual about it?"

Mark explained that Ben was reporting on an incident he had just witnessed. Mark gave David a condensed version of the meeting between Ben and Ayman Al-Khafaji, mentioning that this was the code name of a contact he had been cultivating and now managing for three years. He recounted that, as he had concluded the purely factual part of his report to Mark, Ben had paused and added:

"On a light note, Ayman told me that, when talking to his contacts, he referred to me as a journalist friend of his in Cairo."

David had to interrupt Mark and ask:

"Does this make any sense to you?"

Mark smiled even more broadly and replied after a short pause:

"Yes and no. Let me avoid being the three-handed economist as they say. Yet, I must give you the two sides of the story. On the one hand, I can believe the sequence of events Ayman described. I'll be the first one to accept that there are more than a few coincidences, but, after all, why not? They might be just that, coincidences. Egypt is one of the few places where Iran has surely not managed to gain traction. On the other, it could be a trap or, just as bad, a disinformation effort."

Without missing a beat, David interrupted:

"I think you answered my question. So, what's your recommendation?"

"Well, that's where I feel I need your help, because Ben is asking mine."

"Not sure I follow."

Mark realized he would need to expand on his thoughts to get David onboard. He started with the comment that Ben's initial thought had been to do nothing further:

"In short, he felt he needed to report but did not believe there was much to it."

David interrupted:

"Would agree with him at this time. But I'm sure there's more. Continue."

"That's exactly the point. The moment I asked him an innocuous question, he immediately started to waver."

"What was the question?"

"Simple. I asked him if he would continue to trust Ayman."

Mark paused and seeing David just breaking into a smile, he continued:

"Ben's problem is that he tends to believe Ayman. So, he really worries why someone is willing to be a traitor to an Islamic cause at a time when we surely need to get as much into these groups as we can."

"So far so good . . ."

"Agreed. There's more. He feels that he would fail Ayman, his contact Gamal, and even the fellow who seemed to have defected at the last minute, a certain Mohamed Al-Shenawi, if he, Ben, did nothing."

"Why?"

"I'm getting there. I can understand him. Assume that the incident was no trap, or at least not a trap intended for him. Then the whole thing becomes a great opportunity."

"I'm beginning to see it. Is that all?"

"One thing he added: what if this was a trap for Ayman or even Gamal. Can he let them hang?"

"So?"

Mark leaned forward for a second to grab a drink of the cup of cold coffee which had magically appeared on David's coffee table. He swallowed slowly and explained that his questions and Ben's, to give credit where credit was due, were simple, quoting from memory:

"Can we afford to ignore this? What if this is the first in a series? Will we be lucky enough the next time if there is a next one? Don't we have some debt of gratitude to our local contacts?"

David took his own time to respond. Smiling and looking Mark straight in the eyes, he asked:

"How busy are you currently?"

"As usual; nothing more, nothing less."

"So . . . you could spare a day or two?"

"Yes, I have a number of cases in train, but nothing which requires my personal and direct attention for the next 48 hours or so."

David replied that, in his view, the problem with this issue was probably either of two extremes. It could be something quite innocuous or it could be quite big. He added that, if the latter, this would require him to bring Simon into the loop, taking this even further with the affirmation:

"Simon may even need to take it to the War Cabinet."

He paused to check his logic and concluded:

"So, we don't want to go half-cocked, and we can't ignore something that could be a stroke of luck. After all, we had a bomb explode near a pyramid, and the oldest one in Egypt to boot, and we know someone who had received advance notice. Even more, we've been told of a possible relationship between the Taliban and the Muslim Brotherhood. That's something. Wonderful bait or serious development. We can't ignore it."

Mark told David that, to him at least, the last dimension was the decisive factor. Referring to the manifold activities of Iran against Israel and against the U.S., he could not afford to leave any stone unturned. He brought the meeting to a close:

"Thank you, sir. That tells me what to do. I won't make any major move without keeping you in the loop. In the meantime, I'm gonna fly to Egypt to talk to Ben face-to-face and try to find more."

"Don't hesitate to use one of our military jets. There's no non-stop commercial flight to Cairo. Our embassy in Egypt has entertained many visits from businessmen considering doing business there; many used private jets. One more won't surprise or make any difference to the authorities . . . If asked, you can be one of these businessmen visiting your Vice Consul."

■ ■ ■ ■ ■

Three years earlier, Ben was casually drinking a coffee at Beano's Café right behind the embassy, one of several outfits which the chain has in Cairo and other major cities in Egypt. He noticed that the person seated at the table next to his seemed to be seeking his attention. He turned to the gentleman and asked him if there was something he needed. The gentleman introduced himself as Ayman Al-Khafaji and asked:

"You work here, at the Israeli Embassy?"

Ben decided to provide the simplest, most honest answer, if only because the man could easily find out:

"I do. I am the Vice Consul."

"I need to talk to someone there."

"May I ask why?"

The man seemed to hesitate. Ben tried to calm him down with another simple question:

"Are you looking for a visa? A work permit?"

Ayman sat more upright, though he leaned a bit to his left to get closer to Benjamin when he said:

"I know a few things which I would like to share with someone who could protect me."

Ben did not reply right away as he was mulling the man's comment over. Then, he said:

"I don't think I could help you personally, but I may know someone who might."

Ayman smiled at Benjamin's reply, but somehow did not say anything further. Ostensibly, he was waiting for Benjamin to give him more information. Benjamin offered:

"Would you like me to introduce you to that person?"

Ayman nodded still saying nothing out loud. Benjamin was surprised but still did not want to waste an opportunity:

"When and how would you like to meet him?"

"Would it be safe for me?"

Benjamin wanted to remain positive, though he was starting to smell a rat. He was thinking: *does he simply want me to give him a name and then sell that name to someone else, maybe terrorists? Good ploy, but it will not work with me.* He decided to offer a fail-safe solution:

"What if I gave you a phone number? You could call him directly. He would not know who you are, so you would be safe. Simply tell him that the number was given to you by the Vice Consul."

"No name?"

"Not necessary. Plus, frankly, I don't deal with these matters myself. I have penty to do with my consular duties. So, my name carries less weight than my position."

Ayman smiled and said he would call soon. He added an innocuous comment in parting:

"To tell you the truth, the name I gave you is not my real name, but I assume this is OK, right?"

Ben was still a bit surprised. While it was not unusual at all for contacts to dissimulate their real names, it was certainly not common practice for them to give away that secret so early in the game. Yet, he decided to let that lie, at least for the time being, thinking: *I can always revisit the issue later. By the way, I'll ask Eli to check on that if he can.*

The conversation was over. Ayman, or whatever his name really was, had gotten what he was looking for. He thanked Ben with a smile, got up and walked away to the northeast in the direction of Mostafa Kamel Avenue. Ben eventually did the same, though he walked to the entrance of the embassy. Rather than going straight to his office, he stopped by the cubicle where Eli Goldberg worked. Sitting down on his visitor's chair, he briefed him. To say that both Eli and Ben were unconcerned that a phone call would ever come would be an understatement. Yet, this was not the first time someone had approached Ben, and his job was to make sure he could identify and cultivate any possible source.

■ ■ ■ ■ ■

Ben's personal experience with acquiring and managing information sources in the countries surrounding Israel had taught him that he should not miss any opportunity, but simultaneously should always remain on his guard. A large portion of the population of several Middle Eastern countries were poor, at times because their jobs did not pay well, and in other circumstances because they could not get a steady job. They were thus often looking to sell tidbits of information in exchange for money. That made for a large number of possible sources. At the same time, experience had also taught him that many of these sources were not terribly dependable to say the least. They were ready to sell the same information to several buyers if possible. He had therefore developed an approach which would allow him to proceed, gauge the credibility of the source, and yet never reveal his own real activity.

Tel Aviv had agreed to have a young *Mossad* agent posted in the embassy in a junior diplomatic position. Though everyone would clearly prefer that individual's real activity not be uncovered, there was a feeling that junior agents were easier to move and assign to other missions if ever necessary. Eli Goldberg was the individual currently working alongside Benjamin.

CHAPTER.04

TEL AVIV, ISRAEL; AND CAIRO, EGYPT

Mark's unmarked Israeli military jet landed safely at Sphinx International Airport, located about two hours' drive from Cairo's other airport, Matār El Qāhira El Dawli, best known as Cairo's international airport. It lies 18 miles northeast of the city of Cairo but is showing signs of excessive congestion. After all, it is the second busiest airport in Africa, after Johannesburg in South Africa. Though helping ease the congestion at the main airport, the recently opened Sphinx International Airport was designed to stimulate one-day tourist programs. It is within a few miles of many historical sites such as the Great Egyptian Museum of Giza and the Giza Pyramids area. Tourists could thus easily fly in early in the morning, visit the nearby sites during the day and fly out in the evening, though hotel or resort managers would prefer hosting them for at least a night.

Having been told by the pilot that he would be using the newer, smaller airport and that the airport shared the Giza Plateau with the major archeological sites, Mark had shifted seats in the business jet so that he was able to see the Giza Pyramids and the Sphinx on final approach. Though not totally new to him, he still found the sight exciting. After disembarking, Mark was able to meet Ben Kaplan at the foot of the plane's airstairs, in the area reserved for private jets. Ben was riding in an official embassy car, complete with the Israeli flag on the front right fender. He was the first to speak:

"Welcome."

"Many thanks. The contrast between the desert here and civilization a couple of miles to the east is striking."

Meir Herzog, Ben's driver, had stepped out of the car to take Mark's minimal luggage from the bottom of the jet's staircase. He placed it into the vast trunk of the S series Mercedes and then shut Mark's door on the right side. He let Ben walk around the car and shut his own door on the left. Continuing the conversation started at plane side, Ben replied to Mark's comment:

"You said it. But I might add: civilization and chaos. The new and the old cohabit, but at times it's hard to detect a plan that might have driven the expansion of the city."

He then turned immediately to the reason he had recommended the plane use this newer airport:

"It will allow you a more discrete entry into Egypt than the other airport and the ride to the embassy is only five miles longer. I should add that it should be a more pleasant and scenic ride."

Ben paused for a second and added:

"Just so you know, Meir, our driver is *Mossad* . . . Feel free to speak."

With absolutely no change in his facial expression, Mark simply said:

"Let me take the sights in. We will always have the time to debrief when we reach your office."

■ ■ ■ ■ ■

As they arrived at the embassy, Mark was surprised as Ben suggested:

"Let's first stop at Beano's Café. It's right here, at the embassy's back door. It must be one of the best coffees in Cairo."

Mark simply replied:

"Why not? Sounds interesting. Do you use them a lot?"

"Well, not a lot. We have excellent coffee machines here and they're our main choice whenever we want a cup. But Beano's is a chain throughout Cairo and in quite a few other towns in Egypt; it's a mini-institution here. It's good and quick and it'll give you local color. Plus, it's a way for me to mingle with fellow Cairo residents. That's how I met Ayman."

Coffees in hand, they walked inside the lobby of the embassy, took the elevator to the penultimate floor, and went straight to Ben's office. Ben joked:

"Believe it or not, the builders provided two elevators side by side. The embassy had to have a 'Shabat elevator'."

Mark knew very well that Shabat elevators are set so that, on Shabat, Saturday, the holy day of the week when the most observant Jews are not allowed to use electricity, they can still be used to go from one floor to another. The doors open automatically as the elevator travels from floor to floor up and down without anyone having to press any button.

Mark thought admiringly that though the building was modern, the architect and decorators had worked hard to make the whole thing discreet and as well integrated as possible in the style of the neighborhood. Ben simply remarked that they did not want to impress anyone, adding:

"As I'm sure you know, the relations with the local population are not always super friendly. We don't want to draw attention to ourselves. We'd rather get lost in the crowd."

"I guess the flag is a dead giveaway."

"The flag and the bronze plate. But we sure want to be good neighbors. One more reason to use Beano's occasionally, just like everyone else around here."

Ben's office was spacious, offering a separate sitting area on the far wall. He explained to Mark that his desk was located so snipers could not find a direct line to him if he were sitting there. Mark joked that he had heard that the offices of certain ministers in Jerusalem had been set up in a similar manner. Ben smiled and added:

"No better protection than bullet-proof windows though. With air-conditioning we don't need to open the windows when it's too hot and humid outside."

He then invited Mark to join him in the sitting area, choosing a side chair for himself, leaving the light orange sofa for Mark. Mark immediately started the conversation, going straight to the point:

"Ben, there are many inconsistencies or at least many odd coincidences in the story of the Djoser bomb."

Ben smiled and simply replied:

"You said it, my friend."

Ben then paused to take a sip from the still hot cappuccino he had ordered at Beano's. He readily conceded that the story had potential holes in it. Yet, he started with the observation that you could not reject it out of hand. There was a chance that it might be legitimate. Furthermore, he emphasized that the information about the Taliban which went with the warning about the first bomb was too big to ignore. He added that he had outlined two scenarios when discussing the issue with his contact, Ayman Al-Khafaji. Anxious to get to business, Mark interrupted:

"Let's hear them."

"Before I go there, I should add that there is a third scenario. So far, I've kept it to myself. We should discuss it when we're through with the first two."

Mark nodded his agreement and appeared to be as incredulous as Ben when they discussed the first scenario. It was based on the view offered by Ayman that the terrorists wanted to make a statement and yet made it sufficiently weak so that no irreversible damage occurred. Ben conceded that he understood Ayman's logic but felt that something was amiss. His main concern with that hypothesis was that terrorists do not usually go for half measures. They either act or stay low. Mark nodded his total agreement. They were thus ready to move to the second scenario when Ben offered a thought which he had developed since his conversation with Ayman:

"What if the real new thing here is the alliance with the Taliban?" Mark came right back:

"This was always part of my analysis. What do you mean by saying it might be an additional insight?"

Ben went on to explain that it had been more than 20 years since the Taliban had blown up the two Bamiyan Buddha statues and a dozen years since the Muslim Brotherhood had been out of government and banned as a political organization. The Taliban had a chance to see the world's reaction to its own attacks on anti-Islamic symbols as they saw them destroying the two statues of Buddha. Ben suggested that except for initial, quite vocal outrage, the world did not seem to be too fazed by the bombing, or at the very least ready to forget it as soon as it could. Yet he added:

"The Muslim Brotherhood eventually elected not to follow their plan to raise the height of the Giza plateau with tons and tons of sand to hide the pyramids. Now whether this is because they did not have the time or had doubts, nobody knows for sure. Let's assume they had doubts though they never totally forgot that idea."

Ben paused, seeing clearly that Mark was not getting on board. So, he added:

"I'm talking of the idea of getting rid of the archaeological heritage. That might explain their need for a weak test case to see reactions."

This surely did not seem to sway Mark too much. He agreed that there was some internal logic to the idea but could not get comfortable with it. Ben went further:

"Remember, their original plans, back in 2011 or so, were to bury the great Giza pyramid—a big thing since they would have had to deal with all three pyramids plus the sphinx. They were not ready to destroy. They just wanted to hide them. This time, they seem to have gone after a pyramid which may have more historical symbolic significance, not because it's the first, but one which is not visited often by tourists. Punching a hole in a chapel, hoping to create a hole in the enclosure wall as well, makes a statement, but the destruction is still limited."

He paused for a second and added:

"Grant you, it's no slam dunk, but I can see the logic. I'm sure you know what contradictions you see every day in the Arab world. We don't have to go there."

Mark simply replied:

"Point taken. Now, what about your second scenario?"

Ben understood that Mark, with his comment, had virtually buried the first scenario. He realized that he would have to be more convincing with the second, though, deep down, he was welcoming Mark's feedback: his experience was very useful, and he felt that he could learn a lot from his Tel Aviv colleague. Ben prefaced his statement with the comment that this second scenario had inconsistencies, too:

"That's the reason why I jumped to the third alternative."

Mark smiled and interjected:

"Because you think the first is totally logical. I thought we both agreed that it was, at best, plausible."

Ben smiled back, motioned with his right hand that they were in agreement and then turned to the second scenario. The key assumption there was that the individual who was to place the bomb so that there would be visible damage to the pyramid was suddenly afraid of the consequences. So, trying to avoid destroying Egypt's historic heritage, he decided to choose a different target than originally intended. Ben was careful to note that the scenario fully depended upon the conflicted nature of the mind of the terrorist that placed the bomb. Mark agreed that the conflict was feasible but wondered whether it was truly realistic:

"You're assuming that a fellow would support the Muslim Brotherhood's religious goals but object to its anti-archaeological bias. Correct?"

"To a point. I'm assuming that ideological or religious purity does not require him to blow up his own cultural heritage, though he still wants to be a part of the Muslim Brotherhood."

Mark noted that the fellow, Mohamed, would have to have been quite dumb not to have figured out earlier what the consequences of the bombing would be if he had stuck to the hypothetical original target. He added:

"By the way, I'm not familiar with the Djoser complex. Are there many other possible locations where you could drop a bomb?"

Ben replied that there was a mortuary temple right behind the pyramid and slightly west of its center. He suggested that a form of superstition or religious belief might have motivated the terrorists away from the burial chamber, arguing that the main mortuary chapel was the next best thing. He noted that this would not have brought the pyramid down but would have done real damage.

Mark raised an interesting point:

"By the way, let me throw a curve ball here: isn't the main issue not where the bomb was placed, but rather how big it was?"

Ben agreed replying:

"You're absolutely right. The real inconsistency is that you would have needed a much larger and thus heavier bomb to do serious damage. The key question though would have been how to bring it into the complex without being caught; the enclosure walls are 35 feet tall I'm told."

He surprised himself as he made his next point:

"That takes me back to the first scenario. The terrorists knew they had to use a smaller bomb. Both Djoser and other archaeological sites had real protection that made the use of a much larger explosive device not feasible. So, they first settled on a sort of test to ascertain what they could do. They wanted to see how much damage they could cause with explosives that could be manually carried and what the various reactions would be."

Mark conceded the point, arguing that in effect the two scenarios were but a variant on a single theme. He could see Ben nodding, but then argued that the real inconsistency was elsewhere. In his mind, it did not seem logical that the person picked for the mission would not have total, unquestionable loyalty.

Ben mentioned the excuse he had offered to Ayman that the terrorist might have changed the target within the complex because he was somehow interrupted. Mark agreed it was reasonable, but argued that it told him that the real hypothesis had to be that the terrorists were still in early planning stages:

"Whether you're thinking of a test to learn something or of an action that had to be changed at the last minute because of incomplete planning doesn't really matter. What does matter in my view is that we may well be looking at a very first step on the part of the terrorists. They were halfcocked; if the fellow was interrupted or somehow disturbed, it was simply because they had not done enough research."

Ben asked:

"What do you think of the idea of using only one person to carry out the bombing?"

"Again, I think it's consistent with the idea of a test. They're going to need much more extensive means if they want to do in Egypt what the Taliban did in Afghanistan. Think of the Valley of the Kings or

Abu Simbel. Both carved out of solid rock. Anybody that would want to destroy them would require missiles. I wouldn't think a bomb would be enough, even if it were large, hidden in a truck, and driven into the structure."

Mark saw Ben smile and then asked:

"Now, what is your third scenario?"

Ben simply said:

"What if this were a counterespionage operation?"

Mark's tone of voice went up at least 10 decibels:

"Counterespionage? By whom? The Egyptian secret services? Against whom? Us?"

Ben smiled and signaled to Mark not to worry. He explained that he did not believe this could be an official action by the Egyptian government, adding:

"Way too clumsy for them. I must tell you that the Egyptian secret service is staffed by professionals. If they do anything, they do it well."

He paused to look at Mark's reaction and then added:

"Yet, what if someone, somewhere within the Muslim Brotherhood had entertained a hunch?"

Mark jumped on the idea:

"Of what?"

"That there are leaks within their organization. Even worse; imagine that they've begun to ask themselves if they can fully trust all the members of their network. I don't want to polish our own image, but you know that we have had a couple of big successes in the recent past. A couple of cells which we managed to penetrate and then dismantle. What if they had concluded that *Mossad* had a base in the embassy and that they needed to root it out?"

"Perfectly valid assumption, I should add."

"Exactly. So, they would need to flush out whoever is leaking. How would they do it? Simple, they would plan a minor action with minimal risk to them and would allow a double agent to spread it."

Mark seemed to follow so far, though the concept of a double agent surprised him. Ben continued:

"I'm sure they have planted their people into a number of places. I know that we and many other secret services are quite careful, but it would be a miracle if no bad apple had slipped by."

Mark noticed the idea and asked:

"Are you thinking that you, or, more broadly, we might be one of these networks which they wanted to root out?"

"Doesn't have to be, but why not?"

"If that's the case, the Brotherhood would try and get you identified and be either eliminated or forced to leave Egypt in a hurry. OK, I see that, but there is a weakness in that scenario."

As Mark explained his objection, he noted that Ben was looking more directly at him. He thought, *did I strike a chord*? He went on and argued that it had to be almost common knowledge among both terrorists and the Egyptian establishment that one or several of Israel's diplomats were part of *Mossad*, adding:

"Name an embassy where we are not somehow represented."

Ben nodded and Mark continued his rationale. He argued that the idea of a sudden epiphany about a *Mossad* presence in Cairo did not make sense to him. Further, he maintained that, to him at least, the first priority of terrorists who suspect there are leaks within their group would be to unmask who the leaker or leakers were. He concluded that he would worry less about the risks to Ben than about the risks to any of his informers. Ben conceded:

"Agreed. So, the idea of a counterespionage operation may be sensible, but it would not be directed to the outside but to the inside, from the point of view of the Brotherhood. I should add that this could also be controlled remotely by a foreign influence; Iran anyone?

They might feel that they needed to test the waters before going full speed ahead."

Mark nodded as Ben concluded:

"We need to be careful both for ourselves and for our contacts. We don't want to jeopardize any of them."

CHAPTER.05

Before leaving Cairo, Mark and Ben had another in-depth discussion about the three informers.

Ben first focused on Ayman Al-Khafaji, which Mark considered a logical choice as Ayman was Ben's direct contact. Ben had said he had met him a few years ago in circumstances which might seem odd, as he was the one who approached Ben in the coffee shop at the back of the Embassy. Ben told Mark he had put him through the usual motions, all the while he kept telling Ayman that he had no interest in "special information" exchanged for money. He said that he told Ayman that he could not get involved because of the importance of his role as Vice Consul. He smiled as he finished the thought saying:

"I introduced him as is routine here to Eli Goldberg, as you know, a junior *Katsa*. Bottom line. He checked out very well and I eventually started to manage him. He does not know that I am the senior *Mossad* member here, but he now knows or at least strongly guesses that I have some connection to *Mossad*."

Ben paused for a second and concluded:

"As you know, this does not mean we may not have been mistaken in trusting him. Certain double agents are particularly good at their game. However, the fact that he has provided quite useful information and seems to have played everything straight so far would lead me to believe he is the least likely of the three to be a plant."

"I can buy that, though, like you, I'm always careful particularly when something odd happens. Yet, from what you're saying, I'm guessing that we should probably look elsewhere."

"That is what I've concluded, though my antennas remain up. My motto, borrowed from the late U.S. President Ronald Reagan, is 'trust but verify.' I am not about to forget that."

Mark conceded that Ben's approach looked quite reasonable, He suggested that they could always come back to Ayman and naturally next asked where the loose end might be. Ben replied:

"I assume that by 'loose end' you are referring to the other two men in the loop in this case, and not to weaknesses concerning Ayman."

"Quite right."

Turning first to Ayman's informer, Gamal Al-Sahid, Mark conceded that he had never met him, and, more importantly, had never heard Ayman make mention of him before. He paused for a few seconds and reasoned that there were many people whom Ayman knew and probably used and whom he had never discussed with Ben. He deadpanned:

"He has his informer network, just like we all have ours. The thing that is unusual here, in Egypt, is that it looks as if everyone uses code names. So, in the end, I will be darned if we know half of what we should."

Returning briefly to the Ayman case, Mark looked surprised as he asked:

"You still don't know Ayman's real name?"

"Well. Officially, I do not. But in reality, I do. I don't know if I would have kept going along with him unless I could be sure that I knew who he was."

He paused and added that his colleague, Eli, had been able to find out his real name was Khaled Al-Moghrabi.

"How did he find out?"

"Simple, one day when I was meeting Ayman near the Botanical Garden, Eli and a couple of operatives followed us, and, after I left, trailed him home. He lives in a rowhouse where the ground floor has a souvenir shop and family space at the back—perhaps a kitchen. Upstairs is where the family lives. He appears to have a wife and two sons."

Mark nodded his approval, though as he always thought of all the angles that should be considered, he added:

"Are you comfortable that he did not pick up the tails?"

Ben smiled and simply replied:

"That was not the first time we had tried to track him down. He picked up a classic tail involving two people a couple of times, though I am confident he could not be sure they were *Mossad*. We finally got him when we went to three agents and used highly sophisticated tools, including an arial drone controlled by one of the agents."

Mark smiled back and deadpanned:

"Great training, I see. Will you still be able to investigate him further?"

"Absolutely. Ayman knows that I smelled a rat and that I need to know more. I suspect that I will use Eli Goldberg for that, as I surely don't want to come out in the open. I may, in fact, need to use another *Katsa* as Ayman now knows Eli."

"Makes sense. Now I know we were initially going to talk of Gamal, but I would like to turn first to Mohamed, the guy who we're told warned Gamal and placed the bomb where the damage was not so large."

Ben immediately conceded that he was the most likely loose end if there was one. There were in his view several reasons that would support the case against him. The most critical issue was the inconsistency between the idea that he would be senior or respected enough within his Brotherhood cell to be given the responsibility to place the bomb and the fact that he would actually be a traitor, adding:

"I have never been inside any similar organization, but everything I read or have otherwise learned tells me that they keep spying on one another. They play their cards super close to the vest. How could he have managed to escape their attention?"

Mark agreed that the question was valid, though he offered what one might call the devil's advocate's view:

"What if Mohamed had been somewhat uncomfortable with a move toward more violence, though he might still support anything which would not have human casualties? What if he had further been prepared to condone a bombing campaign if its purpose and scope were to create unease and public unrest all the while avoiding human casualties?"

He paused and quite seriously added:

"I won't tell you anything you don't know when I say that we have agents in a number of terrorist organizations around the world. A few have been caught and a couple at least were hung for their crimes in Iran, for instance."

Ben noted the real sadness in Mark's face as he finished his sentence. He replied to Mark that he could surely see the point and commiserated with the implications when things did not turn out the way they were supposed to. He added, knowing the Taliban connection could not fail to have raised more serious concerns in his mind, concluding with a smile:

"These guys are not known to be gentle. Plus, they worry less about human casualties and more about destroying their targets."

Mark smiled back and replied:

"That has got to be the understatement of the century given what has been reported in the press and what we know from our own sources. But you could imagine that Mohamed stayed put because his fear of the consequences of quitting the group was greater than his concerns about the next few steps. Am I making sense?"

Ben nodded all the while simply saying that the scenario made sense but raised serious questions as to Mohamed's reliability, adding:

"Not sure what it says about Gamal having such a fellow as an informer."

Mark seemed in full agreement and asked:

"Exactly. Now, how about Gamal?"

Ben replied that it was a longer story, though he conceded that, as he went through it in preparation for his meeting Mark, he realized that he did not know as much as he would like. Rhetorically he added with a wink of his eye:

"But, then again, isn't that always the case when you talk of the network of one of your contacts?"

Mark smiled and added:

"For a start you probably don't know his real name."

"Right on. Quite possible, but who knows?"

Ben started with the observation that Ayman said he was vouching for him. Yet, he conceded that he, Ben, had not conducted any detailed investigation of Gamal, if only because he had not even known his name until very recently, adding:

"The same circumstances that led Ayman to learn the identity of Mohamed."

Mark asked Ben what he knew:

"As of now, very little, other than the fact that officially he is a tour guide specialized in pharaonic monuments. I've asked Eli Goldberg to find out whatever he could, all the while remaining very discreet. Remember, Ayman tells me that Gamal is not his real name.

Thankfully, he seems to operate in the Cairo area. We are going to try and use the same trick as with Ayman, though the problem is we have no warning when he and Ayman are about to meet."

Ben paused to see if his initial comment raised any question in Mark's mind. Hearing none, he kept going, making the point that Gamal, if he were the loose end, would be the biggest challenge, as he was the one who knew Ayman and was therefore, at most, one person removed from *Mossad*. Mark asked:

"Have you thought of what his purpose might be if he was indeed a double agent?"

"Well, the obvious one would be to flush out our activity in Egypt. But it begs the question: how would he even know that Ayman had a *Mossad* contact?"

"Totally agree. As we discussed earlier, what's so special about there being a *Mossad* representative in the local Israeli diplomatic corps?"

Mark paused and then surprised Ben with his next question:

"But then would it not mean that Ayman might also somehow not be playing it straight?"

Ben had to concede:

"Hate to tell you that, but the thought did cross my mind. We're on the same wavelength, Mark."

Making a gesture with his hands indicating that they had run out of answers, he added:

"We are going around in circles. That's got to be because we simply don't know enough. As I just said, we've run out of answers but not of questions."

Turning to the vetting of his contact, Ben argued that the *Mossad* protocol represented the state of their art. He conceded that it was not a guarantee against any mistake, though at this point he said he could not see what else he could have done with respect to Ayman, adding:

"I feel that we have been as diligent vetting Ayman as we could have been. So, until proven otherwise, I think I'm back to my initial position: I trust him, but, again, I'm still partially undercover. As for Gamal, I don't know, and I think I need Ayman's help."

▮▮ ▬ ▮▮

On his return to Tel Aviv, Mark sat down with David Heller to fill in his report. He shared the contents of his conversation with Ben about the three informers and then said:

"There are at least three different threads that warranted a deeper analysis, and I think Israel would need to dedicate resources to investigate the incident which Benjamin Kaplan brought to light. However, I must warn you that here more than other places, the devil is gonna be in the detail."

First, there was an absolute need to evaluate whether there was indeed any budding relationship between the Taliban and the Muslim Brotherhood. Coming up with details would be quite challenging, but there were ways and several places where information could be gleaned. Second, in their conversations in Cairo, Ben and Mark had not been able to get to the bottom of what had to be a crucial question: was Mohamed for real or not? Third, if he were not for real, the next question was even more important: what were he and the Muslim Brotherhood up to? Would it have been a trap?

Mark added a final point:

"Whatever we do, and here by 'we' I mean *Mossad* in the largest dimension, we must make absolutely sure that there is no way any finger can point to us. Nothing that we do must risk revealing Ben's real job. I should add that until proven otherwise, we must also protect Ayman."

David immediately agreed, though he added:

"No problem from 30,000 feet up. However, can you clarify what you mean by 'the devil is often in the details'?"

"Sure. We must first make sure that Ben and Ayman are well protected. Any investigation which we elect to conduct should involve resources we bring into Egypt and should not be linked to the Embassy."

David came right back:

"Understood, my friend. But why spend resources on this?"

Mark took a good 30 seconds to begin his reply. It did not surprise David, as he knew that Mark was very thoughtful and always wanted to check his logic from multiple angles before replying. When he finally spoke, Mark argued that the entry of the Taliban into Egyptian politics, if proven, would be a game changer, though out of caution he added:

"I don't mean that the game would be totally different. I mean that the game would become more complex and require a response. That response could range from action on our part to simply finding a way to warn the Egyptian secret services. I recall that Countess Renate surely has a way to do that through the head of security in Saudi Arabia"[1]

∎ ∎ ∎ ∎ ∎

Countess Renate was the founder and head of The Shadow Experts.[2] That network was as secret as its leader. It consisted of specialists across a wide variety of disciplines who cooperated with and were directed by Countess Renate to defend "good causes." They ranged from micro-biologists to advanced material engineers, to art experts, to cyber engineers, to electronics gurus, and to other specialties, each as esoteric as the others. All associates knew they were members of the network, but most did not know who the other members were, other than those people with whom they had worked

---

[1] See *Crypto Trap*, by the same author, Barringer Publishing, 2022.
[2] See *The Shadow Experts*, by the same author, Barringer Publishing, 2021.

on one or another assignment. They all knew Renate; most, if not all, had seen her in person or on various video conference calls. Yet, no one could claim that he or she had met with her regularly. These specialists were all "part-time associates" who punctually came into a team to solve a problem and returned to the shadows when they were no longer needed. Besides the honor of being a member of the network, they were all generously rewarded when they participated in a project.

Renate had no board of directors. Her only employees were a handful of individuals who worked for her at the Castle, her residence in the Austrian alps. The castle had a completely hidden lair which allowed Renate to remain linked to everyone without anyone giving away where she was. She even had a corporate jet which had been modified to include vertical take-off and landing capability and could thus be hidden underground. She could leave or return to the castle without anyone seeing how she had flown in or out, as the castle grounds did not include any visible runway. The handful of employees were the only ones who knew of her twin identities—her real name was Princess Alexandra, a wealthy orphan and distant heir to the Habsburg imperial crown. Her husband, Prince Karl, of Danish royal blood, also had a twin identity as he morphed into Captain Frederik, her pilot and all-around aide when she became Countess Renate.

■ ■ ■ ■ ■

David asked point-blank:

"When you say a game changer, you're thinking of Iran getting more and more involved in regional politics, right?"

"Absolutely, sir. You don't miss much, do you?"

He expanded on the thought arguing that Israel already knew that Iran had direct and indirect control over various militias in the region: the Palestinians, whether they be related to Hamas or Hezbollah, the Houthis in Yemen, various organizations in Syria and

Iraq, or possibly a rebirth of ISIS. He then pointed to the increasing Iranian saber rattling and evidence that Iran seemed ever closer to nuclear capabilities. His last point was the probability that Iran had fingers in other places spread throughout Africa and even the Indian sub-continent, and that Iran had cooperation agreements with China and Russia. He concluded:

"The deeper we get, the more any change becomes critical, even though we currently are facing off with Hamas and, there, Iran is no longer in the shadows. We have declared war after their horrendous attack on the Holit Kibbutz among others."

He paused to check himself, quickly adding:

"There is still more. We must assume that there are groups which operate within the supposedly stable Arab kingdoms. A few of these stable kingdoms were, in fact, in negotiations with us for a more visible relationship. They are now hesitating. For instance, what about Qatar: they are supposed to be friendly, but they accept that the leadership of Hamas lives officially in Doha, the capital of the Emirate."

Mark took a deep breath and concluded:

"The real issue is that Iran allowing, and in fact maybe promoting, the entry of the Taliban into Egyptian politics would indicate both a greater willingness to broaden the conflicts and the risk that more extremist positions will be considered. The geopolitical implications of that would be even greater than localized trouble in Egypt. The death of a thousand cuts . . . For a start, you could place it in the context of the Israeli-Palestinian conflict: Egypt is known not to welcome Palestinian refugees. Iran cannot possibly like that."

"I see what you mean. Let me take this up with Simon, particularly if we are going to use The Shadow Experts. I want to get his read before moving further, but my gut tells me you're correct."

CHAPTER.06

TEL AVIV, ISRAEL; CAIRO, EGYPT; AND SOMEWHERE IN THE AUSTRIAN ALPS

Simon was all smiles when David and Mark walked into his office. He had a particular relationship with David Heller. David had been his second-in-command until Simon had succeeded the legendary General Ariel Landau, formerly the Head of *Mossad*, who had retired to spend more time with his wife. Unfortunately, she died before he had the time to retire, but this allowed him to groom Simon and for Simon to groom David for another couple of years before the transition finally took place.

It was late in the afternoon when the three men got together. Instead of the usual coffee or tea, Simon naturally offered what he liked to call "an adult beverage." David was happy to share a single malt scotch with his mentor, but Mark preferred to stick to sparkling water, arguing:

"I don't want to break my promise to Minoo that I will never have more than one drink before dinner. And she expects us to have one together."

Mark could afford to speak so openly of his wife before David and Simon as she had once been a *Mossad* agent[3] and had worked quite closely with Simon.

Simon asked:

"So, gentlemen, what can I do for you? David gave me a 30,000-foot review as he called it, and I must say I found this quite interesting. More than that really: intriguing and worrisome."

David invited Mark to take Simon through the general outline of the case, suggesting in the end that, in an ideal world, he would probably have chosen to wait before bringing this up to Simon so early in the process.

"Don't tell me that Mark forced your hand, David. I know both of you and I wouldn't believe it."

David and Mark responded with a smile to Simon's own as he made the remark. Mark conceded that the issue in his mind was still quite confused. Yet, the deciding factor that pushed him to bring David into the loop was that they had uncovered something which might be important for the *Mukhabarat*, Egypt's General Intelligence Service, or GIS as it is often called. Both David and Mark concluded that they could not afford to wait; they needed to act. Simon replied: "Let me guess. You think we should ask Countess Renate to open that communication line for us?"

"Bingo."

Having said that, David paused and added the obvious next question:

"By the way, don't you have a direct line with Saudi Arabia's chief of security?"

Simon had a quick laugh and replied:

"Yes and no. I can certainly call Abdul Al-Wahabi, Saudi Arabia's chief of security, directly. We have worked together several times. In

---

[3] By the same author, see *Operation Kovesh*, Barringer Publishing 2020.

fact, he once told me that he owed me a big debt of gratitude. On the other hand, though I suspect I've met the head of *Mukhabarat* at some point, I cannot remember when or in what circumstances. So, I think an introduction would be needed for the two of us to chat. Abdul Al-Wahabi or Countess Renate would be the best for that. But what am I to tell him?"

David took over from Mark for a few minutes. He wanted to make the point that the only thing that could be done now was to offer a warning. He articulated his rationale quite simply:

"We know that a bomb had exploded. We know that our contact knew about it before it blew up, though he was not able to convey the warning before it was too late."

He paused and added:

"We know that Egyptian police investigated. We know the way the news hit the papers was, at best, sanitized. For instance, in the local press, the bombing was described as a minor snafu. That must mean that just after the incident or at least after the police reported it, the Egyptian government, and the head of the *Mukhabarat* must have been made aware."

Simon smiled and motioned to David to continue as he surely could not doubt any of his logical steps so far. David went on:

"The real key is this: there is one element the Egyptian authorities might not know—the alleged connection between the Muslim Brotherhood and the Taliban."

Very much in character, Simon asked:

"Are we really sure of that?"

Mark preempted David and simply replied:

"What do you mean, Simon? Are we sure of the fact that there is a connection or are we sure that Egyptian authorities do not know of the connection?"

Laconically, Simon fired straight back: "The former."

Mark replied that the only element which was incontrovertible was that a contact had told an informer that there was a connection. Additionally, the same contact's warning about the bombing proved to be correct, both in terms of location and timing. He cautiously added:

"Note that there is still no certainty here. For instance, I could build a case which says the reference to the Taliban was meant by our informer's contact to wet our informer's appetite. In short, we have absolutely no proof of anything; just a number of indices, but enough smoke that someone ought to be looking for the fire."

He paused again to check his logic and then said:

"However, there is the fact that this is the first bombing aimed at an archaeological site in a long time. Even if you go back 10 to 15 years, the targets were tourists, not the sites themselves for all we know. Remember Dayr al-Bahri, the archaeological site located across the Nile from the city of Luxor, six shooters killed 58 foreign nationals and four Egyptians in November 1997. Same purpose in terms of hurting the country, but no damage to the country's touristic assets. So, at this point, we cannot say any more. In fact, if Benjamin Kaplan's third scenario were to be the correct one, you could easily argue that this might have been something to get us more interested in what otherwise might just be a minor event."

David added:

"Totally agree. Yet, we do not know what scenario to believe as of now. That's why I think we should share the information with the Egyptians, as a gesture of good will, all the while providing all the necessary caveats."

Simon asked:

"OK. Now, if you were me, what would you do . . .go directly to Abdul Al-Wahabi or ask Countess Renate to make the contact?"

David was going to reply first, but he took his time to reflect. Simon knew David well enough to be fully aware of the fact that

David was an excellent chess player; as such, his thoughtfulness required him to think everything through. Simon quietly waited for David to be ready, until he eventually said:

"If I were the one making the call, I would go through Countess Renate."

Simon was smiling, encouraging him with his smile and body language to continue his thoughts. David argued that he saw at least three reasons for his recommendation. The first was that she might or might not need to disclose that the party she 'represented' was *Mossad*, adding:

"Abdul Al-Wahabi would know that you head up *Mossad*. So, Countess Renate may offer a screen for us. There will always be time later for us to come out in the open as and when appropriate."

Returning to his rationale, David reasoned that Countess Renate might or might not have her own direct connection to the head of the *Mukhabarat*. He added:

"Why go through a third party, if she already has a direct line?" David's third reason was that it had to be easier for her to retain a measure of objectivity concerning the credibility of the sources of information on which *Mossad* relied.

Simon smiled and simply said:

"Wow. You've gotten me used to complete answers, but this one takes the prize. You've won, my friend. Glad we are both on the same team."

Turning to Mark for a second, Simon added:

"I do not mean to forget your role here, Mark. But let me assure you that you are in excellent hands with David as your boss and mentor!"

David nodded with a wide smile and asked:

"Will you take this to the Prime Minister? Do you need us to prepare anything for you?"

"I will probably speak to the Prime Minister and to Moshe and Eli."

■ ■ ■ ■ ■

Simon was referring to Moshe Shamir, the foreign minister, and Eli Spielberg, the defense minister.

Less than a week later, Countess Renate was back on a video-conference call with David and Mark. Her tone of voice immediately told the *Mossad* officers that she was happy with the result of her endeavor:

"Gentlemen, I have decent news to report."

■ ■ ■ ■ ■

Countess Renate had first called her former client and by then reasonably close acquaintance Abdul Al-Wahabi, Saudi Arabia's head of security, to ask for an introduction. She had taken the liberty to give him a short briefing, as agreed between her, Simon, and David:

"Abdul, thanks for taking my call."

"Countess, you know you are a friend, both of mine and, more importantly, of the Kingdom."

"Much too nice, Abdul. I pride myself on trying to help worthy causes and, as you know, I've always found you on the side of good causes."

Countess Renate knew Abdul well enough to know that he had an iron fist in a velvet glove. She knew that he would help her if she could show she was definitely on the right side of an issue from Saudi Arabia's point of view. However, she also knew that he was totally loyal to the Crown Prince and did not like wasting his time. So, she simply said:

"Let me give it to you straight: I need to contact the Head of the *Mukhabarat*. Is there a way you can help me?"

"Menes Al-Soliman?"

"Is that his name?"

"Yes. I know him well, though we do not work terribly closely together. The security problems which Egypt faces are generally somewhat different from those of the Kingdom."

He paused for a second and corrected himself:

"Except that Iran is often behind the problems, Egypt's and ours. Tell me, why do you need to talk to him?"

Countess Renate explained that, as Abdul well knew, she had to keep many things quite close to the vest. Abdul interrupted:

"I know. I have come to accept that this is probably why you're successful."

Seemingly veering off topic, while still very much focused on the question, he asked matter-of-factly:

"Anyway, can you tell me if your Israeli friends are involved?"

"Unfortunately, my friend, I cannot. I'm pretty sure that they are now or will soon be somewhere in the loop, but I am calling on my own."

"I thought you would say something like that. Let me go back to my earlier question if I may: can you tell me anything about why you need to talk to Menes?"

Adbul could hear a short laugh at the end of the line. The countess then proceeded to tell him that someone she knew had heard a rumor which they believed was profoundly serious if true. Abdul asked:

"Why now? Why not wait until it's more than a rumor?"

"That's the real problem, my friend."

She explained that the issue could be so important that her contact felt they had to warn Egypt now, all the while conceding that the rumor might be false. Turning to the rumor itself, she argued that it had been presented as a fact to someone who reported it to her contact. Further, that someone had indicated that a bomb would be placed near a pyramid. She completed her logical explanation:

"And a bomb did explode in the complex surrounding the step pyramid of Djoser. I've got to admit that I'm told the damage was not as significant as one might have expected. However, there is one thing for sure. The source mentioned a couple of items: the rumor and an advance warning of the bombing. One was unquestionably true. Shouldn't we take the second one—the rumor—seriously?"

"Interesting. Actually, I had not heard any of that. Wonder why the Egyptians kept it out of the papers. Are you sure a bomb exploded there?"

"Positive. My source showed me pictures of the damage. As I said, nothing huge. The pyramid is unscathed, but there was damage to another structure within the complex. So, as I just said, the rumor of the bomb panned out."

"So, if I understand your point, you're saying that your contact received two tips, one of which definitively proved right. For the other, it must remain at the rumor stage, but your source is inclined to believe it."

"Yes and no. Let us say that my source believes that the warning should be passed on."

"What's the rumor?"

"Believe it or not, my source heard that the Taliban is working with some branch of the Muslim Brotherhood."

Abdul interrupted with a higher than usual tone of voice:

"The Taliban?"

"Absolutely. That's what makes this serious."

She paused and concluded:

"And the place where the bomb was placed reminded everyone of the Taliban's bombing of the Bamiyan Buddhas in Afghanistan in 2001."

Abdul's demeanor and voice tone had changed radically. He said he understood the decision made by Countess Renate's contact and would be happy to introduce Menes Al-Soliman. He added:

"I'm sure that this is top secret. May I mention it to the Crown Prince?"

"Please don't. We do not want to disturb him with what might be a false rumor. Yet, I guess that at some point, we'll find out whether it is founded or not. Then I guess it is your prerogative to keep him fully informed."

"I see. But even if I'm the only one knowing, I'm sure you will not mind if I do a bit of digging, particularly on whether there has been any trace of Taliban infiltration in Saudi Arabia. Iran is not our best friend, you know?"

Countess Renate simply replied:

"Be my guest."

"Let me do one more thing, Countess. At the risk of stealing your thunder, would you mind if I first called Menes to introduce you and tell him that you shared a rumor with me, and that I was the one who recommended you call him?"

"No problem, but I would prefer if you did not share what the rumor is."

"Goes without saying."

CHAPTER.07

The next day, Countess Renate received an email message from Abdul Al-Wahabi with a copy to Menes Al-Soliman. It was confirmation that Menes would call her later that afternoon at 4 o'clock Cairo time. The message, also being read by Menes, added that Abdul had total confidence in the countess and her network.

At the agreed time, her cell phone rang. She knew, but Menes did not, that the call had ricocheted across a number of different lines to make the call untraceable. She picked it up and said:

"Menes Al-Soliman, I presume . . ."

"Quite right, Countess Renate. My friend, Abdul Al-Wahabi told me that you needed to talk to me. In fact, he mentioned that you had information that I should hear."

Countess Renate quickly responded that she was delighted to talk to Menes, though she did not want to overemphasize the importance of the information she had received from a client. She cautioned that she and her client had only one real data point, which would be considered quite insufficient in normal circumstances. Yet, given the nature of the rumor, she felt that it would be better to have transmitted the information even if it turned out to be wrong than to have sat on it and it turned out to be right. Menes thanked her and agreed with her analysis. He added that, if the rumor proved to be true, he hoped that he would have an opportunity to thank her client in person. Countess Renate politely replied with a charming smile, which Menes could obviously not see since they were not on a videoconference phone:

"I would hope so, but certain clients of ours are quite secretive. But why don't we cross that bridge when we get there?"

She then simply said:

"Let me tell you the rumor. After all, that is the point of this call, right?"

She did not let Menes reply to her rhetorical questions and went on:

"A client of mine heard from an informer in Egypt that there had been some form of a cooperation agreement between the Muslim Brotherhood and the Taliban."

Menes interrupted:

"That is incredible. We have not heard of that on our end. What makes you believe that it is something more than loose talk?"

"Well, my client also heard from the same source, and at the same time, that a bomb was going to be placed . . ."

"In the Djoser pyramid complex?"

"Exactly. And very importantly, my client was subsequently able to verify that a bomb did explode there, although I was told that the damage was not significant."

Menes audibly breathed in and simply said:

"And you know that this is exactly what happened, don't you?"

Countess Renate said that she had not been able to verify the damage herself. She did not think there was any need to mention the photos which Ben had been able to take with his "special *Mossad* glasses" and transmitted to Tel Aviv. She did say, however, that she understood the prediction her client had heard was indeed correct.

She added that her client was hesitant initially for her to take the news further. She explained:

"He said that there was something in the series of events that did not compute."

Menes asked what that was, and Countess Renate quickly replied: "While attacking some historical, non-Islamic archeological treasure fits with Taliban practices, my client saw at least two issues. The first is that the Muslim Brotherhood had talked back in 2011 or so of burying the great pyramids in sand to hide them as they were unislamic, but never carried the idea out. The second, which is even more important, is that the damage caused by the recent bombing was minimal."

"I'll grant you that. Frankly, I tend to think this may in fact be a false alarm, too."

Countess Renate felt she could mention the logic which Ben had initially suggested to Ayman, without providing any attribution.

"What if the terrorist had somehow been disturbed and was forced to drop his bomb in a different location than originally planned?"

Countess Renate was surprised to hear Menes agree that this could happen as he said:

"Particularly at the time at which the bomb exploded! That would suggest the bomb had been dropped around the time the guards made their last round before lunch and take a one-hour rest after that."

Yet, he noted that even if placed in the most sensitive spot within the complex, a bomb of that size would not have done real material damage. He concluded:

"Frankly, I agree with you and your client. That there was a bomb is not debatable. That it did damage is not debatable either. However, it makes little sense to go through the trouble and the risk of placing a bomb if it's going to be as weak as this one was. Something indeed does not compute. I wonder what we are missing."

He paused for a few seconds pondering his last statement and quickly added:

"But I still thank you and my friend Abdul Al-Wahabi. I very much appreciate your call. I would rather have 10 indices which do not produce actual results rather than miss one that proves to be very important."

Countess apologized for having disturbed Menes for such a minor matter and was going to continue when he interrupted her:

"From what Abdul tells me, you have surely contributed a lot to his work in Saudi Arabia. I will not ignore your warning, and I owe you a debt of thanks."

He paused and then asked:

"Can you give me any lead as to the identity of your client?"

The countess replied that she could not, though she was willing to commit that she would reach out to Menes if she heard anything more on the topic, adding:

"In due course, I would not be surprised if you got to meet my client."

∎ ∎ ∎ ∎ ∎

Having heard Countess Renate's report from her conversations with Menes Al-Soliman, David asked:

"Were you surprised by his reaction?"

"A bit. He was so polite and calm. That bit I fully expected. The thing that surprised me, though, is that he seemed almost nonplussed. A bit as if nothing important had been discussed."

"That could be what we might call the 'Al-Wahabi' effect."

"Indeed. Menes seemed so reasonable."

David asked:

"Did you discuss our idea that this might have been a test?"

"I did. I did. He made me take him through the whole logic. Interestingly, he seemed more convinced by the hypothesis the bomb was not intended to be placed where it eventually was. To him, even as small a bomb as this one would have done much more damage if it had been placed in the mortuary temple. He argued more archaeological work had been done and therefore the damage would have been more significant. He said that there were places within the whole structure that were weaker than others."

Mark asked:

"So, where did you leave it?"

"In short, he thanked me for the tip, as he called it. He told me he believed he had things under control yet asked me to reach back to him if I heard anything new."

She paused and both *Mossad* officers could see her waving her hand in front of her face as she concluded:

"To me, you have done what you could and so have I. I suspect he will not go any further, but in risk management terms, you've definitely done your duty and could not be accused of anything if there were further developments."

■ ■ ■ ■ ■

Though he wanted to call Ben, Ayman had decided he needed to have a conversation with his informer, Gamal Al-Sahid, first. They agreed to get together near the Cairo Tower, a concrete tower inspired by lotus flowers. It was made up of eight million mosaic lozenges and had long been the tallest structure in Cairo and even in Africa. It was one of Cairo's best-known modern monuments, sometimes considered second only in popularity behind the Great Pyramid of Giza. Interestingly, a local Islamic group issued a *fatwa* against it in the 1990s, vowing to destroy it because it could be perceived as a phallic symbol. It was located on man-made Gezira Island, in the Zamalek part of town. The area was home to cultural powerhouses, both official and private. Ayman wanted to talk to Gamal about the points which Ben had raised when, still in the Djoser pyramid complex.

He had pointed out to Ayman a few inconsistencies in the story of the bombing. Gamal was surprised by Ayman's line of questioning, and he replied with a trace of anger in his voice:

"Wait a minute, Ammon. There was a bomb, right? So, what's the problem?"

Ayman, aka Ammon, calmly explained to Gamal that the issue did not relate to the bomb itself. Yet, he reminded Gamal that his "tip" had comprised two crucial elements. The first had to do with the imminent bombing of the Djoser Pyramid. The second talked of the possible alliance between the Muslim Brotherhood and the Taliban. Gamal was furiously nodding as if to say, "So what?" Ayman did not allow his friend's reaction to detract him from his train of thought, asking:

"Two questions. First, why would they place the bomb in a place where the damage was about as little as could be anywhere within the complex?"

Gamal seemed to want to reply, but Ayman motioned with a wave his right hand that he was not through as he posed the second half of his question:

"Further, given the limited amount of damage, the bomb had to be quite small. What were they trying to achieve?"

After hearing the second half of the question, Gamal's urge to reply appeared to fade. Rather than blurting out his answer, he pondered the twin questions for a short while and replied:

"You know, Ammon, these are excellent questions. I've asked them myself."

Ayman interrupted despite Gamal's hand signal that he was not through and asked:

"You talked to Mohamed?"

"No. No, I have not. I mean, I've been asking myself these questions. The only reasonable explanation I could produce was that this was either a signal or a test."

"Hold it. I've thought about that. How could it be a signal if they did not leave any trace of who was behind the bombing, take any credit for it, or make any threat of further action?"

"I know. That's the problem. One question I'm asking myself is whether my friend, Mohamed, is truly with us."

He paused long enough for Ayman to ask:

"What do you mean?"

"Well, what if he was still totally dedicated to the Brotherhood cause? What if his warning me was their way of letting the world know this was a Muslim Brotherhood act, though it was conveniently too late for me to do anything to prevent it I should add?"

Ayman looked like he was thinking for a minute or so and then replied:

"Interesting hypothesis. Telling you ahead of time but still too late was their way of taking credit for it."

He paused for a second and continued:

"However, why do you say you could not have done anything? Instead of calling me, couldn't you have called the authorities? Warned security people at the complex?"

"I've thought about that. First, why would anyone believe me? Second, how would I get to anyone. I live in Cairo, remember? I have no contact with the people that watch over the Djoser complex."

Ayman seemed only marginally moved by Gamal's reply. Still, he kept silent to see what Gamal would say next. Gamal's next point was, by contrast, totally believable:

"Remember that I am not out of the Brotherhood. I'm on record being in favor of focusing on Islam rather than political goals. Yet, my going directly against the Brotherhood would have made me a sitting duck. I was painting a target on the back of my *djellaba!*"

Ayman's face displayed both concern and the onset of a smile as he was wondering how one could paint a target on the back of one's *djellaba*. Typically, a loose cloak with a hood, a *djellaba* has a hood at the back when it is not worn on the head: the target would have to be low enough not to be partially obscured by the hood. Setting that thought aside, he still said:

"OK. I get that. But there is something I still don't know and worry about. Does Mohamed know about me?"

"No. Not about you. Not about anybody else. Yet, he knows that besides my main tourist business, I have contacts who are willing to give me money for the odd tip. So, he must have assumed that this was big enough news that I would pass it on. Whoever got my message would not be able to act fast enough to prevent the explosion. In other words, they would achieve their goal. There would be damage to the pyramid complex. And responsibility for the bomb would be attributed to the Brotherhood."

Ayman remained silent for at least a minute, as he appeared lost in his thoughts. Eventually, he came back with two more questions for Gamal:

"I get your point, but it does not resolve my problem in full. First, why would they place the bomb where the damage would be so minimal? To my knowledge, you haven't told me of any menace or demand they might have made."

Gamal appeared set to reply when Ayman added:

"Wait a second. Let me give you the second part to that question. Isn't this a huge risk that the government would react even more strongly against the Brotherhood? After all, they are still banned, as are the various offshoots we hear about, like Islamic Jihad and several others. So, any indication they give that they are prepared to go after our archeological heritage, and to disturb the flow of the tourist revenues that come with it, would be a perfect excuse to launch a massive clean-up operation by the police, maybe even the army. It's not as if the leaders aren't known, right?"

For the first time, Gamal looked confused and even embarrassed. Ayman interpreted his look as a reflection of the fact that he had not thought the whole thing through. This feeling was reinforced when Gamal simply replied:

"You know, my friend, I think I must do some more thinking. You raise several excellent questions. Are you a professional spy?"

"Me a spy? You're kidding. Hell, no! You know my activities well enough. Just like you, I am a tourist guide. The difference is that I'm married and have a couple of sons, while you're still single. So, I also have a souvenir shop which my wife runs so that the whole family can have a decent lifestyle."

He paused and added:

"I've got two main concerns. First, I need Egypt to prosper so that my business can continue to support me and my family. Second, I want Islam to grow so that more people will be saved by following the Prophet."

"I see. But what do you do with the stuff I tell you?"

"I've told you before. I have a couple of friends who are journalists. They help me get free, or at least cheap, advertising in the press for my business, particularly in the English language sheets which are placed in many hotels. On my end, I help them with a scoop here or there."

"Understood. Though I must tell you that I haven't seen any article in the Arab press that discussed any of the points we discussed ahead of the bombing. They just mentioned the bomb and the fact that the damage was limited to a small building outside which would be closed to the public until further notice. In fact, the only news was in the local press. Nothing in the Cairo papers."

Ayman fired straight back:

"Have you checked the better tourist hotels?"

Gamal did not respond, but sheepishly shook his head. Ayman had the odd feeling that Gamal was trying to turn the tables on him; was he questioning the actual impact that Ayman's passing the story on to one or two of his journalist contacts could possibly have? Was he trying to signal that their cooperation might end? At any rate, Ayman did not like the situation. Yet, he felt proud of his idea of asking his last question. This was exactly what he would have done if he had any inkling that an informer's cover was losing credibility. In the end, going back to Gamal's questions as to why he had seen nothing about the bombing in the press, he simply concluded:

"Gamal, I'm not a journalist. And I know that neither are you. Yet, I know that journalists operate under the control of an editor and a publisher. I would not be in the least bit surprised if the people to whom I talked had been told to keep these details quiet while the editor or the publisher reported them to the police or the *Mukhabarat*."

CHAPTER.08

CAIRO, EGYPT

Benjamin Kaplan was sitting at his desk finishing the cappuccino he had purchased at Beano's Café less than a half hour earlier as he arrived at the embassy. One of his cell phones rang, and he noted that it was the one which he used to connect with his informers in general and Ayman Al-Khafaji in particular. As he was picking it up, he wondered: *what in the world can he want to talk about?*

"Sayyid Ben?"

"Yes, Ayman. What can I do for you?"

"Any chance we could meet today?"

"Why? Did you pick up another rumor?"

"No. No rumor. Much more important. Facts. Unpleasant facts."

"And you don't want to discuss any of this over the phone?"

"Yes, Sayyid Ben."

"OK. Can you be near the entrance to the amusement park on Maadi Island at 3:00 p.m. today?"

"Sure. Can't it be any earlier?"

"Afraid not, I do have a day job . . ."

With a clear tone of partial dejection in his voice, Ayman reluctantly replied:

"OK, See you there."

I I ■ I I

Ben was quite impressed by what Ayman had just told him. He was surprised and happy that Ayman had, by himself, thought of the need to question Gamal a bit further. He recognized that most critical questions had been asked, though he noted that Gamal had avoided answering a couple of them. He pointed out potential further avenues of questioning to Ayman, all the while congratulating him. Afterwards, he felt he needed to hear what Ayman made of what Gamal told and did not tell him, asking:

"Any important implication?"

Ayman had ample time to revisit his recollections of the questions and answers and to identify what helped and what did not. He first said that he found Gamal's objections reasonable, though he felt that it would seem odd for the Brotherhood to risk the wrath of the government with an action that did not project any real strength. Ben interrupted:

"We are back at the point where the size of the bomb and the spot where it was placed were apparently chosen not to impress. However, their going from secret meetings to actions, however modest, exposes them to serious political consequences."

Ayman could only agree:

"Absolutely. That does not make as much sense as I would like."

Ben could only repeat his earlier question:

"So, what do you make of it?"

Ayman conceded that he had plenty of time to consider what he called "multiple conspiracy theories." Ben smiled, encouraging him to say more:

"Well, for a start, the people behind the bomb could be a splinter group within the extremist arm. They might have planned the whole thing, including the Taliban rumor, precisely to get the government to go after the Brotherhood. Just a thought: imagine that there is a split within the Brotherhood between those who are truly focused on Islam and others who are seeking to overthrow the government for the benefit of some foreign power?"

"Interesting and credible. That would explain the small bomb and the limited damage. Do enough to attract attention, but don't do too much to hurt the archaeological heritage. Any other theory?"

Ayman continued:

"Could be a test to see how strongly the government might react. They have plenty of things on their minds as we speak. Anything short of a massive response could indicate a government weakness that the Brotherhood as a whole or the foreign-influenced faction could exploit."

Ayman paused again, turning his various thoughts into his head to make sure he said enough but never too much. He suggested:

"Given what's happening in and around Gaza, you could also argue that Iran is trying to widen the conflict and wake up 'Arab street' as the press calls us."

"I see that. Could it be a test of who you are and what you do, Ayman?"

Ayman's face suddenly displayed surprise and worry:

"Why would they do that?"

"Who said 'they'? Could your friend, Gamal, be under orders to assess you?"

Ben casually explained that Ayman's help had surely been useful in a couple of recent operations. Someone might have noticed and wondered if there was one coincidence too many. He asked again:

"Could this be trying to flush you out as they say?"

"Sayyid Ben, that's theoretically possible, but there's a flaw in the logic."

"What?"

"Gamal was not involved in either of those two prior situations."

"Ha! That's a critical point. Good. Thank you. However, do you have any reason to think that the section of the Brotherhood to which Gamal belongs could have been involved in those two earlier situations?"

"I really don't know. But I see what you mean. I guess it's possible. What should I do?"

"At this point, nothing. Keep yourself covered and remain careful. Don't take any unnecessary risk."

Without a pause, Ben asked:

"Now let me ask you a last question. Is there any way to find out more about Mohamed?"

I I ■ I I

Less than a week later, Ben Kaplan was surprised by the phone call he had just received from Ayman. In fact, he did not expect anything from him, after having had one additional meeting, this time in Cairo, after their common trip to Djoser. Ayman's voice seemed a bit different from usual, a bit distressed, a lot less fluent than normal as he said:

"Sayyid Ben?"

"Hey, Ayman. What's up?"

"Any chance we can sit down for a few minutes later today. I have a couple of pieces of news I would rather not discuss on the phone."

"You're in Cairo, right?"

"Oh, yes. No need for either of us to drive terribly far. Can we meet near the entrance to the botanical gardens, you know, by Nahdet Misr."

"Feel more comfortable in a crowd? I promise I will not be carrying my gun."

I I ■ I I

Less than a couple of hours later, they met at the foot of the statue of Nahdet Misr, the Sphinx and the woman supposed to represent Egyptian essence. Ayman had been able to identify Ben from afar as he stood taller than average. The crowd around the statue was as usual quite large. It took Ayman a good minute to be able to make his way to Ben, as people were pushing and shoving just to stay on track to where they wanted to go. They greeted each other, first shaking hands and, as is customary for friends and at times for people who know each other well, kissing on both cheeks, adding a hug and a back slap. Nobody in the crowd around them could suspect that there was anything more than a "normal" relationship between the two of them. They crossed the street and casually entered the Orman Botanical Garden. With the hot and still humid climate often prevailing in Egypt along the Nile, the greenery was in full force and seasonal flowers in bloom. Numerous birds were flying around, fighting to collect whatever seeds had fallen. Ayman asked Ben to keep walking rather than using one of the many benches they immediately encountered. He surprised Ben further by taking him along a convoluted path that got them after five minutes back to almost exactly where they had started.

"Are you lost?"

"Lost? No. I just wanted to make sure that we were not followed."

"Why so much more caution than usual?"

Ben may not have noticed it as they were still both walking, but Ayman's face took on a more serious and even sad look as he said:

"Remember Mohamed Al-Shenawi?"

"I think I do. Isn't he the contact who told your informer Gamal of the two bombings?"

"Absolutely, but we can't say that anymore."

Though the context gave Ben a good sense of what Ayman was talking about, he could not control his reflex action as he exclaimed:

"What?"

Ayman stopped and looking directly into Ben's eyes, he simply said:

"He was murdered."

"Murdered?"

"Yes, murdered and most likely tortured before that. His bruised body was dropped in front of the front door of his house yesterday in the late afternoon. He had been shot, but the body also showed signs of torture. I'll spare you the gory details, I'm sure you understand."

Ben nodded and, following his training, he skipped over details of the murder itself and asked:

"How did you find out?"

Matter-of-factly, Ayman replied that Gamal had called him with the news. Ben was still not satisfied:

"Did you ask him how he found out?"

"Sure. The first thing I asked as a matter-of-fact. He told me that one of Mohamed's sons called him. From what Gamal told me, the son said that Mohamed had apparently forgotten his cell phone at home when he went to meet whoever killed him."

Ayman looked emotional and Ben let him regain his composure. Ayman continued:

"Mahmoud, Mohamed's eldest son, decided to go through the numbers of the last few calls his father had made on the cell phone he found. That's how he happened onto Gamal's phone number."

Ben cringed as he was hearing Ayman's explanation, thinking that he could see breaches of spying etiquette every step of the way. Yet, he only said:

"I guess we're lucky that Mohamed forgot his cell phone."

He suddenly stopped and then added an afterthought:

"Unless he 'forgot' it on purpose."

Ayman's face abruptly displayed a look which told Ben that he did not follow Ben's train of thought; Ben had "lost" him. So, he felt he needed to expand on his earlier point:

"We should try and find out if he had more than one cell phone. There might be one that he used to communicate with Gamal and another which he used to make and receive other, so-called 'normal' calls. That would mean that his murderers would know about his usual contacts, if he had his other phone with him, but not the numbers of people who were supposed to remain anonymous. So, maybe, he had intentionally left at home the phone with which he made or received the really sensitive calls."

Ayman was impressed by Ben's quick thinking. He commented that was exactly what he did when he went to visit with someone. He would take his personal phone, as he called it, but not a phone that he used for, what he termed, his "other business." Ben did not react to Ayman's comment with more than a mild nod and immediately asked:

"Did Mohamed know about you?"

Ayman smiled briefly, though his mood quickly returned to its prior seriousness as he said:

"No. But, under torture, he could have talked of Gamal."

Ayman paused for a brief second and added the obvious next inference:

"And Gamal knows about me."

"I see. What a mess!"

Ben paused for a short while and asked:

"Is there anything we can do?"

"Well, for Mohamed or his family, not really. But for Gamal, we need to find a way for him to disappear for a while."

By then, Ben noted that Ayman seemed to be back in full control of his emotions. He went back over the story which Ayman had just told him and said:

"Hold it, my friend. One thing is either incomplete or makes no sense. How would Mohamed's son know which of the various numbers he found on his father's cell phone to call? Wouldn't you think that there were quite a few?"

"I asked the question, Sayyid. Gamal said he did not know. He told me that they had spoken recently, given the bombing we know about. Maybe Gamal's phone number was the one which appeared the most, or the most recently."

Ben allowed himself a weak nod, only saying:

"Possible, I guess."

Ben paused and signaled for Ayman to stop walking. They were at the foot of a specimen sycamore fig tree, a plant often mentioned in the Bible because the small orange fruits are excellent food for animals. Additionally, the bark, leaves, and milky latex of the sycamore fig all have medicinal value. The tree under which they stood was particularly large and well-developed, with a height of close to 60 feet and a girth at the base nearing 50 feet. Ben went on:

"The only real issue would be if Mohamed only had one phone. How sure are you that he had two?"

Ayman was surprised but had to reply:

"I don't know."

"Didn't you ask Gamal?"

"I did. He replied that he wasn't sure. He said that he always emphasized the need for a separate cell phone with which he conducted his informer activities. But he could not remember whether Mohamed ever confirmed that he did."

Ayman paused and added:

"The one thing that still worries me, Sayyid Ben, is that Gamal presented him as a friend rather than a contact. Do you see what I mean?"

"Wouldn't you do the same thing?"

"Not quite. I use a different word. See, for a friend I would say *alealam lisadiyq*, while I would add *muqarab* for a close friend. Gamal seemed to say that Mohamed was a close friend, not just a friend."

"Ha. We're back to square one. We do not know which phone Mohamed's son found and what names could have been on its contact list."

Ben's mind was busy thinking of how protection for Gamal could be organized if needed. He realized that whatever needed to be done to help Gamal should in no way bring Ben or *Mossad* into the open, nor should it disclose that Ayman had a relationship with an Israeli diplomat. His conversation with Ayman was not over. He felt that he needed to be quite direct with his informers. On the other hand, he knew very well that it was his duty to protect Ayman. Ayman's raising the issue of Gamal's safety created a real challenge. He could see that Ayman was emotionally affected by Mohamed's murder and thus knew he had to be careful how he approached the issue of his implicit plea.

"Has Gamal told you that he needs to flee or hide?"

"No, but I'm sure it's something which must be on his mind. If not, is it not my responsibility to take care of him anyway?"

Ben did not want to give a yes or no answer. He argued that there were two dimensions to the problem. One involved providing protection to Gamal to ensure his safety and that of his family. The other had to do with wanting him safe so that there was no risk of him pointing the finger at Ayman if he should, in turn, be captured and questioned. Facing Ayman directly, Ben told him that there were ways Gamal could be protected, even if it meant that he and his direct family were to fly overseas for a few days or weeks, adding:

"This applies to you as well, my friend. Your safety is our responsibility. You've taken the risk to help us; we will pay you back with our protection. The problem with Gamal is that from what you tell me he does not know of the connection to Israel. Is that correct?"

"Absolutely."

"That is what makes this whole thing a bit more difficult. We cannot do anything which would reveal that connection. You'd be burned, and I'd have to leave Egypt as well."

Ben paused for a short second as he could see Ayman having difficulties understanding the connection Ben was making. He explained to Ayman that anything that was done to protect Gamal and involved anyone from Israel, diplomat or otherwise, would reveal that Ayman had a connection with Israel as well. That would finger him as the next person to be "punished" and would then expose Ben. He added:

"I would have to return to Israel as I would be persona non grata in the Arab world. You see?"

Ben jokingly added:

"There are plenty of vice consuls or even consul positions for Israel around the globe. But I do like Egypt and enjoy the Arab culture."

Ayman nodded his having understood, though he mumbled:

"I should have thought of that earlier."

Ben immediately realized that Ayman was losing it and offered:

"First of all, let us avoid any form of panic. Panicked people make stupid mistakes, and we don't want that. Right?"

"Agreed, but . . ."

"At this point, I would suggest that you play everything very safe. For a start, do not call Gamal from your cell phone. Use a public phone and do not call him from close to your home."

"Understood, Sayyid Ben. But he already has my cell number. What if he calls me?"

"Don't worry. I have a plan. Listen."

Ben explained that his plan comprised two steps. The first was for Ayman to call Gamal from a public phone. The purpose of the call would be to ask how he was and get a sense of what was happening, what he was worried about, and whether he wanted to continue to serve as a contact for a while. Second, during that call, Ayman should inform Gamal that he had lost his cell phone. He would then immediately give him a new number. That number would correspond to a new phone which Ben would give Ayman later that day. It would not allow most forms of geolocation. Ben added:

"In short, whether you initiate the call or receive it, the call cannot be traced."

"But what about my family and my friends?"

"Why should that be a problem? Don't tell me that you only have one cell phone, right? I've always thought you had three."

Ayman conceded that he had three cell phones, one for his personal and business use, the other for anything that dealt with his "other activities" as he called them, and one reserved for communications with Ben. Ben jumped on that statement:

"Hold it. I'm sure you have more than one informer, right?"

"Yes."

"Are you using the same phone to talk to all of them?"

Ayman let go of a weak sigh as he had to admit that he did. Ben replied:

"We will have to fix this later. But at this point, that does not create any problem for your family and your friends. Agreed?"

Ayman appeared to be breathing a sigh of relief as he realized that the mess was much less deep than he feared. He still asked:

"What if whoever murdered Mohamed keeps tracking my old 'ancillary business' number?"

"Why would they? You've told them you've lost the phone?"

Ben could see that Ayman still seemed to hesitate and asked him directly:

"What's the problem, Ayman?"

Ayman replied that he could see that the protection suggested by Ben made sense for him and his family, but he was not ready to throw Gamal to the wolves:

"I really worry for him."

"Understood. That's a very honorable feeling for you to have. Now, let me suggest this. He knows his business and you have to assume that he will know how to protect himself. Plus, we know that he does not have a wife or children. Let's wait and see. Let me know immediately if he tells you that he needs help. I'm sure there are ways that he could be protected without us getting caught in the middle. The key is that he cannot know of a connection between you and me."

Ben paused and asked:

"How about any other contacts that you have? Do any of them know Gamal?"

Ayman smiled and simply replied:

"The world is exceedingly small in Egypt, Sayyid Ben. We treat friends a bit as extended family, and business associates a bit as friends. So, it's quite possible that a contact of mine may have met Gamal."

But he paused and emphatically stressed the point that Gamal knew nothing of Ayman's real name and a fortiori of his address. He knew the outline of his activities. He knew that there was a wife and two sons, but that was it. Ayman added:

"Remember, in the kind of activities I have, we know better. So, I do the same thing with any informer. They don't know who the real me is. So, there is no chance that they could have met Gamal as an informer of mine, though they might have met him as an individual, among others. Let me take it further. I don't use my real name with them either."

He paused and conceded:

"The only weakness I can think of is that I use the same name with all of them."

"And what is it, if I may ask?"

"Sorry, Sayyid Ben, but do you really need to know that?"

Ben waved his own question away, realizing that Ayman was quite capable of thinking on his feet; though he also noted that Ayman seemed to have forgotten he had implicitly given Ben his other code name when he recalled a conversation with Gamal. He filed that thought in his mind, as he kept wondering how Ayman could simultaneously seem almost broken at one instant and back to his normal calculating self the next. Yet Ben added:

"So, the only vague connection that someone else might pick up between you and Gamal would be if either of them revealed they knew someone named whatever name you won't tell me. Correct?"

"Yes, but that's a bit farfetched."

Ben conceded the point and concluded:

"I understand. Yet, my recommendation still holds. Lay low yourself and make sure any link you have with Gamal is through the new phone I will give you. By the way, he doesn't know about your 'BB' cell phone, your 'Ben Business' third phone that you should only use to talk to me, right?"

"Never."

"That's good. But this demonstrates to you the importance of not mixing 'business' and pleasure. Keep that phone strictly for yourself. It's even more important now than ever."

Ayman quietly walked back across Nahdet Misr Street and then across Charles de Gaulle Street to a parking spot right behind the Austrian Embassy, where he had left the scooter he used to travel within Cairo when not using the underground or buses. A two-wheeler was quite a bit more convenient to navigate Cairo's at times mind-blowing traffic. He agreed to meet Ben later that afternoon near the entrance to the amusement park on Maadi Island which they had already used as a rendezvous place to pick up his new phone reserved for dealing with Gamal.

CHAPTER.09

TEL AVIV, ISRAEL; AND CAIRO, EGYPT

Back in his office at the Embassy, Ben immediately called Mark Levi in Tel Aviv on a videoconference:

"Hey, Mark. Important news, here."

"Shoot."

"Remember Mohamed Al-Shenawi?"

"I think I do. He's the fellow we think placed the bomb at the Djoser Pyramid, so it did not do too much damage. Right?"

"Yeah!"

Ben paused and simply said:

"Well, I just heard that he was killed, and that his body was 'deposited' in front of his home, and that there were signs he had been tortured."

Mark made a face and could only say:

"Messy! Messier and messier!"

"Exactly how I felt."

Ben went on to argue that Mohamed's death and the manner of his death shed light on the issues they had been discussing but also raised new ones. Mark's face did not display any disagreement, which was Ben's clue to keep going. He focused first on what he called the new issue:

"We need to find a way to protect Ayman, our agent. Though he talks as if he is most worried about Gamal, my guess is that is quite worried for himself as well."

"You're going to explain that, right?"

"Sure."

Ben explained that the basic assumption had to be that Mohamed eventually talked as the murderers tortured him. They must only have killed him when they had what they needed or at least wanted. If Mohamed talked, he should have revealed Gamal's identity, adding:

"He is the one person we know he knew. He had told him about the Taliban story, and he had warned him about the bomb which he placed at Djoser."

Mark asked:

"There might be others that he knew as well, I guess?"

"Maybe yes, maybe not. We've been told that he was very worried, so he may have been very careful and only talked to the one person he thought would be able to use the information. Remember, we are still assuming that he warned of the bombing and may have sabotaged the location of the bomb because he had fallen out with the attacks on the Egyptian national patrimony."

"Back to your prior train of thought, Ben, which explains why Ayman would be worried about his safety. What's the real danger?"

"The usual, I'm afraid, but also the unusual. For one, Gamal has not asked for Ayman's help. So, we don't know whether he is worried or not. Also, we know that Ayman has at least three different identities, the one he uses with us, the one he uses with Gamal and his real one, which, as I told you a while back, we know, but he doesn't know we know."

Ben paused and smiled, realizing how convoluted his last sentence had been. He then continued:

"He tells me that he assumes that Gamal has at least two identities, since he is convinced that Gamal Al-Sahid is not his real name."

Ben paused and took his logic a couple of steps further. He explained that he had to assume that Gamal used his real identity with the Muslim Brotherhood. So, to Ben, the key question was whether Mohamed and Gamal were in the same Brotherhood cell. Seeing that Mark was struggling with the detail, Ben clarified his point:

"If the two of them were in the same cell, then you have to argue that things don't look too good for Gamal. Mohamed would have known his real name, and he would have been able to say he was the individual in whom he had confided about his discomfort with the violence. And to whom he had leaked the Taliban connection and the impending bombing of Djoser."

He paused for a second and continued:

"Now, assume that Gamal and Mohamed were not in the same Brotherhood cell, then the problem is much less critical. There is no more reason for Mohamed to know Gamal's real name than for Gamal to know Ayman's real name, which we know he doesn't. I don't worry about the fact that Gamal is also in the tour guide business; they are a dime a dozen in Cairo and, in fact, throughout most of Egypt."

Mark simply asked:

"So, on that front, you're taking a wait-and-see approach?"

"I am because I really don't want to bring Gamal into the *Mossad* loop."

Mark thought for a few seconds and out of the blue asked:

"Wait a minute. Let's go back to the bomb. What if it was, in fact, a ploy for the Brotherhood to penetrate your network, our network in Egypt?"

"I did think of that, as you know. At this point, as you yourself argued, it looks a bit farfetched, but it cannot be conclusively rejected. So, the last thing I want to do is allow Gamal to find out about us. That means that any help we may provide to protect him will have to be local and with no connection to the embassy. No need to do anything at this point, but we may need your help."

Mark looked surprised as he said:

"My help?"

"Yes. You might use David's contacts in Washington, for instance, to ask the CIA to help protect him. The Americans can do a lot more than we can; they're a lot bigger."

"Great thought; it's now on my notepad. Do you know anyone there?"

"I do, but it might be more powerful if the request came from higher up, if you see what I mean."

"I see. But what about Ayman?"

Ben argued that there were at least a couple of scenarios which he needed to consider to make the link. The first involved assuming that, whomever the terrorists are, they would come after Gamal and that he, in turn, would talk. He concluded:

"That could mean that Ayman might be the next name to 'drop' but that would assume that Gamal has somehow pierced Ayman's identity. If we could do it, why couldn't Gamal do it, other than my original belief that he would not have access to the sophisticated equipment and resources we have?"

Ben paused after his rhetorical question and simply said:

"I guess if Gamal did not have the resources we used to tail Ayman, the risk that Gamal would somehow point to Ayman remains possible, as does the risk that I am next. But the risk must be low."

The speed of Mark's reaction surprised Ben as he said:

"We cannot have that. Cannot take any risk, even if it's small. What's your second scenario?"

Ben replied:

"That's where it becomes cloudy, and I did not share that logic with Ayman."

"Why?"

"You'll see. It relates to Gamal and how Ayman stands by him."

"I see."

"What if Gamal was a double agent?"

"A double agent? Didn't we cover this already?"

"We mentioned it but did not discuss it. I mean that he would be providing his services both to us and to the Muslim Brotherhood."

"Why?"

Ben initially replied that he had absolutely no ground on which to suspect Gamal, other than the episode of the bomb in Djoser. He repeated his point that the place the terrorists chose to place the bomb did not make sense. More specifically, he argued:

"Why place the bomb where they did, in a place where the damage would have been peripheral to the main architectural attraction, the Djoser Pyramid itself?"

Mark was about to interrupt, but he saw Ben's wave of the hand and let him finish his thought.

"The only logic I could understand behind a weak bomb would be a warning. However, what good is a warning if it is not accompanied either by a press release claiming responsibility or by tracts left near the site of the bombing?"

Ben paused again and simply concluded:

"Let's stop this. We've been around that bush a number of times. This tells me that we need more information to go any further."

Mark smiled and simply said:

"Well done, my friend. You are indeed onto something. We know that Mohamed was for real, i.e. really trying to help someone outside of the Brotherhood. That cost him his life. But we don't know the role played by the intermediary, Gamal. I would still love to know who killed Mohamed and why. Back to Gamal's role, we don't know it for as long as you stand by Ayman."

Ben interrupted to repeat his original comment:

"I trust Ayman. In fact, of the three characters he has to be the one I trust since he's the only one I know. But I'm not prepared to rule him totally out of the loop. As I said earlier, 'trust but verify'."

"A worthwhile precaution."

Ben then mentioned to Mark the plan he was hatching for Ayman. He explained to Mark one option would be to try and hide him in Alexandria. Mark interrupted:

"Why Alexandria?"

"It's the only other Egyptian town in which we have a diplomatic representation, a consulate. I have a couple of informers there and they have good contacts."

Mark congratulated Ben:

"Looks like you have the situation in hand, my friend."

■ ■ ■ ■ ■

Later that afternoon, as Ayman and Ben met near the entrance to the amusement park so Ben could give him the new telephone, Ayman surprised Ben again:

"I got a call from Gamal."

"Hold it! We had agreed that you would not pick up on your old cell phone."

"Oh! I did not. I saw his caller-ID and let the call go into voice mail."

Ben appeared relieved, but Ayman was not finished with his story. He explained to Ben that he then listened to the message which Gamal had left him. Ben raised his eyebrows in anticipation of what was coming next. Ayman was shaking when he continued:

"He told me that he had received an anonymous phone call telling him that he was to report to the place where the *usra*, the family or the cell, used to meet. He said the *naqib*, or captain, the head of the cell wanted to see him."

Ben immediately understood Ayman's problem and decided on the spot that he would speed up the process of relocating him and his family to Alexandria. In the meantime, his advice to Ayman was to do nothing, arguing that they had agreed he would say he had lost his cell phone. Thus, he could not possibly have heard the message. Ayman asked if he should call Gamal. Ben conceded that this was reasonable yet made Ayman commit not to agree to anything:

"I'm still quite confused about what has happened. I know how you feel vis-à-vis Gamal, but I cannot share your feelings at this point. He remains a suspect."

"But why, Sayyid Ben? We know that Mohamed was the problem. Don't we?"

"Sorry, my friend, but I disagree. We're told that Mohamed died. But he certainly did not mean to set a trap for us. Right?"

Without waiting for Ayman to reply, Ben continued:

"If anything, he died because he tried to protect the Djoser treasures. Now, I would suggest two possible scenarios, only one of which leaves Gamal reasonably dependable."

Ben proceeded to argue that there was a scenario which would have Mohamed inform Gamal of the impending terror act. Mohamed would tinker with the bomb to minimize the damage or place it in a less harmful location than planned. Ayman looked surprised, and Ben explained:

"Imagine he was instructed to place it at the base of the pyramid. He was afraid this would cause too much damage even if the bomb was weak and thus decided to drop it in the chapel far away from the pyramid."

He paused and verified that Ayman was following; then he concluded:

"In that case, Mohamed would be a bit of a martyr, as you call those who suffer for a cause, and Gamal could be in the clear."

Ayman was smiling. Ben moved onto the second scenario saying:

"Now imagine that Mohamed was betrayed by someone, and why not Gamal, by the way? In fact, we don't need Mohamed to have existed. Gamal's old *usra* is trying to find out about you and possibly about whomever you work with. He calls you, inventing the whole story. You come, see the damage and the results of the explosion, and you bring your contact, me in this case, into the loop. I'm sure glad I wore that heavy disguise when I was in the Djoser complex with you. They would have a really hard time connecting any picture someone might have taken with the real me."

He paused for a second and returned to the flow of the hypothesis:

"Gamal tries to infiltrate our network by claiming to be in danger when, in fact for all I know, he may even be the *naqib* of the *usra*. Once he is in, he serves as a double agent for as long as it helps him and eventually blows you up and possibly me as well. In that case, there's a reasonable chance that Mohamed never existed . . . Gamal or another crony would have likely planted the bomb."

By the time Ben finished with his description, Ayman was certainly no longer smiling. He was in shock. He had never really thought that his friend Gamal might be a double agent, at least since he had vetted him as a worthwhile contact. Now that edifice seemed to have a few structural cracks. Meekly, he said:

"But, Sayyid Ben, what if he is legitimate?"

Ben conceded that this was a perfectly reasonable scenario as well and suggested that Ayman should help Gamal if he requested it. Yet, everything should be done away from the Israeli connection. Seeing the worried look on Ayman's face, Ben felt it would be OK for him to share with Ayman the idea he had discussed with Mark:

"We may need to ask for help from the Americans. They have a bigger local network and might be willing to hide Gamal for a considerable time. Whatever we do, he CANNOT be made aware of your connection with an Israeli diplomat."

CHAPTER.10

TEL AVIV, ISRAEL; AND CAIRO, EGYPT

Back at *Mossad* headquarters, Mark felt he needed to report to David. Things had reached the point where he did not believe he should pursue the project on his own. The *Mossad* campus was located in the north of Tel Aviv, about three miles north of Hayarkon Park. The headquarters occupied a modern structure angled to face to the northwest; the complex was made up of seven individual but inter-connected structures, five of which were arranged as the two sides of a right angle. Each of these five towers looked somewhere between square and hexagonal and had a large internal light well which provided natural light to most rooms without windows to the outside. All the offices facing the outside and to the northwest had a nice, unobstructed view of the Mediterranean and of the Herzliya Marina across the Glilot Ma'arav Interchange.

So, though he knew he was still missing critical information, Mark felt he was facing a quandary. He could keep going on his own and quite conceivably start wild goose chases. On the other hand, the severity of what it might mean to have an alliance, however informal or even embryonic, between the Muslim Brotherhood and the Taliban did not leave much room for error.

David's initial reaction was predictable. Mark had been very careful to give him first a short executive summary, and only then to take him down into the details which he thought David needed to know. The one element on which David zeroed in was that there was one believable scenario which would possibly diminish, if not totally eliminate, the role of the Taliban. As he had wisely observed:

"The idea of attacking, if that's the right word, an archaeological treasure might have come from the Taliban. But frankly, between the two of us, the Muslim Brotherhood would not have needed the Taliban to come up with the idea. What was done in Afghanistan in 2001 had made headlines in most of the world."

Mark immediately conceded that the scenario which David suggested was unfortunately totally plausible. In fact, he reminded him that the Brotherhood had had plans along the same line when they were in power in 2011. Yet, at the same time he made the point that it would have been quite a far-fetched reference if the only goal were to find out the identity of Ayman's upstream contact, adding:

"From what we know, and Ayman is the source, Ayman never disclosed his connection with Ben. In fact, I would not rule out the possibility that Ayman initially might have tried to serve more than one master. He hasn't demonstrated any particular affinity or even care for Israel. His principal focus as far as we can tell is that he wants to fight the extreme violence promoted by Muslim Brotherhood."

David could not disagree. They therefore discussed what the options were that they could investigate. Mark first reminded David they had earlier decided that any local investigation in Egypt could not involve Ben or any of his operatives. The risk of breaking his diplomatic cover was too great. Any investigation would have to involve Mark and some member or members of his Tel Aviv team. They knew that contact had been established with the Egyptian secret services through Countess Renate, though the contact just involved a warning based on the rumor of the possible alliance between the

Taliban and the Muslim Brotherhood. David further noted that the one issue which they needed to ponder was to what extent they could conduct their own investigations since the Egyptian Secret Service, the General Intelligence Service or the *Mukhabarat* when they use its Arabic name, was on at least a part of the case. David asked:

"Why would we need to remain involved?"

"Well, I think there are at least two, possibly three, reasons. They're called Benjamin Kaplan, Ayman Al-Khafaji and maybe Gamal Al-Sahid! We must make sure they can keep operating safely and, with respect to Gamal, determine whether he is clean or dirty."

"Good point. Tell you what. Go back to Cairo and work with Ben in the shadows for at most a week or so. See what you can dig up. Then the two of us can regroup and decide whether it is time for us to place a call to Countess Renate."

■ ■ ■ ■ ■

Meanwhile, in Cairo, Ayman had placed a call to his informer, Gamal. The first thing which Gamal said after Ayman's salutation was:

"Ammon, you got my message?"

"What message?"

"I left you a voicemail a couple of hours ago?"

"Ha. I see. Well, I'm not surprised I never got it. I'm calling now to tell you that either I lost my cell phone, or someone stole it from me."

The inherent cynicism of Gamal immediately took over:

"Wait. How are you calling me then?"

"Come on, Gamal. You should not be asking these kinds of questions. In today's world, you can get a new phone in minutes."

He paused and added:

"Just got myself a new phone. The caller-ID shows you the new number. Please use that one to call me from now on."

Ayman waited for some reaction from Gamal, thinking to himself that the first half of the plan, Ben's plan, had worked smoothly. He then asked:

"You said you called earlier."

"I did. I'm in trouble. I received an anonymous phone call asking me to report to the place where the *usra* to which I belong usually meets. Apparently, the *naqib* wants to see me."

Ayman had to summon all his acting capabilities, which were, in fact, significant, to appear surprised and react the way he would have had he taken the call before talking to Ben:

"What? Anonymous? The *naqib*? That's serious. What do you think he wants?"

"I'm sure Mohamed talked. He probably said that he had warned me of the impending bombing."

"Wait a minute. Even if he talked to you, there is no proof that you talked to anybody else, OK? The bomb did go off, didn't it? So, you don't need to worry, right?"

"That is my hope. It might not go any further. However, as we both know, the bombing did not do the damage I think was anticipated. So, they may want to know if I talked."

"Wait a second. How about the idea Mohamed had to place the bomb in a different spot because he was disturbed by something?"

"That'd be OK if it is true. But why would they kill him if he gave that reason? So, I must assume he did not say it or said it in a way that was not credible."

"Wait, you wouldn't reveal anything, would you? It would be your death warrant."

"And trouble for whomever I mention. You're right. Normally, I would not talk. However, what if they start to threaten me? Then I may talk, too."

"You're thinking torture? Why would they go directly there?"

"Who knows? But it's got to be a risk. Don't you agree?"

Ayman was troubled. On the one hand, if Gamal was the solid contact he always thought he was, Gamal's phone call was innocuous. Ayman would not be expected to promise to protect Gamal this early in the game, simply because in reality he did not have much to offer. On the other hand, if Gamal was the double agent which Ben had suggested he could be, then Gamal's indication that he might talk under pressure could surely be viewed as some form of extortion: *you help me, or I spill your name.* At that point, though he still leaned toward viewing Gamal as a trusted informer, he could not take any risk. He felt he needed to remain believable and so asked:

"What did you tell the anonymous caller?"

"I simply reminded the nameless caller that I long ago stopped attending meetings and thought they would not want me as a member of the *usra*, though I totally shared their Islamic ideals."

"Isn't that true?"

"Absolutely. Anyway, I said I would be happy to meet the *naqib* if he wanted to see me, but that he would have to call me himself."

"Smart, quite smart. You did not ask what he wanted to talk about?"

Gamal replied that he could not believe there was any friendly subject to discuss, adding:

"I must assume that he thinks I know of Mohamed's death, and probably of how he died. I can't believe the call would be a simple coincidence."

"Wait a second, Gamal. What if the *naqib* simply wants to know what Mohamed told you?"

"Who is he going to believe? A guy he had tortured who was hoping to save his skin or me? I think I would be walking into a trap."

"So, you don't really want to meet him?"

Gamal went back to his discreet blackmail game:

"I'd prefer not to, but how can I avoid it?"

Ayman asked whether Gamal had family or friends he could visit away from Cairo, suggesting that he could disappear for a short while, leaving his phone behind so that any call from the *naqib* would go into voicemail. He added:

"Just had a thought. You could change your voicemail message to say that you are leaving on a short trip where you will not have your cell phone with you. Ask any caller to leave a voicemail with their name, phone number, and a short message, and say that you will return the call when you are back in a week or so."

"What will the extra week or so do for me?"

Ayman was increasingly confused. He knew the cultural practices within Egypt. He believed that Gamal as a trusted informer would naturally ask for some form of hospitality. Why was he, therefore, not coming out with a straight request for protection? He still decided to keep playing the game until Gamal showed his hand:

"A week is a week. Many things can happen."

Gamal became emotional. He accused Ayman of being too cold:

"How could you stay calm when there is a risk to my life?"

Ayman thought *here we go.* He calmly replied, gratifying Gamal by calling him a friend:

"Gamal, you are my friend, and I want to help you. Now, what can I do? You're welcome to come and stay for a few days at my house."

Ayman knew that the option was not valid as Gamal did not know his real name or where he lived. Yet, at the time, it was the easiest offer for him to make. He was not going to mention that he would probably be on his way to a safe place as per Ben's promise. Gamal did not need to know that. Surprisingly, Gamal seemed to calm down as he said:

"That might be a solution. But I'm putting you in danger."

He paused for a second and added:

"Plus, I don't have huge financial reserves. So, if I am with you, hidden, I can't keep on with my business and we will run out of money. And if I keep taking calls from tourists either on my site on the internet or on my business cell phone, it would be child's play to find me."

"Wait a minute. Do you conduct your business under the Gamal Al-Sahid name?"

"Sure, why not?"

Ayman thought that it was time to bring the conversation to a close. They were going around in circles. He simply said:

"Tell you what, Gamal. Wait a day or so. Either you're going to get a call from the *naqib,* or you will not. If you do, call me immediately on this new number and we will work out a solution. If you don't, let's try to find out more about the anonymous caller. Deal?"

CHAPTER.11

TEL AVIV, ISRAEL; LUXOR AND CAIRO, EGYPT; AND SOMEWHERE IN THE AUSTRIAN ALPS

Ayman Al-Khafaji was awakened early in the morning by yet another phone call from his informer Gamal Al-Sahid:

"Sorry to disturb you this early, but I have worrisome news for you."

Ayman sat up and got out of bed, walking quickly to the living room next door. He knew that the vibration of the phone might well have awakened his wife, but he hoped that she would be able to go back to sleep quickly:

"The *naqib* has called you back? I thought you were going to go away."

"No. It's not that. No call from the Brotherhood."

"Ha. Good. So, what is it then?"

"Another contact just called me. There is another bombing coming. This time, they are aiming for the Colossi of Memnon, you know near Luxor, 400 miles or so south from here."

Gamal was referring to two massive statues, both representing the Pharaoh Amenhotep III. They stood in a large field, at the front of where the ruins of the Pharaoh's mortuary temple were located. The temple was constructed a couple of miles away from the Valley of the Kings, which was located almost due east of the ruins. The Colossi and the Valley of the Kings were part of an area close to 20 square miles, replete with a huge quantity of archaeological treasures. The Colossi, the statues, both faced toward the Nile, which flowed east-southeast of the site. A well-maintained, paved road ran the full length of the south side of the site where the statues stood. Also, though there was a low wall most of the way, there were several entrances allowing cars, or most likely trucks, to go into or out of the complex. The formal entrance with a large parking lot was found at the west end of the complex.

The statues were made from blocks of sandstone, which were said to have been quarried near Cairo (at *el Gabal el-Ahmar*) and transported overland to Thebes, (now Luxor), 420 miles to the south along the Nile. These statues, each of which stood on a stone platform about 13 feet high, were massive. They were about 60 feet tall and stood about 60 feet from each other. Two smaller statues were carved into the front throne alongside the Pharaoh's legs and were said to be Amenhotep III's wife and his mother. Experts believed that each statue weighed approximately 720 tons. Thus, they thought that the stones were too heavy to have been brought from the quarry by boat. They had to have come by road. One could imagine the immensity of the work needed for such a feat.

■ ■ ■ ■ ■

Ayman could not believe his ears:

"They are huge, but they are not in great shape. A strong enough bomb could easily topple them. That would be terrible. Luxor and the Valley of the Kings is such a huge tourist attraction."

Gamal replied he was only reporting what his contact had told him. Ayman asked:

"How do you know him?"

"He was a friend of Mohamed's before he moved to the Luxor area. He's a tour guide like most of us and he felt the field was too crowded in Giza. He's been enjoying his work there."

"How well do you know him?"

"Well enough. That is all I can say."

"You said the bombing is scheduled for tomorrow?"

"I suspect it will take place just after *Fajr*, the prayer that we must make before dawn. At that time, there should not be too many people around. I guess the terrorists are seeking to destroy the statues, not to kill tourists or our fellow Egyptians who work at the site."

■ ■ ■ ■ ■

Ayman could not go back to sleep but did not feel he could call Ben right away. He took care of his morning ablutions, cooked himself a simple breakfast, and eventually placed the call, thinking that though not at the embassy yet, Ben had to be up.

"Sayyid Ben?"

"Yes. Ayman, what's up so early in the morning?"

"Just heard from Gamal."

"Ha, how bad is it?"

"Not about him. More worrisome news. There will be another explosion tomorrow, probably right after dawn, after *Fajr*."

"Where?"

"The Colossi of Memnon, near Luxor."

"Did he give you any more detail?"

"No, but I would bet the explosion will be more powerful."

"Hold it, the statues are what? Sixty feet apart they say, right? That means that either there will be two bombs, or they will be targeting only one of them. Correct?"

"Or there would be just one bomb, but more powerful. Anyway, I don't know. Let me think. How about placing the bomb in between the two statues?"

"Unless it's much stronger than the last time, it won't do much."

"That's why I said it should be stronger, unless they're only trying to convey a message."

Ben kept thinking for a few seconds and, almost as an afterthought, asked:

"Do you know if you can drive a car or a truck onto the site?"

Ayman thought for a second and replied:

"There is an entrance near the west end of the site. It's meant for heavy equipment."

"How far is it from where the statues are?"

"I'd say nearly a thousand feet."

"Is it easy to drive around the site from that entrance to the field where the statues are?"

"Not sure."

By now, certainly fully awake, Ben suddenly had a thought:

"Hold a second, Ayman. Let me fire up my computer."

"How is it going to help you?"

Confidently, Ben simply said:

"You'll see."

Ben waited for less than a minute for his laptop to come on and connect to the internet. That done, he called Google Earth and looked for the Colossi of Memnon. He then zoomed in until the site took the whole of his screen and said:

"Ha, Ha! Here we go. I have got the site right in front of my eyes. I see your heavy equipment entrance, but it looks as if the wall that separates the complex from the road stops about 250 feet east of where the statues are."

He paused and as he had finished measuring the distance on the screen said:

"That's it. You can drive a car through the sand between the road and the statues. If the car is full of explosives, it would surely topple them."

Ayman tried to say something, but Ben continued:

"Thanks, Ayman. I will call you later. Until then, do nothing and make sure that people see you milling about your normal business. Do you have any tourist clients today?"

"No."

"Good. Stay at the shop and be sure people can see you are there."

■ ■ ■ ■ ■

Ben threw a blue, button-down collar shirt on his back and jumped into a pair of grey linen slacks. He then went straight for the room he used as a den. He called Tel Aviv on a safe line, seeking to speak to Mark. He told him as quickly as he could what he had just heard and offered his own take on what the terrorists were about to try:

"My guess is that they are going to use the period before dawn to drive some sort of a car or van onto the site and park it between the two statues. They will set it up to explode after dawn but before the complex opens to the public."

"Why?"

"At this point, I don't think they need or want to make enemies within the local population. They want to destruct treasures, not to hurt common Egyptians."

"Makes sense. Let me brief David and then we'll call Countess Renate. She will have to give a warning to her friend, Menes Al-Soliman. I'll get back to you. By the way, how about Ayman?"

"I told him to remain as visible as possible near his shop; but I also told him to keep his eyes wide open. There should be plenty of people who could testify that they saw him at various hours of the day."

"Perfect."

Mark paused for a second and as an afterthought he asked:

"What if this one is fake, too?"

Ben thought for a second and replied:

"We cannot take the risk. If Gamal is a double agent, then Ayman will be in danger. I'm gonna send a couple of people he doesn't know to look after his safety by milling around his shop. They may have to buy a few trinkets if they're asked why they're spending so much time looking . . ."

■ ■ ■ ■ ■

Countess Renate called Mark to report on her conversation with Menes Al-Soliman, the Head of the *Mukhabarat*. Mark had made sure that David was in on the conference call. Countess Renate started with what sounded like a joke:

"Well, gentlemen, this time I think Menes took me quite seriously."

David asked:

"What did you tell him?"

"The whole story as you know it, except for two details. First, he does not know that you and your vice consul in Egypt are involved. My client is still anonymous. Second, he has no idea how my client got the information."

Mark was elated:

"Super. So, our people are staying fully in the background. They're protected, right?"

"They are."

Countess Renate paused for a second and quickly corrected herself saying:

"I guess they're as protected as they can be."

Mark changed tack and asked:

"What is he, Menes, going to do?"

Countess Renate conceded that Menes Al-Soliman had not told her anything, other than:

"We can't have that!"

She concluded that they might well try to intercept the bomber, whatever manner he was going to operate. David asked whether she had mentioned the scenario which Ben had developed, and her reply said it all:

"He knows, but I have no idea whether he believed me or how he would prevent it."

Mark chimed in for David's benefit:

"Ben's scenario is that a van full of explosives will be parked in the vicinity of the statues and explode when the driver has had a chance to flee, ostensibly being picked up by his colleagues near the site."

"That's what I told him, but he remained tight-lipped. The one thing he let slip was that he wasn't so sure that the driver would not be a suicide bomber."

"What did he mean by that?"

"Well, David, again, he did not say much. But reading between the lines, my guess is that they would try to stop the van before it reaches a position where it can damage the statues."

Mark noted with a heavy dose of cynicism:

"Well, the driver might not have started as a suicide bomber, but he might well still end up dead!"

■ ■ ■ ■ ■

Right after *Isha*, the prayers which Muslims recite at nighttime, usually before 2:00 a.m., a truck drove into the parking lot at the west end of the Memnon complex. As it was still pitch dark, it would have been very hard for anyone to see what was happening. But the vehicle clearly belonged to the military. A careful observer would note that three groups of two soldiers each moved quickly and set up positions at some distance from the Colossi, but close enough to see what was happening. The first group walked toward what looked like a dirt path located at the southwest corner of the overall complex. From there they could see the two statues. Bushes and a couple of tall trees protected them. The second group walked only a few feet to stand under two palm trees at the back of the parking lot. From there, they had a perfect view of the front of the two statues and thus whatever might eventually be parked between them. The third group walked furthest, all the way to the front of a lone farmhouse located along the northern border of the site. Separating the farmhouse from the ruins was a dense hedge comprising both bushes and three palm trees. A careful observer would note that all three groups had a unique perspective of the statues, but no two of them could possibly hit another group as long as they kept shooting forward and in a narrow angle.

The heavy case which each group carried had these contents: a mid-size machine gun, Barrett M82s with tripods, six 10-round magazines, and a sound suppressor. Weighing just over 30 pounds, the M82s had an effective range of one mile, much more than enough as the position that was furthest from the statues was not more than 350 feet. Though principally used in Egypt for special marine operations, the guns offered a good compromise between more powerful but much heavier machine guns and the sniper rifles which might not accomplish the task.

Once the three military groups were in position, the truck that brought them drove out of the complex and toward the east and then turned north after passing the ruins of Amenhotep III's mortuary temple. It stopped within the Al-Asasif necropolis near the temple of Merpentan, the fourth pharaoh of the 19th dynasty of Egypt and the pharaoh that is said to have been ruling at the time of the Exodus recounted in the Bible, though many scholars believe that the pharaoh of the Exodus was in fact Ramses II.

■ ■ ■ ■ ■

"Ayman? Ben here."

"Sayyid Ben? Anything new?"

"I should be asking you, my friend. Have you heard from Gamal?"

"Nothing since the warning for Luxor!"

"Good. The message has been transmitted. The Egyptian government has it under control, they say. So, stay close to home and as I said earlier, be visible to your customers and friends."

CHAPTER.12

LUXOR, EGYPT

Meanwhile, near Amenhotep III's mortuary temple, the night was still quite dark, with only a sliver of moon, which was surely not sufficient to allow anyone to see much. This would be particularly true if one wished to walk on the uneven, sandy ground within the whole complex, with the Temple at one end and the two Colossi of Memnon near the other. The three two-man military units which had taken their positions earlier had the ability to see as each had one pair of night-vision goggles. They could see and not be seen unless the enemy wore night vision goggles as well.

Demonstrating the efficacy of their training, an observer who had been able to watch them would have been impressed that all three groups were doing about the same thing at the same time. They were part of a mission which, at the outset, did not differentiate between the duties of each unit. Omar, the lieutenant in charge, had wanted three units so the area they were protecting would be well covered, so each unit would have a different point of view, and so no unit would be in the line of fire of the other two if they had to use their guns. The soldier manning the machine gun had taken a semi-crouched position and was using the gun's infrared sight to scan the area. Next to his left hand, he placed two spare magazines on a piece of cloth on the ground to ensure no sand would interfere with the mechanism. Together, the three magazines for the soldiers provided up to 30 rounds each. Lieutenant Omar thought that should be sufficient unless the situation deteriorated into a wild shooting match. In that case, he was still confident of his team's superiority as he and his extra soldiers were a few miles away with more ammunition.

The main reason for having a lighter machine gun was for the soldiers to be able to stop what might come: an explosive-filled car or van which would be driven and positioned near the two statues. In fact, the plan was for the gunner of one of the teams to shoot the van or car filled with explosives far enough away from the statues and other preserved structures to minimize damage. At that point, so early in the process, no team knew who would need to do the shooting. Lieutenant Omar had stressed the obvious:

"Nobody shoots before my order. You may use your handgun if you need it to defend yourselves. I want to make sure that whoever shoots does not have anyone in the line of fire. We don't want any friendly casualties."

Behind and on the left of each gunner, their teammate was standing upright. He was the one using the night-vision goggles to survey a broader area than what his partner could see through the gun sight. He could then warn his partner as well as the other units if there was anything suspicious. He also was the one speaking in a soft voice into the field radio of each unit so that Lieutenant Omar and all units were fully informed in real time.

Unit One, the team that was furthest from the colossi, was tasked with the surveillance of the heavy equipment entrance at the north of the complex. Though the unit was hidden a good 600 feet from the entrance, that position allowed them an unobstructed line of sight. Admittedly, there were a couple of trees, in fact, a lone tree and another surrounded by low bushes which limited the range he could observe. Yet, Lieutenant Omar had decided the other two units could complement Unit One's observation and allowed him to have all three units close enough to the statues. After all, he thought the few seconds' advance warning he might miss were not terribly important compared to the much better odds of stopping the car or van before it got to the statues. At the same time, Lieutenant Omar did not want any unit too close to the statues or to the spot where he expected to blow up the van or car filled with explosives. He did not know how powerful the bomb would be, but, assuming it was meant to hit two statues that were 60 feet apart, he did not want anyone closer than a good 150 feet, if not more, when the bomb exploded.

After his Unit One teammate, Gunner Ashraf, had found a comfortable position from which he could hit his target, Sergeant Baashir handed his goggles to him. Gunner Ashraf was not surprised. He knew that Sergeant Baashir was tasked with doing a rapid inspection of the surroundings. Both he and Lieutenant Omar knew there was a farmhouse right behind the location assigned to their unit. Baashir had to make sure that the area was secure, so he approached the farmhouse. He was not concerned there would be any danger from the occupants of the house. Yet, two worries were on his mind concerning the plans originally developed. First, he needed to make sure the enemy had not anticipated a disruption to their operation, having a car or a small group of soldiers near the farm which would also threaten the safety of the farmhouse occupants. Second, he needed to wake them up and warn them about the possible need to evacuate quickly if the need came. He did not tell them about the bomb that could explode near their home, but they were sufficiently impressed by the presence of Sergeant Baashir in full combat uniform that they nodded their agreement.

While doing his round, Baashir was still in constant radio contact with his gunner and the rest of the units, including Lieutenant Omar who had stayed with the truck, with two additional soldiers, and the driver. They were ready to race back to the complex when needed. Baashir quietly whispered in his microphone:

"Farmhouse occupants warned and no unexpected presence nearby. I'm back with Ashraf. Unit One standing ready to move the occupants of the farmhouse away from the site if the bomber comes close to our location."

The two other units and Lieutenant Omar, all of whom wore modern earbuds to communicate among themselves, acknowledged the call. Nothing happened for the next 30 minutes, leading Lieutenant Omar to ask:

"To all units: make sure you stay as sharp as possible. We expect action within an hour and possibly less than that."

In fact, about 15 minutes later, around 2:45 a.m., Unit Three, stationed at the back of the parking lot near the east end of the complex, was the first to notice something:

"Two headlights from the southeast on the main road. They just drove suspiciously by our position. In fact, we saw them drive at much too slow a speed to be an ordinary car passing by; plus, they briefly stopped and started again. They must have been checking that the area was clear for them. Unit One, do you have them?"

"We just got them. They stopped in front of the heavy equipment entrance."

A few seconds later, Baashir added:

"Wait. They're now driving into the complex. It's a panel van. It has stopped in the vast area in front of the ruins. It's remained quite close to the road. I wonder why they are staying there. They could easily drive 100 feet or more into the complex. They would be better hidden from the road."

Lieutenant Omar asked:

"Anyone have any idea why?"

Ashraf replied:

"Is their vehicle so heavy with explosives that they fear getting stuck in the sand?"

Lieutenant Omar thought for a few seconds and gave his order into the microphone:

"Lieutenant Omar here. Don't change the plan, but we will probably need to shoot at the van sooner. If it is so full of explosives, we cannot allow it to get within 600 feet of the statues."

He paused for a second and added:

"By the way, that means that none of you should be closer than that when the bomb explodes."

"Sergeant Baashir here. The van is not proceeding forward. The front right passenger is exiting. I see a light coming on in the cabin. There's at least one more person in there, the driver, but there could be more. The man who's exiting is holding a flashlight. They're clumsy; everybody can see them. He's walking to the back of the van. Hey, he's just opened the back doors. Now there are two sources of light coming from there: the man with the flashlight and the light inside the cargo area of the van. Wonder what they're doing."

Lieutenant Omar took vocal control:

"Operation Statue Save is on! All units, be flexible as we may be looking at a different kind of attack."

Speaking to his driver, he added:

"Ahmed, move the truck slowly back toward the main location. No driving lights. Stop just before the left-hand curve."

"Yes, sir."

The man at the back of the terrorist vehicle was now leaning his upper body into the van. It looked as if he were grabbing something and pulling it out of the van. Sergeant Baashir announced:

"All units, the man is grabbing something that looks like a truck ramp. That's it; that's what it is. He's now positioning it right at the back of the van as if he were waiting for something to roll off the van. Does it mean that the bomb is not the van itself but something else?"

Lieutenant Omar asked:

"Can you see what's rolling off the van?"

"Not yet, sir. The man walked away from the back of the van. I can't see him as clearly as I'd like. The tree and the bushes to the left of my line of sight are hiding him. Jabari, Unit Three, do you see anything?"

"I see the man, but nothing else. The van is oriented toward the north. I cannot see inside."

Baashir came back on the line:

"Hold it. It looks as if the man is holding a control box in his hand. I can see a faint red light moving right at the back door of the van. It's coming down the ramp. Hey, it seems to be an LED light at the tip of an antenna."

He paused and added:

"That's got to be a remote-controlled vehicle rolling out from the van. That's it. They are not going to blow up the van. Bet you the bomb is the remote-controlled unit or it's something on the remote-controlled unit."

"Lieutenant Omar here: all units keep your eyes on the small red light. I agree with you, Sergeant Baashir. They must have been afraid the van could not go through the complex. Cannot understand why."

"Could they fear they'd get stuck in the sand?"

"I guess, but it makes no sense. There is a real dirt path. The loose sand is on the side. Baashir, are you getting a better picture?"

"Yes, sir. No doubt, it is a remote-controlled vehicle. Looks like a cart, with some big load in the middle of it and an engine behind it. The load in the middle has to be the bomb. Hey, the wheels are larger than normal."

Lieutenant Omar opined:

"Must be because of the sandy surface. They don't want their contraption to get stuck. Watch out, all units. This may mean that the vehicle will not stay on the compacted dirt path but may well hide among the ruins, in the sand."

Baashir replied first before the other two units:

"Agreed Lieutenant."

Baashir continued:

"The man is piloting the bomb platform diagonally toward the northwest. Actually, I see it much better now, no ruin to obstruct my view."

"Jabari, Unit Three here. The van is reversing. Looks like it is coming out of the complex. It's indeed exiting; just turned to its left. Coming toward us all."

"Unit One, Baashir, here. Unit Two take over from me. I must go and warn the occupants of the farmhouse. The bomb looks like it's going to drive quite close to us. Much too close. Gunner Ashraf must move, too. Lieutenant, Ashraf is moving west toward Unit Two. I'll join him there."

"Agreed. Make sure the civilians are safe. Ashraf, take position so that Units Two and Three are not in your line of fire."

"Yes, Lieutenant."

"Sergeant Hossam here, Unit Two. I can see the bomb platform. Wait, the man controlling it is no longer behind it."

He paused as he was looking for the man and continued:

"Ha. I have him. He left the platform on the dirt path to the north of the complex. He walked south to be close to the side of the main road. Wonder why? It looks like he stayed on the complex's side of the small wall that runs alongside the road. He can see the platform from where he is. He is walking toward us and following the platform. They're about 200 yards away."

Hossam paused and suddenly exclaimed:

"Baashir, Ashraf, watch out. If the platform keeps going straight, it's going to pass less than 50 feet from your position."

Lieutenant Omar came on the line:

"Baashir, can you see it well."

"No problem, sir. In fact, I think the vehicle will veer to its right about 100 yards from us. That's where the ruins with the tree and bushes are. I can't believe he would take the risk of getting stuck there. It's much simpler and clearer closer to the middle of the empty space. Ready to move further away if we have too."

"OK. Keep us informed. Hossam, anything worth reporting?"

"Yes. The terrorist van has stopped by the side of the road, on the other side of the wall. It's right behind the lone tree."

"Baashir, do you see why?"

"Not yet, Lieutenant. However, we had found that the dirt path on which they must be driving the bomb platform was not always level when we inspected the place earlier on. That's got to be the answer. In fact, Jabari, Unit Three, can you cover for me? The platform is getting too close to a clump of trees, and I am losing it. Plus, Unit One needs to move further east, still on the north side of the complex. Jabari, you should have a better angle."

"No problem."

Lieutenant Omar gave instructions to his driver:

"Ahmed, move the truck forward slowly. Still, no lights at all. I want to see the van. Don't get any closer than 500 feet. Stop when you get to the heavy equipment entrance. Baashir, report on the occupants of the farmhouse."

"I was able to get them out of the house. We are now standing to the north of the building. They are safe. I told them not to move. I'm getting back to Ashraf."

Lieutenant Omar replied:

"Ashraf, move toward Unit Two. Baashir, join him there."

Baashir replied:

"Yes, sir. Jabari, I'm back and can see the action. There's no question as to the terrorists' plan. They're going to drive the bomb close enough to the statues and detonate it. Lieutenant? When should we blow it up?"

Laconically, Lieutenant Omar stated:

"All units, we are almost ready. Ahmed, drive forward. Looks like the van stopped a bit further on. Bet you it is following the man who's controlling the platform. Switch your headlights on and drive past the van. Stop at the main parking lot. Men behind me be ready to shoot at and capture the terrorists. I want them to be alive, if possible. Shoot at the tires of the van first. Gunner Ashraf, you seem to have the best line. Shoot at the bomb; keep shooting until it blows up. All units, take cover. We don't know how powerful it is."

CHAPTER.13

TEL AVIV, ISRAEL

Simon had asked David for a detailed briefing on the latest development in Egypt. David had invited Mark to join him, as he had been the one who followed the situation the most closely. Simon asked Mark to summarize what *Mossad* knew of the bombing near Luxor in particular, as he had already been told of the "Djoser mini bomb" issue. Mark started with a general comment:

"We are all glad that it failed, in that the bomb did not cause any damage to either statue. It did leave a small crater just short of 400-500 feet behind them. Thankfully, that area of the site has no monument or sign of archaeological excavations. So, we have burned bushes, a crater less than a couple of feet deep, and numerous displaced stones that tumbled from the various ruins. Nothing that cannot easily be corrected."

Mark explained further that the bomb-carrying cart had been hit almost 500 feet from the statues as the crow flies, adding:

"For it to get to the statues directly, the cart would have had to travel another 100 feet or so, in a southerly direction. Ashraf, the gunner, was himself about 300 feet away, with a straight line to the bomb."

He mentioned that both Ashraf and Baashir had moved from near the farmhouse to a spot protected by a tall tree 100 feet away from their original location. The tree provided cover for Ashraf to move not more than 30 feet to his left at which point he had a straight line to the cart, aiming between the lone tree and the tree with the mid-height bushes around it. He could see the two small headlights which allowed the man controlling it remotely to see the surface of the dirt path right in front of him, through the onboard camera which broadcast to his remote-control unit. Ashraf fired the first two rounds aiming at the lights and then discharged the remaining eight about a foot higher, which was enough to trigger the explosion of the bomb carried on the cart, remote-controlled by the terrorists. A couple of straight hits caused the bombs to explode, though it was fortunately not close enough to the statues to do any damage to them. As he was recounting the event, Mark added:

"By the way, we all owe a great debt of thanks to Ben Kaplan."

He could see Simon perk up, while David's facial expression did not change, as he had already heard the details of the story. Mark explained that all the details he got on whatever happened at the site were due to a crucial individual whom Ben had cultivated over time. He was buried deep within the *Mukhabarat*. That source provided both a copy of the report that had been filed by Lieutenant Omar, and which detailed what happened in the field and a summary of the information gleaned from the interrogation of the two terrorists. With a discreet smile he added:

"I can't vouch that the secret service men followed all the requirements of the Geneva convention in their interrogations. Our 'man' was not in the room when the two terrorists were questioned. The point, however, is that they did talk and offer quite a lot of actionable information."

Simon asked about the main points contained in the interrogation report. Mark noted that a common theme was how close the stories each man told were even though they were not allowed to talk to each other from the moment they were captured. He added:

"This tells me they are probably of similar ranks within their organization, as it did not seem that there was anything that was known to one and not to the other."

David smiled and cynically added:

"Or they were well-trained and knew what they could and could not say."

"Absolutely. But as you will see when I dig a bit further, I cannot believe they were coached to say a few of the things they said."

Mark went on to say that both men confirmed that they belonged to a local, Luxor-based section of the Muslim Brotherhood. They confessed that their mission had been dictated from what they called "higher up," though they claimed not to know who ordered it. The interrogation report inferred from their statements that the local section executed a project which was ordered from Cairo or wherever the Brotherhood leadership was hiding. They were even able to name the *naqib*, the captain of their local Luxor section. The police had unfortunately not managed to apprehend him. He was able to vanish in the countryside as soon as he heard the news the bombing had been thwarted. Mark noted this probably meant there was at least one outside observer the security services did not see and arrest, adding:

"Otherwise, who would have told the captain that the bombing had failed to destroy its target?"

David suggested:

"It's totally possible that the captain himself was somewhere in the distant neighborhood. From what we've seen of the pictures of the site, there was space to hide far enough away from the statues to be OK and yet close enough to survey the damage. Remember, these people often travel on bikes or mopeds. They can hide anywhere."

Simon offered a third possible explanation, arguing that the captain may have gone to inspect the site after the explosion had been due to occur and could either see his people being arrested or that the statues were still sitting. Mark concluded with a smile:

"The fellow had to be quite unhappy. But I guess we should not be surprised that he fled and went into hiding. I suspect that the *Mukhabarat* also has its share of spies or informers within the Muslim Brotherhood, so I suspect that they will eventually catch the man, unless he is allowed to flee abroad."

He stopped, cleared his throat, and added:

"Though I would think that he is not senior enough for that kind of first-class treatment. Yet who knows? Let me turn to the main element from our point of view and you'll see there may be reasons to think the fellow will indeed hide abroad for a while."

Mark could clearly see that Simon was on board, though his demeanor told him that David must have given him a preview of that element. Thus, as somewhat of an anticlimax, Mark reported that both men were still able to point to the Taliban as being a part of the picture, though they could not be specific on any details. He noted that the report suggested that the man had only reluctantly made that comment, adding:

"I guess the report cannot discuss what kind of coercion was applied, but we probably all get the picture."

Back to his earlier flow, he said the men related there had initially been debate as to whether the bombing was a good idea. Apparently, many of the members of that section, which seemed to include more than a single *usra* or group, worked in the tourist trade, which is very active in the Luxor area. It has often been called the world's largest open-air museum.

■ ■ ■ ■ ■

Originally known as Waset in ancient Egypt and Thebes to ancient Greeks, the part of Luxor located on the west bank of the Nile, opposite today's modern city of Luxor, was a true archaeological paradise, comprising numerous pharaoh tombs, temples and many other sites such as the Valley of the Kings, the Valley of the Queens, the memorial Temple of Rameses III and many others. Equally important, one can find two of the holiest temple sites in Egypt: Karnak and Luxor. Karnak was the second largest ancient religious site in the world, second only to Angkor Wat in Cambodia, and had been dated back more than 37 centuries to the reign of Senusret I, the second pharaoh of the 12th Dynasty. Both Karnak and Luxor boast massive statues, a number of obelisks, and architectural wonders, often covered in hieroglyphs.

■ ■ ■ ■ ■

Thus, as Mark continued his report, he said that the police learned that several of the active working brothers (ach'amal) resisted the idea of the bombing of a site which tourists wanted to visit. They argued that any form of terrorism around the archaeological sites could be quite damaging to their businesses. From their point of view, the issue seemed not to be the need to protect the colossi, which were already quite damaged by the passing of time so that the heads were hard, if not impossible, to recognize. Rather, they wanted to preserve the flow of tourists to the area where they earned their living. They recalled how difficult it had been for them to survive 10-15 years earlier when terrorists targeted historical sites, frightening away tourists, and felt that this was not something they wanted. Mark paused and added:

"Apparently, they were only convinced when the leadership vowed to avoid the most extreme tactics of the Taliban or of the Muslim Brotherhood under President Sisi, arguing that the goals of the current campaign were not as ideological. The decisive factor was when the leadership was quoted as saying the targeting of archaeological sites to be bombed was designed to avoid massive damage and only to attract attention to their cause."

"What do you make of that last statement, Mark?"

"At this point, Simon, I really can't tell. There are plenty of possible interpretations. At one end of the spectrum, they might want to remind the world they exist, feeling that Palestinian terrorists are attracting a lot of attention to themselves. At the other end, it might be a warning to the Egyptian government to prevent it moving to a more accommodating stance with Israel. As you know, they have been talking quite tough, but they also have been relatively gentle in their actions. They might want to slow down if not stop the movement of middle-of-the-road Arab countries to seek accommodation with Israel. The really nasty interpretation is that there are links between the Muslim Brotherhood and Iran, and that Iran wants to sow trouble to add pressure on Israel to settle with Hamas."

Looking at both Mark and David, Simon simply said:

"Well, my friends, this is excellent, and I should add not a surprise to me. I tend to see Iran's hands all over the place. I want to bring this up to the Prime Minister to get his reading. Though most of what has happened is really none of our business as it's all within Egypt, there might be a case that offers useful opportunities for disruption."

He was smiling as he said this last word, given the fact that the branch of *Mossad* for which David was responsible was precisely called: Disruption.

■ ■ ■ ■ ■

Simon set up an appointment with Jesse Benaroya, Israel's Prime Minister, traveling to Jerusalem to see him. Jesse's office was in Jerusalem, in the government center on the same hill as the *Knesset*, which dominated a part of Jerusalem's skyline. His office is practically divided in three distinct zones. First was the area where Jesse's desk was located, which allowed him to see Government Hill through two windows with impact resistant glass protecting him from any attacks. Then there was a working table area which took care of small conferences that did not warrant the use of the Cabinet Room next door. Finally, there was a sitting area with a sofa and three chairs, two opposite the sofa and one at a right angle to it. The coffee table in front of the sofa was complemented by end tables next to each chair, giving everyone easy access to his or her beverage.

Jesse greeted Simon with a wide smile and, having thanked him for making the trip to Jerusalem, invited him to take a seat on the cream leather sofa. Simon's main message was couched in careful terms, as there were still loose ends, if not holes, in the story. His conclusion called for a serious evaluation:

"As you know, Jesse, Iran has been trying to get to us. They've only done it through proxies so they could avoid declaring any official responsibility."

Jesse interrupted and cynically added:

"Frankly, given the state of the world and of the United Nations, I'm not even sure that they would not get away with a direct attack provided it was non-nuclear and only did physical damage."

Simon elected to let the statement pass without a direct response. He knew it was characteristic of Jesse's demeanor to launch into one of his broad ideas even when he was discussing a very specific issue. Iran and the state of the world was one of them. Simon had no intention of starting a new thread to the conversation. He veered toward one of the apparent lessons of the events that had taken place in Egypt:

"I can't believe the Taliban would be moving any closer to the Muslim Brotherhood not only without the permission of Iran, but in fact with even some formal incentive."

"Can't fault that, though we have no proof. Correct?"

"Absolutely. In fact, so far, an American lawyer would say that we are only dealing with hearsay and information most likely obtained illegally."

"Illegally?"

"Under duress."

Jesse nodded his head having now understood and said:

"I see. What do you think we should do?"

Simon thought for a short second, although he had prepared his conversation quite extensively on the helicopter ride from Tel Aviv. He simply asked:

"Should we be thinking of retaliatory actions against one or several of the various proxies or even against Iran if the opportunity presents itself?"

"You don't mean anything official, I'm sure?"

"Surely not. I suspect that there are a few things that we can do, here and there, which could be conducted by David Heller's Disruption Group."

"Your old hunting ground, Simon."

"Absolutely. We need to be quite careful, quite original, and very well-prepared. But I wonder whether something that would hurt these proxies in their domestic activities might not make Iran think. And an even better idea would be to hit at Iran directly."

"I think I see where you're going, Simon. Yet, you know this has to remain totally unattributable to us . . . forever."

"That has to be a *sine qua non*, sir."

Jesse seemed to pause and then blurted out:

"Come to think of it, I would want the War Cabinet involved. I don't need to tell you it has its hands full at present."

"Which I read to mean that nothing should be done before having had yours and their OK."

"You don't miss many, do you, my friend?"

CHAPTER.14

TEL AVIV, ISRAEL

Less than a week later, after the Prime Minister and his War Cabinet had met and come to a decision, Simon got together again with his two associates and simply said:

"My friends, the instructions from the Prime Minister, and by the way the War Cabinet as well, are clear: devise means to punish Iran for its meddling in the domestic affairs of several countries in the region."

Simon paused and exhaled before continuing:

"I give you *carte blanche* to come up with ideas but remember the key requirement, and this comes directly from the PM: nothing can conclusively point to Israel, now or ever."

Mark and David did not miss the emphasis that Simon placed on his last point. They listened as Simon continued:

"You know and I know we will surely be blamed one way or another, but there can be absolutely no proof."

David smiled at Simon's last comment and simply said:

"Par for the course, I guess."

He took a sip of sparkling water that was on the end table to his right and asked:

"Are you able to share a bit more color with us?"

Simon smiled and told David that the whole agenda of the latest War Cabinet meeting was obviously top secret. However, he felt comfortable telling David the point bringing the group to the need to act was the confirmation that the Taliban had something to do with the second bombing aimed at the Colossi of Memnon. At the same time, he offered:

"I don't need to tell you the first military priority at present is with respect to Hamas and Gaza, although we are whiskers away from extension of the conflict with Hezbollah and insurgents in Syria. So far, there have been skirmishes along the Lebanese border, but they have not been much different from what we are used to. Further, the Americans are dealing directly with threats and attacks aimed at various installations in Syria and Iraq."

He paused and quite seriously concluded:

"Our maneuvering room is limited because we don't have the first call on the country's military resources. So, my recommendation is to design a small number of pinpointed operations, with the idea of implementing only one at a time. Am I making sense?"

Mark replied:

"Totally. Let me get to it, have David opine on them, request any change he needs, and then we'll be back to you with a short list."

David was about to get up from the cream-colored leather sofa in Simon's office when Simon asked him:

"Have you considered having Mark travel again to Cairo?"

"No. Should he?"

"Well, I don't want to be a prophet of bad luck, but I feel we should stay on top of what happens to Ben Kaplan's sources."

He paused briefly and surprised David saying:

"I am thinking of Ayman Al-Khafaji in particular. Whoever his source is, Gamal, if I remember correctly, must be in a difficult spot. The failed Colossi of Memnon bombing is apparently the second time there has been a leak within the Muslim Brotherhood. They must be asking themselves a lot of questions."

■ ■ ■ ■ ■

David and Mark spent the morning ruminating over the actions they could undertake to "punish" Iran without any traceability to Israel. They quickly decided that for operations to retain the anonymity they sought, they had to avoid any direct military campaign. Mark added:

"This does not mean that we cannot benefit from or use equipment that belongs to Tsahal (the Hebrew acronym for Israeli Defense Forces—*Tsvah Haganah L'Yisrael*)."

"Totally agree. Let me add one element which we will ignore only if absolutely necessary. I would rather target militia or terrorist organizations rather than an official state."

"Makes all the sense in the world, although I would immediately suggest an exception."

David looked a bit surprised and asked:

"Which one?"

"Given the role of the Taliban in the two bombings we have seen in Egypt, I would have no issue hitting Afghanistan directly."

"Agreed. But it cannot be a military action."

David raised his eyebrows, though he quickly figured out what Mark meant. Whatever they did had to be local sabotage operations which did not use the military. He understood that the distance between Israel and Afghanistan precluded the Air Force or the Navy from conducting an operation without being immediately unmasked. Noting that David was now on board, Mark concluded:

"For sure. I would also think that we should prioritize actions which would benefit others than just Israel, though our mission remains first and foremost to protect Israel."

David concurred and asked Mark to work with a couple of senior leaders within his team to produce specific "projects" as he called them. As Mark was leaving his office, David added with a broad smile:

"I suspect that one of your first visits will be to Marvin Goldstein."

Mark smiled right back:

"You are almost right, sir. I'll have to see him eventually, but not immediately. I need to know what I want to ask. As you know, with Marvin, you run a real risk of technobabble overdose!"

A veteran of the service, Marvin was responsible for all technological development for *Mossad*. He had an encyclopedic knowledge of the capabilities of each of the branches of Tsahal. He also knew exactly what was being planned and what research directions were emphasized and those that were not. Truth be told, he was often the initiator of several key innovations since the various branches of the Israeli Defense Forces did not always realize how new or emerging technology could enhance their capabilities. At 52, Marvin had worked with all the key players in the service. He knew his stuff better than anyone and had a mind that thrived on challenges. He loved innovation, even if it were going to stretch his own capabilities nearly to the breaking point. He was a man of vision, and his vision focused on technology. His only well-known shortcoming was that he loved technology so much that he would often extend his explanations to levels of detail that many considered unnecessary, and he often veered away from common Hebrew, or English, to speak in technobabble. Yet, most people still gave him a pass on those, as he was so good at everything else.

Mark and his team quickly drew up two lists. The first involved projects that focused on already well-understood targets, particularly the various incarnations of the Palestinian resistance. The second had four projects. One was aimed at dealing blows to Iran's nuclear industry, which had substantially rebuilt since Israel's last attack.[4] Another looked at any means to disturb Iran's oil and gas production. The third concerned the Houthis in Yemen as they were known to have fired at least one ballistic missile toward Israel. And the fourth focused on Afghanistan as a means of retaliating against the Taliban. From the start, Mark's task force as he called it had agreed on one additional condition that should govern any actions they undertook: they would make every effort to abide by the laws of war, by which they would endeavor to minimize civilian casualties and would refrain from any form of biological or chemical warfare. Mark had summarized his reasoning, though he was preaching to the choir since his two associates had no difficulty agreeing with him:

"We are fighting regimes, not civilians. I am almost certain David and Simon would immediately agree with me, but, even in the unlikely event they don't, I'm ready to defend this choice."

I I ■ I I

Once Mark and his small team had refined their list, it was time for Mark to visit Marvin Goldstein. Marvin's office was just as one would have expected—messy like the office one would know belonged to the proverbial absent-minded professor or scientist. The wide bay window offered a beautiful view of the Mediterranean and of the Herzliya marina. Inside the office, he had drawings, blueprints, mock-ups, and detailed models of several of his current works-in-progress. The coffee table in front of his visitors' sofa was littered with technical

---

4 By the same author, see *Operation Kovesh*, Barringer Publishing 2020.

magazines and papers or articles that he had not yet read or wanted to read again before deciding what to do with them.

There were even a few folders on the floor in the general area of his desk; only Marvin knew what was in them . . .

Yet, Mark immediately noticed the two orchid plants which Marvin had placed on his credenza. They were a talking point within the whole office and had been given various nicknames: "Marvin's Zen Island," "the flowery side of the mad scientist," "Marvin's internal contradictions in full view," and several others, not always immediately printable. Everybody had his or her own label, always meant as a joke, as Marvin was held in extremely high esteem by all, whether high or low on the totem pole. To most people, he was "the visionary." The orchids had enough sunlight to satisfy their need for some light but not too much that they might have died. Marvin took care of their weekly watering himself and everyone knew not to tinker with them. They were his and not *Mossad's*. To Mark, they exuded a sense of calm and peacefulness in the middle of what could only be called a cluttered office. David had told Mark that Marvin would soak the orchids in water for 30 minutes, wipe the pots dry afterwards, and promptly place them back where they belonged.

Mark initiated the conversation with a brief summary of the mission given to him by Simon and David. He told Marvin he totally understood that more than two-thirds of the possible projects on the lists would not be realized, or at least not in the near future. Yet, he said he wanted the agenda to be as comprehensive as it could be so he would be sure he had not left something out.

Marvin asked as he almost always did when he started any conversation:

"So, what can I do for you?"

"Well, as you go down the lists, can you eyeball the projects that simply require too many resources at present or those that simply make no operational sense. I'll grant you, my team and I allowed our collective imagination to go as wild as we could and only started applying reasonableness tests afterwards."

Marvin took his time processing through the two lists. Mark was surprised to see him once or twice come quite close to giggling. He certainly was not about to interrupt the master of innovation, but the giggling made him worry. When he saw Marvin had run through the lists, he asked:

"Marvin, I saw you suppress a giggle or two at one point. Is there something really silly?"

"No. Absolutely not. Your main plan for Afghanistan is incredibly ingenious."

"It is realistic?"

"Well, one part of it is in the field of biochemistry and we are not particularly great in that area. Yet, I'm quite sure Countess Renate of the Shadow Experts might be able to help. I'm ready to find a way to help you if you can get the raw materials, my friend. But I'm not sure how we could organize safe and anonymous delivery."

"How about the others?"

"Well, I won't surprise you saying there is nothing terribly new with respect to the Palestinians. Plus, at this point, we're not involved in surreptitious guerrilla warfare. We are fighting a war. So, I would lay those aside."

He paused and shifted back to what Mark and his team called the first list:

"I like your idea with respect to the Houthis and to Yemen, but I'm not sure we have the capabilities to project our forces so far at present. I'm sure a special force team could do the job, but I can't imagine Simon or David agreeing to send a small team with only minimal backup. Things tend to go wrong when you least expect and can least afford it."

Shifting to the Iranian list, Marvin smiled. He argued that there was no time to organize something new on the nuclear front, adding:

"You know that based on reports which we have never confirmed, we have used virtually every trick in the book. Plus, I'm sure that's where they would expect you to hit. The really interesting idea you have has to do with the oil and gas disruption. I suspect they have not realized that something could be done. We need to look at your idea in more detail."

Mark thanked Marvin profusely and told him that he would now take the edited lists to David and Simon, mischievously adding:

"Come to think of it, I'll talk to David first before I suggest we go to Simon."

"Smart. Very smart."

■ ■ ■ ■ ■

Mark's meeting with David to go over the edited list of projects from his visit with Marvin was relatively uneventful, although David kept congratulating Mark and his team for their imagination. For the sake of simplicity, at the outset at least, Mark chose to keep only three projects, noting that there was ample room to expand the list if the opportunity presented itself or if it became more relevant. The three projects were labelled by the country in which they would be carried out; so, he called them Afghanistan, Iran and Yemen. He did note, however, that he reserved powder to deal with the three most dangerous Palestinian organizations: Hamas, Hezbollah, and Islamic Jihad.

David was quite complimentary regarding the work done, asking many questions concerning how the projects would be conducted and by whom. In the end, it became abundantly clear there were several missing elements. Mark himself replied:

"As I said at the outset, the only 'outside' resource on which our team called was Marvin. And you understand that I say 'outside' because he is not a part of the Disruption group."

"Understood."

"Now, Marvin was quite clear there would be several practical issues which included but were not limited to equipment. In other words, we know there are holes in our plan, but we did not want to go beyond our *Disruption* group before having at least your OK and, possibly Simon's if you thought we needed to."

David replied that Mark's strategy was quite sensible, though he asked:

"Where do you see the biggest holes?"

"Unquestionably, they have to do with Afghanistan and Iran. In both cases, we are assuming some substance exists which we could use, and Marvin agreed with that assumption, though he did not call it an assumption, but a speculation. In fact, the only project where we have everything we need, except the backup, is with respect to Yemen."

"How do you plan on acquiring these substances, as you call them?"

"I wanted to talk to you about a conversation with Countess Renate."

"You're correct. Let me get Simon's clearance. This said, I suspect he will not object, though he will probably tell me to be quite prudent."

CHAPTER.15

*TEL AVIV, ISRAEL; AND SOMEWHERE
IN THE AUSTRIAN ALPS*

Countess Renate was only mildly surprised when she saw the invitation to a Zoom videoconference with David Heller and Mark Levi. She had already been a part of the current adventure through the help she provided when the issue was to contact Menes Al-Soliman. But she quickly assumed that either there was another case for which she might help or that there were additional needs in the current case. Unbeknownst to her, she was correct about the latter idea, but she was mildly surprised that the request David and Mark were making differed from the normal pattern of their interactions.

Though her relationship with David's group, and *Mossad* more broadly, had always remained totally on the professional level, both the Shadow Experts and *Mossad's* Disruption Group had understood a vast number of synergies could be created when they worked together. Thus, while the initial joint-efforts had so far always started after *Mossad* had developed most, if not all, aspects of their planned scenarios, the recent past had seen a few initial conversations that would fall under a feasibility study header.

Bringing Countess Renate and the Shadow Experts earlier into the deliberations would surely make certain new things possible. On the other hand, it might require David and his team to disclose elements that were top secret. In fact, David's invitation clearly indicated the current plans were not much more than half-baked ideas. He even indicated that the topic of their conversation would include certain details which even the Prime Minister didn't know about.

"David and Mark, how nice to see you two. What can I do for you today?"

David replied:

"Great to see you, too, Countess. Thanks again for all the help with respect to Menes. Here, I'm going to let Mark carry the ball most of the time today, as he is the one investigating the feasibility of the projects we want to discuss with you."

"No problem. Mark, I'm all ears."

Before Mark even had a chance to start his reply, David prefaced his comments further with a crucial caveat:

"Sorry to cut Mark off after what I just said, but I must add an important note of caution. A part of Mark's comments that is absolutely top-secret and is only 90% verified is that the Taliban are helping The Muslim Brotherhood in Egypt. But I'm only saying this to remind you, since we've already discussed this with you when we needed to connect with the head of the *Mukhabarat*."

"I remember it well. Any further development since then?"

"Yes. There was a second attempt, which was foiled by Menes Al-Soliman, the head of the *Mukhabarat*."

Countess Renate replied:

"I'm sure at this point I don't need to know the details but let me assure you that you have surely stirred my feminine curiosity. Now, Mark, I cannot wait to hear what you have to say."

Mark took over the conversation and proceeded to describe the idea behind the plans to punish the Houthis of Yemen, to hurt Iran directly, and to disrupt things in Afghanistan. Both he and David could clearly see the smiles and, even at times, the giggles of Renate as he was going through the details of what he wanted to do. When Mark was through, she simply said:

"Well, gentlemen, I think we may be able to help. I need to talk to a few people within my network, but I believe I am aware of a couple of experiments which might produce the kind of results you are seeking. I would love to talk about how you plan on bringing these substances to bear, but I suspect this is premature. After all, you say you know nothing about them other than their desired outcomes, and neither do I."

■ ■ ■ ■ ■

Less than a week later, the same three people were back on the video conference phone, with Countess Renate the initiator of the meeting. She was happy to announce that she had met with some success concerning one of the questions, though she was still investigating the other.

She described a substance which she felt could certainly help strike at Afghanistan. She explained she knew quite well a scientist based in Melbourne, Australia. The gentleman, named Stuart Harvey, had started as an analyst, and had eventually grown into one of the most recognized names in the field of biochemistry as applied to agriculture in Australia and elsewhere in the world. He worked at CSIRO, though he also had teaching and consulting responsibilities.

She explained:

"Let me give you a brief introduction of the entity for which he works. CSIRO is an acronym for Commonwealth Scientific and Industrial Research Organization. Its own website gives the best description of who they are. So, I'd rather quote it than invent something just to paraphrase. 'CSIRO is an Australian Government statutory authority constituted and operating under the provisions of the Science and Industry Research Act 1949. CSIRO's primary functions under the Act are to carry out scientific research to benefit Australian industry and the community, and to contribute to the achievement of national objectives.' The element which might be of interest here is the focus they have developed to fight against undesirable plants that threaten crops."

She went on to argue that the introduction into Australia, an island continent, of undesirable species had been one of its most constant concerns over the years. She mentioned one of the funnier examples:

"Cats probably first arrived in Australia as pets of European settlers during the 18th century. But later, they were deliberately introduced more broadly in an attempt to control rabbits and rodents. Well, now feral cats are considered a plague that needs to be controlled as rabbits once were. Similar stories could be told about foxes or cane toads, but let's dispense with that. What has been true for animals is even truer for plants and that's where Stuart Harvey comes in."

She paused and added:

"One of Stuart's most recent achievements involves a substance which remains secret."

She explained that when dropped on an undesirable plant, the substance prevents it from developing its usual reproductive capabilities.

Countess Renate turned to the example of opium as a primary crop in Afghanistan. She pointed out poppy seeds are harvested from dried poppy pods. She explained that, without them, without having seeds, farmers could not keep up annual planting. She added with a smile that most seeds are in the ground by November in the Northern Hemisphere concluding:

"The flowers usually appear within 90 days."

She then turned to opium harvesting and seed production, telling David and Mark:

"Once the petals of the crimson flowers have fallen, the pods are 'scored' just like tappers slice a small groove in the bark of rubber tree trunks and then peel back the bark so that the latex can seep out. The same is true for poppies: after the opium has been scraped from the bulbs, the pods are cut from the plant and allowed to dry. When they have dried, the pods are cut open and the seeds are removed and sun-dried for the following year's season."

Concluding her short presentation, Countess Renate said there would be no usable seed to collect if anything or anyone were to hinder the development of the plant's reproductive organs. She paused and added:

"You know what? The next time I talk to Stuart Harvey, I must ask him if the substance would also inhibit the production of opium."

Mark was ecstatic and asked whether the substance would be the same for all plants. Countess Renate replied that the substance had to be adapted to each plant, but she had been told the process was not particularly time-consuming, once you knew what to do and how to do it. Mark concluded:

"So, if we could get our hand on the substance, we would be able to punish Afghanistan by making it harder to grow the poppies it needs to feed its opium industry."

David asked:

"Do we know how bulky and heavy that substance would be to deal say with one acre or one hectare?"

"At this point I don't, but I could find out quite quickly."

David concluded:

"Let's find out and, in the meantime, Mark and I will work on logistics."

■ ■ ▓ ■ ■

Mark's major goal at this stage of the project was to deal with what he euphemistically called "technical difficulties." In his mind, technical difficulties were those elements of a potential solution that were not currently available. In fact, David had kidded him when he first used the phrase, saying:

"You call them technical difficulties; I call them hurdles."

"Can't disagree with you, but I need to be optimistic. I think I have found solutions, or rather workarounds, but I need to know first, if they are feasible, and second, how quickly they could be made to work."

"That's one of the things I like about you, Mark: your optimism. Just make sure you do not try to square a circle. Others have tried, and no one has succeeded."

"So far, David, so far!"

■ ■ ■ ■ ■

One of Mark's first decisions was to abandon the idea of attacking Iran's nuclear industry, arguing to his team:

"We've been after it in so many different ways that I suspect they are prepared for us."

He added:

"That does not mean we will not keep trying, but until we come up with something radically new and feasible in these times of constrained resources, we shall focus our attention elsewhere."

While he was thus prepared to focus away from Iran's nuclear industry, Mark and his two close associates, Nathan Heimer and Elias Schneeberg, were determined to strike at the country's oil industry. They had correctly observed Iran had no trouble raising foreign currency by selling oil despite all the sanctions against it. Mark had thought of a three-pronged attack which would require three discrete, though somehow, related operations. Indeed, while the operations would be carried out by three different teams, they were supposed to occur simultaneously to create more confusion in the enemy's ranks. David had approved the outline of the plan and suggested to Mark he did not need him to be on the call when Mark spoke with Countess Renate. Indeed, though two of the attacks would call upon *Mossad* internal capabilities, both in terms of materials and execution, the third required help from the Shadow Experts.

Mark was, as usual, captivated by the always joyful and partially throaty sound of Countess Renate's voice as she said:

"Mark, how can we help you this time?"

"Well, Countess, we have devised a plan to hurt Iran's oil industry, unfortunately not permanently, but certainly for some time. But one of the key elements of the plan requires the help of Wong Hai Chock, your cyber expert in Singapore."

"Wonderful. I'm sure he will be delighted. Now can you give me a quick outline?"

Mark proceeded to describe the full extent of the proposed attack, though he warned Renate that he would withhold all unnecessary details, not because they were secret, but because they might be confusing. He could clearly see from Countess Renate's face on the screen she was comfortable with that, though she asked:

"Will you allow me to ask questions if I get lost?"

"Sure. Goes without saying, Countess."

"Thank you."

Turning to the need for Wong Hai Chock, Mark explained that he wanted as many computerized controls as possible at work within Iran's oilfield operations to fail. Countess Renate asked whether Mark had an entry into the relevant computer systems. He replied that *Mossad* had a deeply buried agent within the regional directorate who could provide the entry. Correcting himself, he added he actually had several contacts who could do the job. Referring to whomever would be entrusted with the task, he added matter-of-factly:

"He would allow us to infect his computer, which then would in turn infect the whole network."

He paused for a quick second and mentioned the crucial missing link:

"However, we cannot allow any trace of any intrusion to remain. That's where we will need Hai Chock. Someone must erase any trace of invasion on that computer immediately afterwards, and I know this capability is already in his toolbox."[5]

"I know exactly what you mean. In fact, he might be able to call on his friend Nathan Sharon who, as you know, is particularly good at finding entry points into networks."

"Could be interesting, though we might not need him since we have our entry point already."

"I understand that, Mark, but what if you wanted to extend the reach of your disruption?"

Mark nodded and conceded he had not considered that option as an arrow in his quiver. Countess Renate wondered how disrupting the computer network of Iran's oil industry played into the project he had outlined. Mark replied the question was excellent and explained that the goal of the other two physical activities, as he called them, was to interrupt the flow of oil. The various "explosions" which he was planning would create the need to stop operations, failing which a massive oil spill could develop. The way the various explosions would be conducted would also create auxiliary serious difficulties at the time normal operations returned. He added:

"Without going into too much detail, what we're planning to do should force Iran to shut down production for more than a few hours. We may not be talking weeks or months, but we surely are talking days."

Mark paused to check that the countess was still on board. Having verified she was, he continued:

---

[5] By the same author, see *Escaping the Bear*, Barringer Publishing 2023.

"The idea is we've been told that shutting down several wells for some time is feasible but may create tensions within the oil reservoir. In fact, the only thing that you do when you shut a well down is like turning a spigot off. Yet, the pressure within the well and the reservoir does not fall; in fact, it keeps rising as the oil is no longer allowed to flow out. I'm told that water or something equivalent is pumped into the well to equalize the pressure, but there are limits."

"I see. But I assume that this requires the stoppage to be sufficiently broad, otherwise you could compensate the temporary shutting down of a well by allowing a greater flow from neighboring wells."

"Correct. Or by directing production toward holding tanks rather than being allowed to flow through pipelines. And that's the key. We are planning to cut off that option."

Countess Renate smiled broadly and interrupted:

"I bet you want a computer failure to prevent any form of orderly shutdown or the onset of compensatory measures."

"Yes, but there is more, Countess. And that could be the spectacular part!"

CHAPTER.16

Simon picked up his phone and as usual for him only said: "Simon here . . ."

David Heller was calling Simon to ask for some of his time. He needed to find out whether access to a couple of secret, or at least semi-secret, Navy resources[6] could be available. David was referring to a couple of vessels that looked like supply ships where the bridge was toward the front half of the boat and the middle and aft sections above deck were suitable for carrying different loads, including drilling pipes, for instance. However, they could, within a minute, be made to look like fishing boats when the crane that would normally lie horizontally on the aft deck was raised. In short, they were a lot more than supply boats.

■ ■ ■ ■ ■

---

6 By the same author, see *Below the Surface*, Barringer Publishing, 2021.

The first crucial difference between these vessels and regular boats was they could reach considerably higher speeds since they could transform into hydrofoils with a couple of simple maneuvers.

The foils, which at rest were folded into the hull at the bow of the boat, could be extended; at speed, the boat riding on these foils would rise higher on the water and create less friction with the water and thus more speed. To accommodate the fact that the boat could rise higher on the water, the angle and length of the two propeller shafts could also be altered so they would still operate at full power and with full effect at top speed. That alone made them quite different from any supply boat and would allow them to outrun virtually any boat, particularly as their twin engines were double the power which boats of that size would normally have. Unfortunately, with the need for more power came the requirement that fuel capacity be increased as well. They weighed more, but that would not be visible to someone from the outside, as the extra space for fuel was taken from the cargo-carrying capacity below deck.

Another series of modifications would never be visible except to those who knew where to look. First, the vessels were equipped with an air lock which allowed the boat to pick up or deliver loads underwater. Usually, this feature was used to transfer cargo from one boat to another, but it also allowed the boats to be resupplied in food or water from a submarine without the operations being visible to anyone above water. Also, the lower level of the front deck, under the bridge tower, hid a full gamut of electronic surveillance equipment. It offered space for a couple of operators to work while allowing them to move from that space to the modest living quarters on the bridge without stepping out in the open. Only the equipment that required placement on top of the bridge would be visible, but even there, many fishing boats have similarly complex navigation gear.

Finally, the vessels could easily change identity. They each had three names on rotating supports on each side of the bow of the ship.

Simply rotating the support would allow the ship to change its name. At the same time, each of the names corresponded to a country of registration. Currently, they were using Malta, Panama, and Gibraltar, but any other country flag could be substituted if needed. Thus, the flagpole at the very aft of the ship would display the flag corresponding to the registered name through a clever mechanism inspired from the multi-color ballpoint pens of the past: each flag would roll around its own axis and the whole retract into a sheave. The captain could therefore "dial up" the flag he wanted. The ultimate disguise, however, dealt with the color of the hull's middle section. The top of the hull would always be white, while the bottom, the part most often immersed into the water, would always be black. The middle section, however, comprised small-section vertical rotating equilateral triangles which could display one of three colors: red, dark green, and white.

■ ■ ■ ■ ■

Simon confirmed the boats would be available with their usual captains, Barack Decker, and Moshe Aaron. Barack Decker's boat carried three names, with three different pavilions, and three different mid-hull colors: the white-hulled *Charm of the Sea* with her Malta flag, the dark-green-hulled *Sea Dragon* and her Panama flag, or the red-hulled *Sailing Joy* with her Gibraltar flag. Moshe Aaron's ship had the same variations: the white-hulled *Sailing Princess* with her Gibraltar flag, the red-hulled *Sea Riches* with her Panama flag, and the dark-green-hulled *Flying Dolphin* with her Malta flag.

■ ■ ■ ■ ■

As he had been planning this particular attack, Mark had one option that centered exclusively on unmanned submarines. While Israel had been relying solely on Orca drones until recently, Mark decided to shift to a newer, though smaller, design, code named, the Emerald Whale. To differentiate, the Orca was an unmanned submarine with diesel engines. It had a range of 6,500 nautical miles and could run completely alone for months at a time. Basically, it was a 51-foot-long circular tube measuring nine feet in diameter. The version which Israel was using could incorporate an additional payload module that added 34 feet to the length of the submarine drone but allowed an extra carrying capacity of eight tons. An important feature of its appeal to Israel was that the Orca had a hybrid powertrain. It used diesel engines when at or near the surface but could also switch to battery power when stealth was the most crucial need.

The Emerald Whale was an Israeli "version" of the Orca with two crucial differences. It was about half the size of the Orca when the latter carried its extra payload module, making it more discreet, but that also reduced the amount of payload it could carry. The second difference was it was all electric, reducing the endurance of the vessel. This was in keeping with the priorities which the Israeli Navy had for its equipment: it would never be accused of building complexity for the sake of it. Its commanding officers all knew that simplicity reduced the risk of failure, as well as the cost of any program.

The prototype which Mark would be using, named Whale for short, incorporated at least three important additional features. The first feature was an air lock that allowed cargo to be placed into the submarine while underwater. The other two, which were more important, involved a double remote-control capability, which was different from most unmanned underwater vehicles that typically followed pre-programmed routes. The Emerald Whale could be controlled by radio when the submarine's telescopic mast was close enough to the surface, but it could also be controlled through sonar signals when it was underwater. In many ways, this feature was conceptually similar to the software controlling the Eitan flying drone. Though it could be operated entirely through pre-programmed instructions, it could also be remote-controlled.

The only additional challenge created by a submarine compared to a flying drone was the need to provide both above and underwater communication protocols. Radio signals do not travel underwater, and sonar messages cannot be transmitted through the air. The drone could return to home port whenever all signals were lost. If it could not "hear" a signal underwater, the drone would typically rise close enough to the surface for the telescopic mast to send out a radio signal. This would allow the drone to determine its actual location and software using artificial intelligence could then plot the shortest distance to home port, sending that navigation plan to the control officers at home who could vary its route if there was a need. The only drawback would be if the drone did not have the electrical power to reach its destination, in which case the drone would self-destruct.

Offensively, an Emerald Whale could be equipped with mines to lay down. It could also manage a couple of sea-to-land missiles that could be used to hit port infrastructure. The current mission targeted Hudaydah, Yemen, the fourth largest city in Yemen and its principal port on the Red Sea. In the past, Israel had used flying drones to deliver a variety of bombs or even air-launched torpedoes to places closer than Hudaydah. Though theoretically possible, Israel had no drone capable of carrying this kind of ordnance and flying round-trip back to Israel without refueling. The decision made in an earlier adventure to use an airbase in Saudi Arabia[7] had been crucially dependent then upon the Kingdom being a silent partner in the plans. Here, because of the desire to keep all current actions under wraps, the idea of requesting Saudi Arabia's help was just a non-starter.

■ ■ ■ ■ ■

---

[7] By the same author, see *Glitter and Smoke*, Barringer Publishing, 2023.

Meanwhile, Ayman called Ben to relay a conversation he just had with his informer, Gamal. As he had done in prior instances, he tried to give Ben as faithful a rendition of who said what:

"Ammon? Gamal here?"

"Gamal. Where are you? I haven't heard from you for at least a couple of weeks."

"Doesn't matter where I am. I'm only calling to let you know that I've heard that the Muslim Brotherhood is going to place a bomb at the Temple of Abydos."

"The Temple of Abydos?"

"Yes. That's what I heard."

"Do you mean the temple proper, the Gallery of the Kings, the Osireion, the helicopter hieroglyph? There are so many sites, Gamal?"

Ayman said that Gamal simply replied:

"I don't know, Ammon. The only thing I have heard is that the Muslim Brotherhood will place a bomb there in the next 48 hours."

■ ■ ■ ■ ■

When talking of potential multiple sites, Ayman was referring to the well-known places that visitors tour in the city of Abydos. Located not more than 60 miles to the northwest of Luxor, Abydos was one of the main archaeological sites in Egypt, with several old temples and Umm el-Qa'ab, a royal necropolis. Most visited was the Memorial Temple of Menmaatre Seti I, the second pharaoh of the 19th Dynasty of Egypt. He was the son of Rames I and Sitre, and the father of Rames II. The temple contained an inscription from the 19th Dynasty known as the Abydos King List or the Gallery of the Kings. It listed the most dynastic pharaohs of Egypt from Menes until Seti I. Another curiosity was a site called the "helicopter hieroglyphs." There, sculptors of various generations carved new hieroglyphs on stones that already had been used and it led to an oddity: a series of hieroglyphs which resembled modern weapons such as a helicopter or a submarine. Yet, scientists had proved that distinct parts of different carvings coincidentally came together to create these images. For instance, the helicopter had been shown to be the combination of the arms of Ramses II and the head of Seti I. Turning to the last site which Ayman mentioned, the Osireion was an integral part of the temple of Seti I and was said to have possibly been built to resemble a tomb in the nearby Valley of the Kings.

Interestingly, the one element of the dialog Ayman did not report, though it appeared quite innocuous, was the last comment made by Gamal. He noted in passing that he hoped he had done the right thing, a few days earlier. Unsure of what his contact was referring to, Ayman asked for more information. Gamal simply said that he had seen Ayman talking to a Caucasian individual near the El Galaa Bridge on the Corniche El Nile, adding with a smile:

"Probably not more than 1,000 feet north of the Embassy of the Russian Federation. You must like nice neighborhoods, my friend."

Without allowing any emotion to be visible on his face, Ayman told Gamal that he had been right not to interfere. He explained he had numerous tourist clients who stayed at hotels in that area. Gamal had added he had seen them walk together. Ayman deadpanned that it would not be surprising for him to walk with a client. Gamal had said he had lost sight of them as they had walked together on the Corniche while he was near the square just west of the El Galaa bridge. Ayman finally replied:

"It's always a good thing not to interrupt private conversations. I don't want my contacts to know about you any more than you would want me to know yours."

During the call with Ayman, Ben asked him several of the questions Ayman had asked Gamal, to which Ayman kept replying:

"I've asked the question, Sayyid Ben, and Gamal did not know."

"Did not know or did not say?"

"He told me he did not know."

Ben thanked Ayman and told him he would take steps to monitor and protect the various sites. He had the nagging feeling that something was badly amiss. On the one hand, the time frame of 48 hours seemed odd since it was longer than in prior instances. In the two previous warnings, the bombs had been placed in the early morning or, at the latest, by midday of the day after the warning. Similarly, the fact that the announced location covered not one but two adjacent sites and several possible spots within these sites left a lot of room for error. Yet, the two prior warnings had been correct, and Ben did not feel the option of staying put and saying nothing was even a remote possibility. Ben called Mark with the news and suggested that Countess Renate might take the appropriate next steps.

■ ■ ■ ■ ■

Predictably, given the accuracy of Countess Renate's prior warnings, Menes Al-Soliman quickly organized all the necessary precautions based on this news. He dispatched Lieutenant Omar and four of his two-man patrols to the general area. Instead of covering all the specific valuable locations within the two sites, Lieutenant Omar decided he would place his patrols at each of the crossroads one would have to use to get to the sites. He assumed the terrorists would have to come by car since the nature of the ruins would require powerful bombs to create any real damage. He and the truck in which he was riding controlled the fifth of the five locations that he identified as inevitable passage points for the terrorists to reach any of their possible targets by car or truck.

Once the four patrols had set up at their respective stations, Lieutenant Omar surprised the three soldiers who were left with him. In the back of their military truck, he opened a wooden case which had been placed between the two rows of seats, near the cabin where he and his driver, Azriel, sat. The men had earlier complained the box limited the room available for their feet. The top of the case removed, the soldiers could see Lieutenant Omar extract what turned out to be a small aerial drone and a computer tablet. He made sure the battery pack connected to the drone was fully charged and then sent the drone flying in a simple pattern over the three most likely places the terrorists would bomb. What the men could not see was that the drone was equipped with cameras designed to show temperature differences.

Lieutenant Omar's reasoning had been that anyone penetrating into either of the sites without using any of the roads would need to use much smaller dirt paths if they used mopeds, bicycles or donkeys. The camera heat-sensors would detect a difference between the temperature of the moving targets and the environment. Men would be warmer than their environment during the evening and the night and cooler during the heat of the day. To him, it meant that no one could get close to the sites. That would mean that any strike would have to use a missile or at least a small rocket, the one form of attack which he felt was unlikely given the nature of the warning and the prior modus operandi of the terrorists.

Having put in place the best defenses he could imagine, Lieutenant Omar told all of his troops to make sure at least one man stayed awake and focused on the mission in each patrol. He also told everyone a new batch of soldiers would come six hours later to relieve those who had been with him.

CHAPTER.17

TEL AVIV, ISRAEL; AND SOMEWHERE IN THE RED SEA

The plan Mark hatched, and David approved for dealing with the Houthi rebels in Yemen did not involve new technology. For once, the challenge centered on having two categories of weapons that had already worked multiple times in tandem. Practice would allow the team to iron out any issue related to coordination.

■ ■ ■ ■ ■

The Houthi movement, loosely affiliated to Iran, was officially known as *Ansa Allah*, "Supporters of God." It was a Shia Islamist political and military group that emerged from the Saada Governorate of Yemen in the 1990s. Currently, Houthi insurgents were in control of Sanaa, the capital of Yemen, and all former North Yemen, except for the Eastern *Marib* Governorate. The two countries, the Republic of Yemen (North Yemen) and South Yemen, were created after the collapse of the Turkish Ottoman Empire. While North Yemen became an independent republic, South Yemen found its origins as a British Colony in 1874, when Britain brought together the British Colony of Aden and the Aden Protectorate. It remained as such until the revolution there forced Britain to move out in November 1967.

In 1990, the two countries, Marxist South Yemen and conservative North Yemen unified to become the Republic of Yemen. The president of North Yemen became the new country's president, and the leader of the South Yemeni Socialist Party, its vice president. The unification did not go smoothly. Economic and political troubles caused the near collapse of the new country. The Marxist South Yemeni leadership had no intention to play a secondary role to anyone. To date, the political situation remained confused with claims to the presidency contested between the chairman of the Houthi Supreme Political Council, who was only recognized by Iran, and the individual who had been officially president since 2022. Not surprisingly, such a potentially explosive political environment had created some measure of lawlessness within the country.

■ ■ ■ ■ ■

Mark's specific target was a Houthi-controlled harbor, Hudaydah, located just north of the Bab Al-Mandab Strait at the Red Sea's southern tip. Somewhat like the Strait of Hormuz at the southern tip of the Persian Gulf, the Bab Al-Mandab Strait was a narrow passageway, a crucial point through which traffic from the Red Sea to the Indian Ocean must sail. Controlled by the Houthis who were further protected by the narrowness of the strait, Hudaydah was the port where ships highjacked by Houthi pirates had been taken. The main goal of Mark's strategy was to inflict sufficient damage to the harbor infrastructure so it could still manage smaller cargo ships bringing necessary supplies to the country, and yet not be usable by the pirates.

The very first wave of the attack planned by Mark had Captain Barack Decker sailing the white-hulled *Charm of the Seas*, flying her Malta Flag, a white eight-pointed cross on a red background, and carrying a precious cargo from Haifa to the lower end of the Red Sea. Simon, David, and Mark had decided the idea of attacking the Houthi rebels in Yemen not only made sense but could be carried out with a high degree of anonymity and relative safety. In their view, shared with Yael Orbach, the Head of Israel's navy, the Emerald Whale prototype was the best tool available to the team, even though it was still barely beyond the prototype stage. They would need, however, to abstain from using certain functions that had not been thoroughly evaluated yet.

The main challenge, however, was that traveling the nearly 1,300 nautical miles separating Haifa from Hudaydah, at a top speed of 10-15 knots, would take more than five days. More importantly, it would use most of the electrical capacity of the submarine drone. Although the Emerald Whale batteries could be recharged at sea, Mark and David thought it would be inconvenient at best. It would force the Whale to be tethered to a boat equipped with an external battery charger. They, therefore, decided it would be easier and more convenient for the drone to be transported closer to the operating theater.

They quickly eliminated the option of flying the submarine drone to the Red Sea. Israel did not have an aircraft carrier. The official reason often cited for that was it would cost too much money to build. The more likely rationale was that a single aircraft carrier patrolling in the Persian Gulf or the Red Sea would be a sitting duck. Both bodies of water contained more enemies of Israel on their borders than friends. Further, patrolling the eastern Mediterranean Sea or the Gulf of Oman would be redundant given the presence of the U.S. Navy. The only viable airborne solution David and Mark briefly discussed was the idea of transporting the drone onto an American aircraft carrier. Loading it would have to take place south of the Bab Al Mandab Straits, since any maneuver within the Red Sea would be so obvious as to defeat the whole purpose. Also, bringing the Americans officially into the loop was at best suboptimal.

Mark came up with the idea of using one of Israel's disguised supply ships, with a simple modification to be carried out while the ship was in Haifa. The ship they would use, the *Charm of the Seas*, was still relatively short in length, measuring about 110 feet. With two-thirds of the vessel's length occupied by the platform aft of the bridge area, there was still plenty of room to carry the Emerald Whale. The problem was, given the shape of the available space in the hull of the *Charm of the Seas* below deck and the girth of the Whale being seven-and-a-half feet in diameter, it was not practical for the Emerald Whale to be concealed under the deck. Mark's plan for hiding the protruding top of the drone was to cover it with a tarpaulin. To further the disguise, he had ordered a tarp cover six feet longer than the drone, adding three feet of coverage at the front and three feet at the back. He had asked for two feet of pipe to extend beyond the edge of the tarp at its front and at its back so anyone looking at the ship, closely or from afar, would see oil pipes sticking out from the tarpaulin. It would look like the *Charm of the Seas* was simply carrying a cargo of oil pipes, possibly destined to an offshore oil platform. As an additional precaution and despite the relatively high cost, he had asked that the tarp be lined with Kevlar so that any stray bullets would not damage the drone.

Captain Decker had agreed to employ a larger crew than usual since more men were needed to conduct the major operations launched from the ship. The plan was first to lay mines at the wide entrance to the port of Hudaydah, in effect allowing only zodiacs or small craft drawing no more than a few feet of water to pass through. Secondarily, the plan involved firing missiles to damage and, if possible, destroy as many of the naval radar stations located along the Yemen coast from Hudaydah to the Bab Al-Mandab Strait. However, the Emerald Whale would not be used for this since it had not been sufficiently evaluated. Mark had devised another means to execute that maneuver.

■ ■ ■ ■ ■

Captain Moshe Aaron of the *Sailing Princess*, the sister ship of the *Charm of the Sea*, had left Haifa a day earlier than Barack Decker. The *Sailing Princess* flew the Gibraltar flag rather than the Malta flag, but the ship had the same white hull as the *Charm of the Sea*. Moshe was heading to the Persian Gulf since he was expected to play a primary role in the attacks directed toward Iran. David and Mark had agreed that the only realistic route for Moshe was to sail through the Suez Canal, the Red Sea, the Gulf of Aden, and the Strait of Hormuz. Therefore, with Hudaydah on the port side before she reached the Bab Al-Mandab Strait, the *Sailing Princess* would play a defensive role in the general vicinity of the *Charm of the Seas*, if needed.

The *Charm of the Seas* could not reasonably be left to operate solo. Marvin Goldstein had made this his main objection originally. No matter how disguised and special her capabilities, a ship like the *Charm of the Seas* had to have some sort of escort. The team had anticipated at least three kinds of attacks the Houthis might make, whether they had identified her as an Israeli vessel, an enemy ship, or simply a good target for piracy. Just like the pirates of Eritrea, located on the opposite bank of the Red Sea, Houthi rebels were known for their well-developed pirating skills, one of the ways they earned their living. They had already attacked numerous ships, large or small, and captured them, usually for ransom. With only one notable exception, any attack had always involved a number of small ships converging on the eventual target.

Barack's ship needed defenses against such a flotilla whose commander's intention was to board the ship and take control of it. Barack's vessel was equipped with machine guns, two at the stern and concealed below deck. When needed, they would be brought into position. The gunners would sit next to the guns and be protected by the shield in front of them. That shield consisted of steel on the lower half and thick bulletproof glass on its upper section.

A second type of pirate attack might involve the use of rockets or missiles fired from shore or, worse, from unmanned arial drones. Commercial vessels had already faced this tactic, so Mark had taken the precaution of envisaging them as an independent attack on Barack's ship. Depending on the size and number of these projectiles, they could overwhelm the target ship in only a minute or so. The *Charm* had to be defended against such a possibility and these defensive duties were assigned to *INS Storm* under the command of Captain Ayel. A Dolphin-class submarine, *INS Storm* carried non-nuclear missiles for this mission. Together with her normal complement of torpedoes, she could come to the rescue of the *Charm of the Seas* if she were ever attacked.

Although *INS Storm* could also defend against a third type of attack involving helicopters, the planners decided to use Moshe's *Sailing Princess* for this third possibility. In the recent past, Houthi rebels had used helicopters to board a commercial ship and take her over after pirates had landed onto the ship's deck. They had been successful once but failed the second time when a U.S. destroyer intervened. Mark had concluded this mode of attack required the ability to shoot down a helicopter away from the target vessel, so Israel's navy had replaced the gun at the stern of Moshe's *Sailing Princess* with one that could shoot down a helicopter. Equally importantly, they equipped the gun with stronger and more powerful aiming tools, including an infra-red visor. The plan was to position Moshe's boat far enough from the action that the rebels would not pay attention to her, yet she would have any helicopter or unmanned arial drone well within her range of fire.

A final line of defense was provided by the U.S. Fifth Fleet which had been responsible for naval forces in the Persian Gulf, Red Sea, Arabian Sea, and parts of the Indian Ocean. It shared a commander and headquarters with U.S. Naval Forces Central Command in Bahrain.

CHAPTER.18

TEL AVIV, ISRAEL

Mark had not yet convinced himself he had designed the best solutions for dealing with the "sanctions" he wanted to inflict on Iran. When it came to his idea of disrupting the Iranian oil producing industry, he felt he could not proceed further without another conversation with Marvin Goldstein. He was sure Marvin had been involved in developing the weapon he wanted to modify for use in this latter plan and, in fact, wondered whether Marvin might have already considered the variation which he needed. Mark knew the damage created by his plan would not be permanent or even semi-permanent, but it would still force the country to manage the disruption with lower petroleum revenues for some time. Iran's need to protect its oil fields and infrastructure would divert money and resources from its support for terrorists near and far.

Mark's idea involved using the so-called sponge bomb, which had been developed by the Israeli Defense Forces. Their original targets were the tunnels drilled throughout the Gaza area by Hamas.

These tunnels had originally been dug under the Philadelphi Route along the border between Egypt and Gaza. They were meant to go around the blockade imposed by Israel and Egypt following Hamas's Gaza takeover in 2007. The blockade was intended to prevent all forms of smuggling, particularly of weapons, but also of fuel, food, and other goods into the Gaza strip and thus to isolate Hamas. Hamas had massively extended the tunnel network over the years. It amounted to a system so vast and reticulated, it had been colloquially referred to as "Gaza metro," a reference to the Paris metro which had been designed so that no point within the city of lights (excluding its suburbs) was never more than 1,500 feet from a subway station.

Comprising a reported length of hundreds of miles, the Gaza tunnel system ran beneath many Gazan towns. Access points were hidden in innocuous places, such as buildings, private homes, or even within structures usually kept away from military activities such as hospitals, mosques, or schools. The tunnels intersected in several places and had multiple branches, so the network virtually constituted a city underground, complete with radio centers, fuel, and food storage depots, even living spaces for both militants and prisoners.

■ ■ ■ ■ ■

Mark wanted to use the "sponge bombs" which were designed to seal the end of a tunnel, named so because they created extremely hard tunnel blockages wherever they were placed. Importantly, when such a bomb was detonated, it did not trigger an explosion that might cause ancillary effects such as landslides or other forms of rock accumulations. They were like a chemical grenade creating a rapidly expanding foam that quickly hardened into matter as hard as solid rock.

A typical bomb comprised a plastic container with two discrete compartments separated by a metallic partition. Each compartment held a specific and still secret polymeric chemical that remained a liquid or gel until it came into contact with the other one. The removal of the metal partition between the two chambers required an operator to intervene manually prior to placing the grenade.

■ ■ ■ ■ ■

When Mark first found out about sponge bombs, his initial reaction combined marvel with disappointment. The main drawback these bombs had when considered for his current plan was the need for a manual operator to remove the metal partition before a bomb "exploded." As he studied weapons to use in the Iranian oil fields, he saw this as a debilitating weakness. The bombs could not be used without modification.

Although the "solution" which Mark had designed in his head did not seem complex, it surely could create a risk of failure. When calling Marvin to set up an appointment, Mark had only planned to ask whether a technological change would be feasible.

Marvin was ready and smiling when Mark arrived in his office. Marvin loved technological challenges. He had reviewed everything he had on the sponge bombs, which given the simplicity of the bomb's design, did not take that long. Yet, Marvin being Marvin, he was excited to adapt a kind of bomb with a specific target to both *Mossad's* purposes in Iran and broader use elsewhere. The prospect of the challenge ahead got Marvin in what he liked to call, "his creative mode."

After having ushered Mark into his "cave" and pointing him to the sofa, he immediately asked:

"Mark, what can I do for you?"

"Well, I don't know how feasible this idea is, but I didn't want to reject it without checking with you first."

Marvin did not wait for any real detail beyond the mere "headline" from Mark but rather launched into a broader discussion:

"As you know, there are two issues really. The first is clearly the question of the feasibility of this 'invention' of yours."

Mark interrupted with a comment that "invention" was quite a strong word. Marvin chose to ignore the remark and continued:

"The second is subtler, but still very important, particularly at the current time. Even if it were feasible, can we muster the required resources? As you know, we are already fighting a war."

Mark nodded his understanding and mentioned the second condition might be more relevant in the current environment. Mark, sitting amid the various papers, magazines, and books piled up on Marvin's sofa, pulled a couple of amateur pencil drawings from the folder he had brought with him. He explained his thought, which he humbly called a "brainwave," in place of Marvin's use of the more grandiose word "invention." He started with a brief review of his understanding of the basic description and operation of the current sponge bombs, though he confessed that he did not know what the two polymer liquids were. Marvin interrupted:

"Not to worry. Very few people know what they are and I, for one, have been sworn to secrecy."

He paused and added with emphasis:

"I'm not even sure that I could reveal what they are to Simon. So, if the overall boss of *Mossad* cannot be told, you can imagine how serious it is. Yet, the one thing I can tell you is the liquid emulsion created when the chemicals combine is hazardous to work with when mishandled. I've been told a few Israeli soldiers lost their eyesight when testing the prototypes."

Mark suddenly perked up further. He was thinking for a few seconds and then said:

"Interesting. Very interesting. You know what? My brainwave, if it works, might help deal with that."

Now, it was Marvin's turn to be impressed. He leaned a bit forward in his chair, as if to listen more closely. Mark first asked a rhetorical question:

"What's the main weakness of the current design?"

Though he could see Marvin was about to reply, he waved his right hand to let him know he wanted to continue. The response to his own question was the bomb could only work with an operator being present at the time of the bombing. He paused and added:

"And you tell me there may even be dangers to the individual. Think of that danger plus the risk of being surprised by the enemy as the operator plants the bomb."

Marvin nodded his understanding. Mark did not give him a chance to comment further as he shifted to his second rhetorical question:

"What if we could find a way to eliminate the need for manually removing the metal partition between the two liquids? In other words, what if this removal and thus the triggering of the chemical reaction could occur in a pre-programmed manner with no one around?"

Marvin jumped up and replied enthusiastically:

"Brilliant. Brilliant. Why didn't anybody think of that?"

Mark was surprised at Marvin's interruption and decided to see where Marvin would go, thinking, *after all, the idea might be more easily accepted if it came from Marvin.* He also thought he wasn't sure no one had thought of his solution. *Maybe, they just rejected it as an unnecessary complexity.* Marvin continued:

"Let me guess: you are thinking of creating a small explosive charge that would be time- or radio-controlled to blow up the partition, correct? The mini explosion destroys the metal partition sufficiently so the liquids mix, the foam expands, and the tunnel is blocked?"

"Precisely, though I had also thought of another trigger beside the mini explosion, a secondary chemical reaction."

Marvin looked inquisitive:

"Secondary chemical reaction?"

"Yes, I don't know if this is the exact chemical that might work but, when we have wanted to destroy certain electronic mechanisms we did not want our enemies to know about, we used a chemical that dissolves metal: aqua regia, you know the mix of hydrochloric acid and nitric acid."

"Absolutely. Aqua regia, it's three parts hydrochloric acid and one part concentrated nitric acid. But they might create secondary reactions with one or both polymers. We would need to investigate. But that might work; don't reject the idea out of hand."

"Great. But if aqua regia is not the answer, could we think of something else?"

Mark was smiling as Marvin said:

"Sure can. Leave it with me."

Marvin, deep in thought for a few seconds, suddenly asked:

"Why is the normal triggering system not suitable for what you have in mind?"

Mark smiled back and replied that his idea was to use the bombs to sabotage oil pipelines or even oil wells. He added:

"But with the present bombs, we would need to set them off one location at a time."

He paused and added this would not work because a single bomb could not do enough damage:

"Another problem is an operator could not loiter in the same area after the first bomb has detonated. Hopefully, we don't have to keep it that way."

Mark argued that, so far, the major means of sabotaging oil production around the world has been to attack pipelines, blocking them, blowing sections up, or setting pumping stations on fire. The problem is each operation can only deal with a small number of sites at a time. He noted there were a few instances where terrorists had set fire to wells in the same field, but the most he had read about were three wells at a time.

He paused to take a sip of sparkling water and continued:

"Assuming that my modification can work, you could place a number of these bombs in a pipeline or somewhere in a pumping station. They would be carried by the flow of oil. You could even 'attack' sections of the same pipeline at the same time."

"How would you do that?"

"Find a pumping station, shut down the flow for a few seconds, drop a bomb, resume the flow for a minute or so, and repeat the operations for as many times as you can get away with. That way the bombs would end up in different spots when triggered, reflecting the different lengths of time they had spent submerged. The only thing you would want is a long enough stretch of pipeline without a pumping station. Then, at some prearranged time, the metal partition dissolves or is otherwise broken, the liquids mix, and the emulsion expands and hardens to stop the flow of oil. With any luck, it might even damage the walls of the pipeline if they cannot withstand the pressure of the expanding foam."

"Ingenious. But that could easily be repaired."

"Easily, maybe not, but it could be repaired. Now, a variant on the theme would be to use the same process to incapacitate producing wells. Same process. Stop the flow of oil, drop the bomb, let it settle sufficiently low in the drill-shaft, and let it explode."

Marvin still had one doubt:

"Now, when we met for the first time about this a week or so ago, you said no finger could point to Israel."

Mark asked:

"Does anyone else have the technology behind these bombs?"

Marvin did not seem overly bothered, though he conceded:

"Great point. I need to discuss this with David, but my initial thought is that it is not as much of a problem as we think. We could have sold the bombs to rebels here or there. The Iranians have pointed the finger at us at least two or three times when we attacked their nuclear installations. They had "proof" as they said that we were involved, but they convinced no one. I am betting that something similar could happen here."

"That would be great, but this is definitely a decision that's above my pay grade."

Marvin smiled as he replied:

"Now maybe, but I wouldn't say 'never' my friend."

CHAPTER.19

TEL AVIV, ISRAEL

David had asked Mark to give him a detailed presentation of his plans concerning the Iranian operations:

"You mentioned you had three targets? Isn't that a bit too complex?"

Mark replied he had seriously considered that question himself, though he eventually elected to stay with the three discrete actions because he realized there was no real option to deliver a massive blow in a single location and retain the anonymity which was required. David still asked whether the resources that needed to be committed were available. Mark thought for a few quick seconds and explained:

"Let me give you the broad outline of my plans. The three targets are accessible and will not require totally new capabilities, except for a slight change in the mechanism of the sponge bombs."

"Sponge bombs?"

"Yes. The one minor change is there would need to be a delayed triggering mechanism."

"I'm not sure I fully understand, but why don't we first cover the outline, and we'll talk details afterwards."

"Sounds just fine. So, my three targets are the Ahvaz oil field, the station at Kharg Island where the oil products are pumped into large storage tanks from which the oil can be exported, and the South Pars complex, the Iranian part of the giant offshore gas deposit which is shared with Qatar."

David asked:

"Geographically, these things are pretty far away from one another, right?"

Mark conceded the point, arguing that he would need three different teams to ensure that the events take place at roughly the same time. He added:

"I have yet to speak to Wong Hai Chock, Countess Renate's cyber expert, to add a couple of interesting twists."

"I see you're not wasting time."

David paused and then asked further:

"Which of the three targets will have the earliest start?"

"Unquestionably the Ahvaz oil field, though the plan is for the team to handle Pars South on the way."

"Let's then focus just on the Ahvaz oil field at this point. We'll discuss the other two later."

"Sounds perfect."

Mark went on to explain that the Ahvaz oil field was one of the two largest fields in Iran, but more importantly, it was at the center of a major oil producing region, adding:

"There are nine other major oilfields, besides Ahvaz, in less than 43 square miles. Together they produce almost 2.5 million barrels per day, accounting for the large bulk of Iran's crude oil output. I'm told that the Iranians have drilled more than 600 wells in the area over time."

Mark continued, mentioning that the fields produce both crude oil and natural gas, mixed with water. As is normal procedure, the output of the wells is put through one of eight degassing units which provide the necessary three-phase separation of oil, natural gas and water. The water is disposed of into disposal wells. Crude oil is sent by pipeline to local refineries or pumping ports and ultimately to Kharg Island for export. Natural gas is returned to production facilities and reinjected into producing wells, for what is called secondary recovery. This reality reflects the fact that most of the fields in that geographical area have moved into what petroleum engineers call the enhanced recovery phase. Unfortunately for Iran, sub-optimal production designs or processes have led the country to need to use secondary recovery earlier than usual—typically it would start after about 10-15% of the oil has been recovered and might allow recovery rates as high as 40-50%. However, in Iran, a shortage of natural gas is limiting the scope of secondary recovery to not more than 20% of its oil reserves.

David asked:

"What's the plan of attack and what resources will you need?"

"Excellent question. I was getting to it."

Mark explained that the mission team would comprise two *Mossad* agents who would first fly to Kuwait City and from there take a bus to Abdali, the last town in Kuwait on the way to Basrah in Iraq where they would cross into Iran. In Abdali, they would take a taxi to Az Zubayr where they would rent a 4x4 SUV. From Az Zubayr, they would drive first to Basrah and then cross the border into Iran just before Khorramshahr where they would spend the night. Early the next morning, they would drive to Bandar e-Mahshahr, about 60 miles southeast of Ahvaz. Mark joked briefly that David knew one of the two agents well, as he had worked with him on an earlier mission[8]. David interrupted:

"Mike?"

---

[8] See *Operation Kovesh*, by the same author, Barringer Publishing, 2020.

"Precisely, Mike Robert, or more correctly as you know, Michel Robert who changed his name to Mike after coming to Israel from France 20 plus years ago. I believe you have been able to verify that he is fluent in Farsi."

"Remember that well. Thank God because my Farsi was a bit rusty at least at the outset. Who is the other *Katsa*?"

"Heim Meister."

"Don't know him well. Tell me more . . ."

Mark replied Heim was ten years younger than Mike but would be an excellent choice, as his studies included a stint in petroleum engineering. He pointed out Mike's experience should combine well with Heim's specific expertise with the oil production industry. Mark further explained the two men would take the identity of two Iranian oil workers who went to work in Kuwait when the Iranian oil industry had slowed down considerably during the embargoes of 2010 and 2012. He paused for an instant and added:

"Our 'technicians' have done a great job creating appropriate passports for them, as well as the right travel history, you know, entry and exit visas and stamps for at least the last five years."

David nodded his understanding and still asked:

"Is their story plausible?"

"Absolutely, we estimate that as many as 10,000 oil workers left Iran when the embargoes crippled the Iranian oil industry. They needed work and oil workers were in great demand from Kuwait to Bahrain, to Saudi Arabia and points further south."

"Excellent. What are the men supposed to do?"

Mark replied they were to use modified sponge bombs to damage pipelines carrying oil from the ten oilfields to Gavaneh, a port city on the Persian Gulf from which the oil was exported through Kharg Island. David smiled and nodded. Mark could see that David was dying to ask a question, so he paused and motioned for him to ask whatever needed clarification:

"That's why you talked of a modification to our current run-of-the mill sponge bombs?"

"Precisely. We feel the bombs, as they currently are, would cause exactly the damage we want to inflict, but we are not comfortable with having the guys present on the scene when they explode. We had two reasons for this. The first is I don't think it's good for their personal safety. The second is we plan on planting several of these bombs in different locations. We want all of them to blow up at about the same time."

David nodded his understanding. Mark went back to explaining his plan without spending any more time on the modification, if only because Marvin had confirmed the alteration was feasible though not fully tested. The men would be expected to arrive in Khorramshahr early in the afternoon and to book a hotel room where they would rest until the middle of the night. Then, on their way to Bandar e-Mahshahr, they would first drive near the south coast of the area, to a place called Arvand Kenar, along the Shatt al-Arab River which separates Iran from Iraq. The river runs for about 120 miles and was formed at the confluence of the Euphrates and Tigris rivers in the town of al-Qurnah in the Basrah Governorate of southern Iraq. David was surprised when Mark showed him a map of the area:

"Wait, why go that far south when they need to travel east?"

"They need a very quiet place, sir. We are going to be using a toy which you also used during Operation Kovesh?"

"Not the Kovesh? Where would it land?"

"Not the Kovesh. The heli-drone."

■ ■ ■ ■ ■

The Kovesh to which David was referring was a Hebrew variant of the RQ-170 Sentinel, which was like a flying, triangle-shaped wing. It had no tail, and its engine took up the middle portion of the wing. The heli-drone, as its name implied, was a small helicopter drone which could be remote-controlled or allowed to operate autonomously when flying longer distances. The drone was not more than 20 feet long and 10 feet high. It looked like a small helicopter, with a large, horizontal rotor at the front and a much smaller one at the end of a triangular steel assembly affixed to the main body of the aircraft. Under the engine, which was located immediately below the main rotor, sat a large bay for ferrying cargo or equipment. The front end of the aircraft was much smaller than usual, as there was no need for a cockpit. The forward space held electronic equipment and the largest of the two gas tanks. A smaller tank, located at the base of the tail assembly, provided balance, maintaining the aircraft's center of gravity within safe limits as the fuel level in the tanks declined. There were also two, 360-degree, infrared cameras, both facing downward, one under the nose and the other right ahead of the rear rotor, and a third camera at the front of the aircraft which fed information to the remote pilots showing them what an onboard pilot would see.

■ ■ ■ ■ ■

Mark explained the mission for the heli-drone. It had been loaded on the *Flying Dolphin* in a box on the main deck and would fly a reconnaissance mission near Arvand Kenar, at night, to make sure the place was truly deserted. The operators would initially fly over the south end of the Shadegan nature reserve which should be deserted given the early morning hour and because it almost always was. The drone would then turn west over the salt marshes almost due east of Arvand Kenar. Once they found a landing site accessible by road, the remote pilots on the *Flying Dolphin*, Captains Albert Schoenberg and Barack Leven, would send a message to Mike and Heim to give them the specific coordinates of the heli-drone. At the rendezvous, Mike would open the cargo doors of the heli-drone and pick up the bombs it carried, at which point the heli-drone would fly back to the *Flying Dolphin* and reload. Mark had to add:

"It would need to make another voyage for the next step of the mission."

Mark also mentioned that, as Mike and Heim drove past Abadan, the largest refinery site in Iran, they were to place three sponge bombs in the pipelines exiting the facilities, adding:

"Our local sources indicated to us where the system's main weakness is. The plant design has the pipelines from the refinery go to three main holding tanks, and from there the oil products are pumped into the main pipeline. The plan is to place one bomb in each or just ahead of the holding tanks."

Turning to Bandar e-Mahshahr, the men's next stop, Mark explained it was chosen because it was a central point where the various pipelines from several Khuzestan oil fields got together before they eventually went to Gavaneh and onto Kharg Island. Equally important in their choice of Bandar e-Mahshahr was that there were four refineries in the immediate vicinity. With a wide smile he added:

"We have a local resource there as well. He is studying all four of them and points in between them and the main pipeline to see where we could most easily defeat local security and strike. He has told us he found up to eight possible locations for our bombs. We'll consult him, make the decision, and inform the team as late in the process as we can."

Returning to his narrative, Mark said the local resource identified for the team a secondary road running parallel to highway 96. It went through a desert-like area where there would be an opportunity to resupply Mike and Heim with the second set of sponge bombs. Continuing on that secondary road, the team would drive around the end of the small local airport and back to Highway 96 at the north end of Bandar e-Mahshahr. David interrupted:

"Isn't it a bit dicey to have the heli-drone fly so close to a local airport?"

"I've discussed this with Captains Albert Schoenberg and Barack Leven, and they told me it should be OK since the drone is quite small. They will fly in from the north, being too high to be noticed above the airport. Using the desert that lies to the north, they will fly the heli-drone down quickly and find the team."

Mark paused and added with a broad smile:

"One of the things they can do now is move quickly from autonomous to remote controlled mode. They will be in autonomous mode in their overflight of the airport, which means there will be no radio signal going to or from the heli-drone. They will move back to remote-controlled mode as they execute their descent and then engage the autonomous mode on the return trip until the drone is close to the *Flying Dolphin*."

David had to ask:

"How are Mike and Heim going to escape once their second set of bombs are planted?"

Mark replied the plan had several options, though they all shared three common features. In his words:

"They leave Bandar e-Mahshahr by car before any of the bombs actually explode, so at that point, the risk is minimum. Then, they'll use highway 96 to drive through Cham Galgeh and Hendijan and reach Bandar e-Deylam, about 60 miles south on the coast of the Persian Gulf."

He paused to check if David was still onboard. He then turned to the evacuation of the two agents from Bandar e-Deylam. He argued there were options depending upon the circumstances. He asked:

"David, I've mentioned a couple of the pieces of equipment you all used in Operation Kovesh. You may not believe this, but we've dusted off a third, too."

David looked quite pensive as he motioned with his hand for Mark to let him guess. Smiling he said:

"Given the circumstances, it's gotta be the personal jetpacks."

"Absolutely."

David kept smiling, venturing:

"Ha. I assume there have been quite a few improvements, right?"

"Well, Marvin says so, but frankly we may not need any of them other than the enhanced stealthiness."

"How will the team get access to them?"

"They can be brought to them by the heli-drone."

■ ■ ■ ■ ■

The jetpacks to which Mark referred were relatively light equipment packs individuals wore like a backpack. They had two operating modes. In normal operations, they relied on quiet air jets to move, the power for these coming from the central turbine rotating at low speed. There was also a true jet move, like an ejector seat on a jet plane. It relied on compressed exhaust gases which literally jet the individual wearing the jetpack up at a speed to avoid bullets if discovered and shot at. The fuel reservoirs on each jetpack were sufficient to allow users to travel up to 20 miles.

■ ■ ■ ■ ■

"Mark, you said several options."

"Yes, there are three. Ideally, they escape via a zodiac brought in from the *Flying Dolphin*. It's the most discrete solution. But the jetpacks and the heli-drone give us another two. The heli-drone can bring the jetpacks and have the guys jet themselves to the *Flying Dolphin*. The alternative, if the jetpack option looks too risky, is to have the men climb into the cargo space of the heli-drone. Remember, it can carry up to 500 pounds of cargo. So, we'll have close to a 100 pounds to spare."

Mark paused for a brief second to take a sip from a glass of water and added:

"Frankly, we see the jetpacks as the last resort. The enhancements made in the cargo hold of the heli-drone include two notable features that make it a more reliable and more comfortable alternative. First, we have provided a couple of folding jump seats which would allow them to rest their legs. And second, we have added oxygen bottles which should allow them to breathe more comfortably even if the drone had to climb higher than the few thousand feet we would typically use. Remember, it's gonna be a 12-mile run or so to the ship."

"Why bother with the jetpacks then?"

"Excellent question, sir. Let me say I made the decision using the belt and suspender principle. Better safe than sorry: two options are better than one."

CHAPTER.20

*TEL AVIV, ISRAEL; CAIRO, EGYPT; AND
SOMEWHERE IN THE AUSTRIAN ALPS*

Ben who was still focused on the next announced bombing of an archaeological site in Egypt was perplexed as the predicted 48-hour time period, when a bomb was supposed to explode at Abydos, had ended. He was not alone. Lieutenant Omar, whose troops had been rotating every six hours, was shocked. He picked up his phone for instructions from his superior, Menes Al-Soliman, the head of the Egyptian secret services. Menes had asked Lieutenant Omar's commanding officer, Captain Zahur Al-Katib to give him a direct line to Omar to simplify and expedite any required field decision.

"General, we haven't seen any bomb; not only that, we haven't detected any intrusion anywhere around here."

"Very interesting, Lieutenant. My source as you know was correct in previous instances. I wonder what is happening."

Menes paused and asked:

"Do you have enough men and equipment to continue the watch for another 24 hours?"

"Certainly, sir. Consider it done."

■ ■ ■ ■ ■

Ben wanted to call Ayman to ask if he had heard anything from Gamal, but before calling, Ben had played a number of different scenarios in his head and could think of one that might make sense. The plan devised and implemented by Lieutenant Omar had just been too good. The terrorists might have tried to penetrate the perimeter they had initially selected but had seen Lieutenant Omar's forces sufficiently early to escape without planting the bomb. Yet, one question remained unanswered. He asked Ayman:

"Has anything happened to Gamal?" Ayman could only reply:

"I don't know, Sayyid Ben. I just don't know. I haven't heard from him."

Ayman paused and almost immediately continued:

"You know, I was as surprised as you must have been when there was no explosion nor any news that terrorists had been arrested. So, I called Gamal and . . ."

"And . . ."

"Well, he's not picking up his phone. It went straight into voicemail."

Ben took a couple of seconds to process Ayman's reply. He could easily see two explanations, neither of which was terribly good. He knew he would need to discuss them with Mark as soon as he could, but he still wanted to explain his thoughts to Ayman, if only to make sure there was nothing he had forgotten.

He told Ayman that one explanation might be the terrorists had postponed the bombing because they had caught Gamal and were trying to get him to talk. Getting Gamal to confess he was the leak would be an important victory and might ensure that the next bombing would be effective. Following this logic, Ben concluded there might still be remote danger for Ayman. They quickly agreed that they had gone over all this before and felt Ayman was safe, at least for the time being. Ayman blurted out:

"But wait, Sayyid Ben. Doesn't this tell you the bomb might explode at any moment? Once they have obtained what they needed from Gamal, they can go ahead."

"Not so sure, my friend. Not so sure. For a start, Gamal might have already given the location of the next bombing. So, the terrorists would need to identify and plan for another location."

Ben further argued that Gamal really did not have much to give away, since he and Ayman knew that Gamal had no way of knowing who Ayman truly was and where he lived. Rhetorically, Ben asked:

"The only things that Gamal could tell them was to confirm he has leaked information and, second, he has someone, you in this instance, to whom he gives warnings. Would they not suspend their current operation with that information? Wouldn't they expect some form of trap would be set? Wouldn't they think the risk to them was too high? There would be little or no damage and, even worse, they could lose another couple of soldiers, just like in Memnon?"

Ayman agreed on that basis, the explosion might not have taken place when they planned it and more importantly where they planned it. Ben's second explanation was more serious. Gamal would have asked the terrorists to stop the bombing.

"Why would they do that, Sayyid Ben?"

"The one thing I could think of is they might have realized the *Mukhabarat*, and the police would have set up protection because Gamal had warned them."

"How could that happen?"

"We've just agreed that my second hypothesis is that Gamal has warned them. On that basis, the real question is why would this not happen? Further, remember, there are spies around and in both camps."

Ben concluded:

"Call me the moment you hear from Gamal. In the meantime, I'm going to make a couple of calls myself."

He paused and then emphatically added:

"Be very careful. I know that we both feel you are well-covered but the offer to move you out of town for a few days is still on the table.

■ ■ ■ ■ ■

Ben's first call was to his deep source within the *Mukhabarat*. He was not expecting much as his contact would not necessarily be aware of anything planned or executed by the secret services since his principal value was access to all documents. He thought, *doubt that anyone would write a report about that so early in the process, but who knows?* As he expected, the source was aware an important operation was underway but had not heard any news.

Ben then called Mark Levi on a safe line. Mark was surprised when he picked up the telephone and realized who was on the line:

"Ben Kaplan! What is up?"

Ben was not his usual jovial self. After telling Mark the expected bomb had not exploded, he took him through the various steps he had taken. Mark remained pensive for a few seconds and replied:

"I can't think of anything you haven't thought about. Leave it with me. In the meantime, let me know if there is any change."

"Any change?"

"Yes, if you hear the police protection has been removed, if you learn something about Gamal, if there is an explosion in another place."

Ben jumped up from his chair when he heard Mark's last phrase. He blurted out:

"Should we warn our sources?"

He paused and without waiting for a reply from Mark added:

I will call Ayman and ask him to be on the lookout for news or even rumors of another bombing."

"Sounds great to me."

■ ■ ■ ■ ■

Menes was surely surprised when he saw Countess Renate was calling him on his direct line:

"Countess Renate. Do you have news for me?"

"Well, first of all, I don't have news and, second, I am terribly embarrassed the tip my client received proved not to be correct."

"Countess, I hate to tell you this, but a majority of these tips turn out to be false alarms. Also, it might not have been correct, so far. Do you have any thoughts?"

Countess Renate took Menes through the conversation Ben had had with Ayman, as it was relayed to her by Mark. Menes initially seemed a bit grumpy, particularly hearing the hypothesis that Lieutenant Omar's troops might have been exposed. Yet, he did not continue that train of thought and asked the countess what she made of it. Countess Renate said the first hypothesis was very difficult to analyze since she was at least two, if not three or four, steps removed from the informer. Anything that might have happened to him was, therefore, not something on which she could comment. She added, however:

"The second hypothesis is interesting in part because the tip might have been a trap."

"A trap?"

"Yes, General. Imagine the terrorists wanted to execute a mission. Assume they had concluded there was a traitor within their ranks. They would expect that traitor to warn someone who, in turn, warned me and thus you. From what I've heard, the first bomb did explode but with only modest damage."

"In fact, I'd say minimal, but we're splitting hairs; please go on."

"Sure. The second bomb, the one aimed at the Memnon Colossi, could have done a lot more damage. Thank God, your troops caught the terrorists red-handed. Your catching them confirmed to the terrorists that they had to deal with a traitor. More importantly, the traitor was starting to cause them personnel losses."

"Personnel losses?"

"Yes, they must have known you arrested the two people who were involved in the accident?"

"They did, though you could argue they didn't know whether the terrorists were captured or killed in action."

"Grant you that, though they might have found bodies. Yet, as you were saying a minute ago—we're splitting hair. So, in either case, they were people they could not use in the future. However, let's imagine they assume the two terrorists were captured and not killed by your troops and thus talked. I've heard the head of the group seems to have left town."

"Your information is correct. I'm amazed. I'd love to know what your sources are. Sorry, I'm interrupting you. Please continue."

"No problem. Now what if they wanted to know the lay of the land better? Why not appear to decide on a next operation, all the while never having the intention of executing?"

Menes interrupted and argued a requisite assumption in that the latter scenario would suggest the terrorist cell operated on at least two levels. One that included everyone and the other that involved only a select few who made the crucial decisions. Countess Renate replied:

"Absolutely right, sir. You would have to assume that everyone who would normally be in the loop was aware of the operation to explode a bomb, even though the top level never planned to do so. That way the leaders could expect the traitor to warn his masters. Wouldn't that be standard operating procedure?"

Menes finished her thought:

"Agreed. So, we found out about the operation from you and your client; then, we got ready, but the few deciding masters found out that we were planning something and elected to cancel the operation a few hours later."

"Sorry to interrupt, General, but this might be the reason they gave a time period, here 48 hours, rather than a specific time."

"And did not provide a specific target."

Menes paused, feeling quite content he was solving the puzzle and added:

"So, without putting words in your mouth, Countess, but it seems we are in agreement, the terrorists then go on a detailed inspection tour of the area they indicated. They probably do it on mopeds or even bicycles. They happen to see either our troops or even more likely the truck that our field commanding officer uses."

He paused again and jumped up:

"Darn it. Our guys may be sitting ducks as we speak. Thank you, Countess. Now you'll excuse me, but I need to warn our troops."

■ ■ ■ ■ ■

Countess Renate immediately called Mark to discuss Menes's reactions. Mark first congratulated her on the hypotheses she developed, but she interrupted to argue it was not terribly hard to follow whatever thread they had. Her key point was elsewhere:

"What does this mean for your people in the field?"

Mark scratched his throat briefly and argued that the only person in danger was Ayman. He repeated the rationales he and David had discussed in the past and concluded that for Ayman to be in danger one would have to assume that his contacts, Gamal in this instance, would have found a way of tailing him and found out his real identity, adding in passing:

"That's how we did it, but I don't know how many spies-for-a-dime, as I call many of our agents' contacts, have access to drones and to trained agents on foot or with mopeds. The one thing they may have is telephone geolocation, but we have taken care of that for Ayman, unless he has other telephones he has not disclosed."

Countess Renate conceded Mark's logic held, but she ominously added:

"You know, Mark, one of the things that I always care about is the cultural habits of the people with whom I operate. The Arab world is known to be quite open for insiders. I know I am overgeneralizing, but the concept of family is extended, in part because not so long-ago Arabs operated within tribes, which mattered more than families. So, the rumor mill is quite powerful. In the west, we speak of the famous seven-degrees-of-separation as being the maximum distance between two people. In the Arab world, there may be fewer—quite a bit fewer."

She paused and added:

"Hey, I don't want to turn philosophical on you, but my point is that Cairo is small. The tourist guide world is even smaller. So, it's possible your guys are doing their best, but what if their best is not good enough?"

CHAPTER.21

TEL AVIV, ISRAEL; AND SOMEWHERE IN THE RED SEA

Both the *Sailing Princess* and, a day later, the *Charm of the Seas* crossed from the Mediterranean to the Red Sea using the Suez Canal. One can readily assume *INS Storm* did as well. International agreements require Egypt to provide total freedom of navigation there, in both peace and wartime.

The Suez Canal was almost 120 miles long, with a depth of about 25 yards and a width of about 220 yards. The canal itself was a single-lane waterway, with passing places in the Ballah Bypass and the Great Bitter Lake. Ships traveled in two convoys, one southbound and one northbound under regimented conditions, which made it quite difficult for any vessel to deviate from its normal, forward progress. With more than 23,000 ships transiting through the canal each year, it was one of the most important maritime transit points in the world, besides being by far the shortest route to sail from the Mediterranean Sea to the Indian Ocean.

1,000 nautical miles to the south of the canal, on the east coast of the Red Sea, Hudaydah Port was a particularly well-protected natural port. It was the second largest port in Yemen and handled up to 80% of humanitarian supplies, fuels, and commercial goods in Northern

Yemen. The port was taken over by the Houthis in 2015. They had been repeatedly accused of using it to receive arms from Iran. An almost 10-mile-long sandy peninsula jutted out from the town of Hudaydah, forming with the coastline a north-facing "V," with a five-mile-wide mouth. Though there was a "C"-shaped pier and associated harbor facilities at the very top of the mouth of the "V," the bulk of the facilities were found protected by two jetties about four miles into the "V." The space between the two jetties was less than a mile wide and had a depth of about 32 feet.

Mark's team unanimously agreed that no Israeli vessel could run the risk of penetrating the harbor, even at its widest opening. Satellite reconnaissance pictures suggested there were machine gun batteries on both sides of the mouth of the "V" at its widest point and additional defensive positions along the shore on the east side. It was decided that Moshe and Barak, as they were both sailing to Hudaydah from the north, would stop about 150 miles north of Hudaydah, off the coast of Jizan, the capital of the Jizan region, in the southwest corner of Saudi Arabia. The team felt this was a safe place for refueling, using an Israeli tanker coming through the Straits of Tiran from its home port of Eilat, at the top of the Gulf of Acaba.

■ ■ ■ ■ ■

The *Charm of the Seas* and the *Sailing Princess* stopped about 40 nautical miles due west of the Farasan Islands, a small group of coral islands roughly 25 nautical miles off the cost of Jizan, Saudi Arabia. This allowed them to remain in deep enough waters, though still slightly outside of the main shipping channel in the center of the Red Sea. The largest island in the archipelago is Farasan and it is a protected area. It was home to the Arabian Gazelle, though a variety of oceanic animals were also important tourist magnets. They include manta rays, whale sharks and several species of sea turtles, among which one can find the critically endangered green and hawksbill turtles. The Saudi Arabian government provided free ferry rides twice a day between the island and Jizan Port to help maintain the tourist trade which, aside from fishing, was the only major economic activity. The two ships were able to refuel offshore the island and both captains were confident that no indiscreet eyes watched their every move. Once their ships' tanks filled to the brim, they resumed their progress in the direction of Hudaydah using the main shipping channel tracking a 135-degree heading. Moshe slowed down to a crawl as he went past Kumaran Island, the largest Yemeni island in the Red Sea. He dropped anchor to the east of the shipping channel but still about 30 nautical miles from Al Jazirah, a desertic peninsula that seemed to have a single plant, processing food items, on a total area of nearly 12 square miles. Mark had initially taken the precaution of having an Eitan drone take a close look at the area, principally to make sure there were no unexpected military installations within close proximity, but also to get as detailed a map of the whole area as he could. Moshe confirmed the information with a short overflight with the heli-drone. Having concluded there were no threatening military installations, he felt he could anchor for a while, knowing he would eventually need to sail closer to Hudaydah when Barack was ready to start the attack. He knew he was shadowed by *INS Storm* deep under the surface. The submarine would take a position closer to the harbor and sufficiently outside of the shipping channel so it would not be visible on any radar. Captain Ayel had elected to switch his transponder off. He needed to maintain an active sonar as this was the only means of communication he had with both Barack and Moshe, and their respective vessels.

■ ■ ■ ■ ■

The next major challenge was for the *Charm of the Seas* to place the Emerald Whale in the water. Logistically, there was no real difficulty since the crane at the front of the platform right behind the bridge would extend its arm horizontally. That horizontal arm was folded down vertically during the trip for discretion, simplicity, and stability reasons. The crane operator would then attach a harness to four points at the top of the drone and lift it up, so it was out of the hull compartment and high enough to clear the gunwales. He would then rotate the crane and gently lower the drone into the water. Just before releasing the drone fully, the operator would signal the two officers in charge of controlling it remotely so they could take over.

The real challenge, not being logistic, was to conduct the operation without anyone seeing the Emerald Whale being placed into the water. Mark had thought over the problem when he had planned the operation. He had designed, with quite a bit of help from Marvin and his team, a smart countermeasure involving minimal structural work that otherwise would have been expensive and time-consuming. They had attached the starboard side of the tarp covering the drone to two metallic arms lying flat on the deck of the vessel. Rather than rolling the tarpaulin to the side, in this case the port side, they would rotate these two arms vertically, so they held the tarpaulin like a curtain, thus preventing anyone to the port side from seeing the operation. The metallic arms had been simple to manufacture, using telescopic aluminum extrusions, whose motions were controlled by two small electric motors: one would rotate the arms from their horizontal position to stand vertically, perpendicular to the deck. The other would extend the arms so the tarp would be fully extended upwards. The team had also planned the unloading of the drone to be at night with all unnecessary navigation lights turned off. Barack had agreed to the maneuver, though it was technically illegal since he was required to always have navigation lights on, except when at anchor in a harbor. Yet, to his mind, the fact that the *Charm of the Seas* would be far enough from the main shipping channel made the operation reasonable if it did not last too long, and the ship's radar was fully trained on anything that might come into the vicinity.

The drop-off point for the *Whale* had been chosen to minimize the risk of detection. The *Charm of the Seas* had sailed due south when she had passed abeam the *Sailing Princess*, anchored off the Al Jazira peninsula. She went a further 10 nautical miles with a 180-degree heading and stopped, at which point she was about 40 nautical miles from the coastline just north of the mouth of the Hudaydah harbor. Since the *Sailing Princess* would eventually reach a point two miles north of her and *INS Storm* would be in the vicinity, any attempt by small Yemeni pirate boats to come into the area would not be successful. As Barack brought the *Charm of the Seas* to about 12 nautical miles from the mouth of the harbor, the Emerald Whale, loaded with the mines the team planned to use, was immediately submerged and its controllers sailed it toward the mouth of the harbor. The Emerald Whale only had about one hour of underwater sailing before she got to where it would take in order to drop the mines.

■ ■ ■ ■ ■

The mines the team had elected to use were not of a particularly novel design though they incorporated a couple of features to make them more suitable for the environment. They could vary the depth at which they would lay so a typical mine sweeper might not catch them. More realistically, a typical mine sweeper would not catch them all anyway since they had been individually programmed to rise and fall at random time intervals. Thus, there would always be mines that were sitting at or near the bottom of the harbor's entry, while others rested closer to the surface. Marvin had also suggested using a larger number of mines than usual and placing them in three parallel lines.

■ ■ ■ ■ ■

The team knew the number of mines the Emerald Whale could carry would require three different trips between the ship and the mouth of the harbor. Barack would navigate slowly in a wide circle, so that his boat did not attract attention by anchoring for no real reason while waiting for the Emerald Whale to return for a reload. Moshe would follow a similar pattern though the *Sailing Princess* would remain 10 nautical miles from the harbor's entrance. Yet, Moshe knew he could reach Barack's ship within five to ten minutes if needed because of the *Sailing Princess'* hydrofoil capabilities. The *INS* Storm traveled in the same vicinity although the submarine's periscope only marginally breached the water surface from time to time. The team fully expected the Houthi rebels would feel the need to investigate these two supply ships so near their main harbor.

The plan, however, assumed the mines would all be in position before any possible Yemeni reaction. That way, the *Charm of the Seas* could transfer the Emerald Whale back on board before going further south and serving as backup to the *Sailing Princess* as they worked on the Iran oilfield disruption. Unfortunately, the Houthis noticed Barack's ship earlier than expected. Apparently, they had round-the-clock guards to monitor all boats as they passed abeam the harbor. Barack had thought simply changing the identity of the boat before the vessel navigated across the harbor would have reduced suspicion. The rebels sent a half dozen zodiac boats to take a closer look that night. At that moment, the Emerald Whale had completed its third and final mine reloading. It only needed one trip to get back inside of the mouth of the harbor, drop the last cargo of mines, and return to the *Charm of the Seas.* The first vessel to notice the zodiac flotilla was *INS Storm* which was sailing less than a mile closer to shore than the *Charm of the Seas.* Captain Ayel sent a sonar message to Barack: "A few small boats coming in your direction. Speed around 20 knots. Should reach the immediate vicinity of your ship in under a half-hour."

The rebels were used to operating in the near dark and only carried minimal lightning to see where they were going. They had a

GPS signal on a small tablet and could follow their progress in relation to their target's position. They knew the seas well around the area. Once warned by *INS Storm*, both the radars onboard Barack's ship and the eagle eyes of the sailors on duty had little trouble picking up movement in the distance. Barack, who had sped back to the bridge, replied to Captain Ayel:

"Thanks. Activating our passive defenses. Ask Moshe to sail the *Sailing Princess* not more than two miles due north of us, that would be a dozen miles from shore. Still in international waters."

"Aye. Aye. Will do."

Turning to his in-vessel public address system, Barack gave all the orders needed to be ready:

"To all crewmembers. Switch on all underwater lights. Activate all six hull cameras. Make sure that at least two sailors are monitoring them. Everyone who is currently at rest, get up, and be ready in 15 minutes. Prepare to activate bow and stern guns, but only activate them on my signal. Monitor if incoming zodiacs change trajectory when we turned our lights on."

■ ■ ■ ■ ■

The six hull cameras were a recent addition to the equipment on his and Moshe's vessels. Located at roughly 50-foot intervals along the periphery of the boat and about three feet above the highest floatation line, they fastened to a bronze shaft fixed to the white part of the boat's hull. These cameras provided a surround view of the sea. They had infra-red lenses to pick up any source of heat greater than the water temperature. Though the Red Sea waters could get quite warm during the height of the hot season, they never reached a temperature equal to that of humans or even an outboard engine.

The bronze shafts allowed the cameras to be pushed higher up when the waves were stronger. In calm seas, they could drop to only a foot above the surface, yet high enough to avoid going underwater in a small to moderate swell. The cameras could also record objects sailing or floating on the surface. However, the pitch and roll in certain heavier seas did not make them particularly useful when the boat moved at cruising speeds, except when in hydrofoil mode.

■ ■ ■ ■ ■

Having heard that the cameras were all operational, Barack then issued his final order:

"Activate the electrical safety belt."

CHAPTER.22

TEL AVIV, ISRAEL; AND SINGAPORE

As suggested by Countess Renate, Mark contacted Wong Hai Chock, one of the few members of the Shadow Experts who was known, at least to *Mossad*, to be part of the group, and its top cyber security expert. Residing in Singapore, Hai Chock was normally employed as a professor/researcher at the National University of Singapore. He was as honest and straightforward as they come, but he had a passion for puzzles. To him, dealing with hackers and all that was universally known as the "dark web" was of utmost interest, just like solving a puzzle. To Hai Chock, the dark web was a devil that allowed a variety of more or less criminal activities to be conducted behind the scenes. It had to be put out of business, though he recognized that his goal was probably not achievable. As he often said to himself, *criminal minds can be equally smart as honest ones*. Those who knew him would readily concede that Hai Chock had never in the past seen a hack he could not crack and disrupt.

"Mark what a pleasure to speak with you. It's been a while. Thanks for remembering time zones. I can't tell you how often I find myself on a call in the middle of my night."

"I try my best, my friend."

Mark paused for a split second and continued:

"I know Countess Renate has briefed you on our challenge, right?"

"She has, but I wouldn't mind hearing the details directly from the horse's mouth if you pardon the phrase."

"No problem."

Mark went on to give a brief summary of what had led him to design the current project and while mentioning there were at least two, possibly three, other dimensions, he focused specifically on what he wanted to achieve concerning Iran's oil industry. He skipped over the details about how the operations would be carried out but added: "We need to disable or at least dramatically slow down their computers."

"Whose computers are you talking about?"

"The National Iranian Oil Company. As you know, it's a government-owned national oil and natural gas producer. It's also a distributor of hydrocarbons under the direction of the Ministry of Petroleum. They are headquartered in Tehran, on Taleghani Street, not far from the Amir Kabir Technology University."

"I've got to admit I don't know all the details, so the address does not tell me much. However, I've got to think they have to employ tens of thousands of people."

Matter-of-factly, Mark replied:

"An estimated 90 to 95,000 people indeed to be exact."

"That's huge."

Mark conceded it was a huge company but offered its size had to be its weakness. Rhetorically, he asked:

"It must be terribly difficult to control this varied workforce, don't you think?"

Without waiting for Hai Chock to respond, he added:

"Obviously, this is not for publication, but, believe it or not, we, *Mossad*, have at least a half a dozen people imbedded in that structure. It would be much harder for anyone to hide in a smaller organization."

"I'm not surprised, though I always wonder at the courage of people who put their lives on the line like that. I guess that you don't get to slip up more than once before you hang."

"Totally correct and that's why we protect them every way we can."

Mark added that two of the sources worked at the headquarters, while the other four were field officers working closely in the day-to-day operations.

Hai Chock stayed silent for a few seconds and unexpectedly asked:

"You wouldn't be trying to replicate the Stuxnet episode by any chance?"

The Stuxnet worm had been created, allegedly, by Israel and the U.S., and introduced into computers, primarily in Iran. Analysts speculated that it was transmitted through thumb drives and eventually infected tens of thousands of computers. In plain terms, the worm was able to burrow into operating systems and, unlike a virus, which is created to attack computer code, it was designed to take systems over. Once in place, the worm took over key instructions and caused several systems to malfunction. Rumors never confirmed by Iran were that the Stuxnet worm had targeted its uranium enrichment activities and caused damage to centrifuges by getting them to operate in the wrong conditions, such as spinning too fast or not fast enough or operating at too high or too low temperatures. This caused minor explosions and mechanical breakdowns.

Mark smiled and replied:

"Excellent memory, my friend, excellent memory. The bottom line is we're indeed going with the same concept but with two important differences. As you know, we believe that, at least in the nuclear industry, Iran has built strong defenses."

"Let me guess. Are you assuming that their defenses are much less developed in the oil and gas industry?"

"Absolutely, but we don't think it is so because of a choice or absolute neglect. The national oil industry needs to deal with a much greater number of counterparties, and it is not a top national defense priority."

Mark paused and briefly corrected himself:

"I shouldn't say it does not take a high priority. After all, that's the main way, besides arm sales, that Iran manages to earn foreign currencies. The point is that it is not a secret and to our knowledge at least they are not doing anything terribly unusual, other than selling hydrocarbons in violation of the embargo. They're not operating below the radar on this one."

"I can understand that. They have to use foreign contractors for certain high-tech tools or processes, I'm sure."

"That and the fact that the whole oil exploration and production process is well-known and applied uniformly around the world. Not much room for innovation, I'm afraid!"

Hai Chock took Mark back a few steps asking:

"You said two differences, I'm assuming one is the distinction you just drew between the nuclear and the oil sector. What is the second?"

"Good question. I mentioned the second a few minutes ago: we have people in different locations and doing different jobs. They are all connected to the company's central email and intranet, but they have different responsibilities ranging from headquarter jobs, production jobs, and even downstream commercialization jobs. They give us many different points of entry if and when needed."

Hai Chock nodded and congratulated Mark on the penetration. He then asked what the purpose of the intrusion into the computer systems was. Mark replied there were twin goals, with one having a short-term horizon, while the other might offer longer-term benefits. He explained that the short-term goal was linked to a couple of sabotage operations to be carried out in the next several weeks, adding:

"In fact, one of those goals begins as soon as the conditions are in place, and we have at least some control over their computers."

"I see. And the long-term?"

"Well, remember the work which you and Nathan Sharon managed to carry out on Russian computers?"

■ ■ ■ ■ ■

A senior researcher at The Advanced Technology Park, Nathan Sharon[9] might have devised something quite unique. Working closely with the IDF (Israeli Defense Forces), though officially remaining on the academic side, Nathan's focus had principally been on "penetration," the ability to get into other systems or of other systems to get into Israeli installations. Israel is the target of many cyber warfare activities and defending against them meant being sure to catch and quickly fix any entry point that could be available to the enemy. Hai Chock had spent more time working on finding newer and meaner viruses or worms that would allow him to get other systems to do his bidding, since the Singapore Internal Security Department (ISD as it is known in the Republic) was all over the issue of making sure they kept all entry points secure."

■ ■ ■ ■ ■

Hai Chock replied:

---

[9] By the same author, see *Escaping the Bear*, Barringer Publishing, 2023.

"Certainly do. In fact, we have pooled our resources in at least a couple of places so that we simultaneously have highly penetrating and very original viruses or worms."

Hai Chock paused briefly and added:

"Just to be sure, let me reiterate that worms are meant to burrow into operating systems and take them over, while a virus simply attacks the code and prevents it from doing what it is supposed to do. So, here, I suspect you may want both a virus to make the system's response to your attacks faulty and a worm to take the systems over in the future."

"Excellent summary. It would be nice to impose well or pumping station shutdowns when they least expect it, for instance. But for now, we just want their systems to be unable to react to the consequences of our operations."

Hai Chock asked:

"Mark, you said you have quite a number of contacts within the Iranian National Oil Company and in different jobs. What should our next step be?"

Mark replied with a question:

"What do you need to penetrate into their systems?"

Hai Chock responded that he would normally only need an email address. With that, and with the agreement of the recipient of the email to open the attachment, he would be able to do his magic. He added that *Mossad* having people in different positions might give him a stronger hand. He said:

"Assume that they have created what you, in the west, call 'Chinese walls' between various divisions."

Mark did not seem to understand what Hai Chock meant by 'Chinese walls' so Hai Chock explained:

"The official Wikipedia definition of a Chinese wall reads: '*a Chinese wall is an information barrier protocol within an organization designed to prevent exchange of information or communication that could lead to conflicts.'* Most often it refers to the management of conflicts of interests and is thus called an 'ethical wall.' However, I have seen equivalent setups in companies where access to certain information or data was restricted."

Mark nodded and replied:

"Quite useful. Thanks. With that in mind, I think we should use one of our headquarter guys and both of our production people. I know one is located at the main control center of the Ahvaz field while the other is even deeper since he works at one of the eight production units in the field and in its immediate vicinity. Finally, we also have one person who specializes in the pipeline network."

Mark, however, immediately asked:

"Am I correct assuming you could immediately erase any trace of the email you might send to these people?"

"Absolutely and more than that. What Nathan and I have jointly developed is the capability to access any internal audit file within the target system. Thus, our emails have a feature making them invisible to the broader system. So, your contacts would be the only ones who would see them. They would immediately open the attachment, leave it open for 10 seconds, close it, and press 'reply' to respond to the email we sent. That last action activates a secondary virus which erases any trace of the email at their end, though the worm or virus or both contained in the attachment are now at work in the broader system."

He paused and added:

"In fact, your people must know not to erase the email themselves but follow the steps I just outlined. That's crucial."

"What happens if they erase the email?"

"There would be a trace that they received something, as whatever they erased would be in their delete basket, and there would be a trace of some action if they decided to clear out the content of that trashcan."

"That would be terrible, correct?"

"Yes, but not deadly. One thing I can do is have the worm now in their system perform full clean-up functions, even within the audit files. The one negative there is the owner of the system, here the National Oil Company or rather their computer management department, would know something had been amiss. Audit files usually do not self-erase; in fact, that would be dumb since their job is to track all activity. So, having to erase audit files remotely would tell the computer technicians something unusual has happened."

"And?"

Hai Chock simply explained that computer management technicians would typically run a variety of anti-virus software to try to uncover any possible cyberattack. He added:

"Though Nathan and I believe that our intrusions are sufficiently new and unknown, the more people test, the more chances there are they'll find something."

"I see. Let me know when you're ready and I will connect you with the four people to whom you should send your email. On my end, I need to make sure your email gets there several days before our action in the field."

"Quite reasonable."

CHAPTER.23

Back in his office a few days later, David asked:

"Thanks for making the time, Mark. Can you give me a broad outline of your two other expeditions against Iran, as you call them?"

"Sure. Remember the broad setup in the Khuzestan basin around Ahvaz: ten fields, including one called Ahvaz, eight degassing units, and pipelines which take the crude oil from the 3-phase separation units and bring them to local refineries or pumping stations to ports in Kharg Island for export?"

David nodded that he remembered the general outline. Mark smiled and dived into a bit more detail in the last phase of the process he just described, producing a map which he had created to make his explanations more realistic:

"Before reaching Kharg Island, the various oil products transit through Bandar Gavaneh, on the shore of the Persian Gulf. We will call the whole Gavaneh/Kharg area the export complex, as oil for domestic consumption is routed differently. We could have hit Bandar Gavaneh, but we thought better of it. We were convinced that our alternative offered greater ease of operation and significantly reduced risks. So, our second target is the export complex on Kharg Island.

Mark emphasized the final journey of the various oil products took place through three parallel pipelines that ran just short of 30 miles. These operating pipelines travel in a northeast to southwest direction and rest on the seabed for the crossing between the mainland and Kharg. He added:

"One has to assume that though the pipelines could have been shorter if they had been set more directly from Gavaneh to Kharg, in an east-west direction, the longer route was selected because the ocean depths hardly ever reach 300 feet, and, in a few places, the depth is barely 10 feet."

Mark paused and seeing that David seemed fully onboard, he concluded that the plan was to attack the pipelines where they reached Kharg Island, where access would be the easiest, though the place was under heavy guard. He asked:

"Do you need more detail?"

"Just a couple of questions: who will be running that operation and what material will they be using?"

"Perfectly valid! We plan on two agents with strong experience in *Shayetet 13*, the elite naval attack group, Joshua Reiner and Jacob Weinberg. They will be brought to the *Flying Dolphin* by helicopter from Kuwait City. The helicopter belongs to the U.S. Fifth Fleet, though the Americans have not asked, and we have not volunteered, the purpose of their mission."

"Isn't that borderline?"

"Yael Orbach, the overall head of our Navy, tells me it is not unusual for the two navies to help each other that way."

"OK with me if it's OK with Yael. Don't change anything unless you hear from me, but I want to share that detail with Simon."

"No problem. Anyway, the plan is for these two agents to use the Emerald Whale. They will travel in the airlock with their scuba gear. The drone will drop them close to Kharg Island, at a depth of 30 feet or so, and the men will swim to the surface without making any decompression stops. They'll bring three sponge bombs with them."

He further explained that once near the island's shore with the three bombs, they will remove their air bottles and their flippers. Also, they will open the watertight plastic bag carried on their backs, alongside the lone oxygen bottle of their scuba gear, and take out the gun and one extra magazine, as well as a pair of regular light shoes."

Mark paused and added with a smile:

"As a side point but an interesting detail, they will use the light shoes to walk or run over terrain that includes both sand and grass but also rocky surfaces. I'm sure they could deal with it barefoot given their training, but we want them to be as comfortable as possible if they need to escape under duress."

David smiles back. Mark concluded:

"From then, they will walk to the point where they can slip a bomb into each of the pipelines and quickly retrace their steps."

"What if someone happens onto their equipment and removes it?"

"We have thought of that. There will be a third sailor from the *Flying Dolphin* in the Emerald Whale. He will have an underwater scooter with him in the hold. His role will be to collect the men's equipment as soon as they have removed it. He will take the equipment back to the Emerald Whale, wait for them onboard, and bring it back when needed."

He paused and added:

"The men have a radio to talk to Captain Moshe Aaron on the *Flying Dolphin*. And they both have beacons attached to their scuba wetsuits. One way or another, the team will always know where they are."

Mark explained that this contingency was precisely why he picked men with *Shayetet 13* experience, arguing they could dive and stay underwater in apnea longer than people without that training. He concluded:

"Even if we fail to retrieve their equipment one way or another, the Emerald Whale can rise close enough to the surface, say 30 feet or less, and the guys can reach it without equipment. They have a dead reckoning beacon which will guide them directly to the airlock. Once near the Whale, they will use the airlock to get in."

"Correct me if I am wrong, but the main risk there is they get caught, right?"

"Right. By the way, they can only be caught on or very near the island. There are limited risks while they are underwater. Plus, the fellow with the underwater scooter has a couple of underwater harpoons. The motor of the scooter is sufficiently powerful that it could pull all three men if it came to that. Anyway, that's why the operation will occur at night and their landing spot is not more than a mile from where they will plant the bombs."

"Great, and the third location?"

Mark replied the third target was the major natural gas producing complex of South Pars. He added this would be a much more traditional attack, using traditional mines. They would be laid by crew of the Emerald Whale along the seabed and would be remotely triggered to coincide with the other two operations.

■ ■ ■ ■ ■

Mark and David determined that they had to make a decision about Afghanistan. They both felt the solution utilizing the chemical developed by Stuart Harvey in Melbourne, Australia, and proposed by Countess Renate could offer some benefit, though there were shortcomings. The first and most important was that they would be doing a favor to the Taliban rather than hurting that regime. The Taliban indeed banned poppy farming in Afghanistan in April 2022. This led to a 95% decline in cultivated acreage from 580,000 to less than 27,000 acres from 2022 to 2023. The supply of opium correspondingly fell from 6,200 tons to 333 tons in one year.

Now, who knows how much clandestine farming might return over time, but the key point was that hurting the production of opium would hurt the farmers, not the ideologically rigid Taliban. Secondarily, any mission would need an Eitan drone to carry two containers of the substance developed by Harvey. While the Eitan can fly as high as 46,000 feet and travel 4,600 miles without the need for refueling, the long flight time over enemy territory did not seem worth the risk. Mark had indeed argued:

"We have the range to get there and back but flying over Iran for a good three hours each way, to Afghanistan and back, does not seem like a great decision. I know Marvin tells me we can make the containers auto-explode at a given altitude on the way down, eliminating the risk that the Iranians could get their hands on and reverse engineer Harvey's chemical. But again, what do we gain? And what about the drone we might lose?"

David agreed and told Mark that he would advise Simon first and then Countess Renate of that decision.

■ ■ ■ ■ ■

Meanwhile, in Cairo, Ben had called Ayman. The bombing at Abydos about which Ayman had been warned would happen within 48 hours had still not occurred. Now, three days later, it was time to revisit the whole issue. Ben was concerned on at least two counts. The first related to the safety of his contact, and, to some extent, of Ayman's own contact, Gamal. At the same time, he also wanted to be as fully up to speed as possible. Over the prior three days, he had spoken daily with Mark in Tel Aviv, knowing full well that he was likely speaking to Countess Renate. Just the previous day, Mark had told Ben that the *Mukhabarat* had decided to discontinue the surveillance they had put in place at Abydos. Back on the phone with Ayman, Ben asked:

"Any news from Gamal?"

"Still none, Sayyid Ben. I don't know what's going on."

Matter-of-factly, Ben came right back:

"Have you tried to call him?"

"I sure did. At least once a day in the last 72 hours."

He paused and corrected himself:

"In fact, I've tried at least twice a day each day, once in the morning and the other in the afternoon."

"And?"

"Well, the call goes straight to voicemail. The message has not changed."

Ben thought briefly and asked as blandly as he could whether they should assume Gamal was dead. He stopped, immediately realizing he had asked the question too directly. He rephrased it, asking whether he should assume Gamal was somewhere he could not speak, adding:

"He might have been 'arrested' by his comrades."

Ayman, who had sounded somber from the beginning, replied with some emotion that anything was possible. Then, seeming almost depressed, he added:

"Unfortunately, I wouldn't know how to find out. My only communication line with him is the new cell phone number I gave him when I told him I had lost the other one."

Ben, trying to lighten up the conversation, deadpanned:

"And as the only line he has to you, right?"

"Absolutely."

Ben realized he was not going to get much more information on the call. Yet, he wanted to make sure he was doing everything he could to protect Ayman. He first asked him to keep him informed, even if whatever new tidbit seemed secondary. Suddenly, he changed tack and surprised Ayman with his next question:

"Have you talked to any other contact of yours?"

Ayman appeared to regain control over his feelings. Ben wondered if that simply reflected that he was back operating in a "professional" rather than "human" mode. He replied he had talked with a few people, but he immediately added, to his knowledge, nobody had heard anything from the Muslim Brotherhood. He said this was odd though not unprecedented. He argued there might be an explanation. Ben jumped on it and asked what he meant. Ayman replied:

"I wonder whether they may not have been so surprised by the police activity at the Colossi of Memnon and then at the Temple of Abydos. If you remember, we still do not know whether the bomb at the Djoser pyramid was or was not meant to do more damage. So, it may have surprised the Brotherhood's leadership, but they would not have needed to change their plans. Then came the clear defeat they experienced at the Colossi. There was no question as to what they were trying to do, and they failed."

He paused and Ben encouraged him to continue, saying he had followed the analysis so far:

"They planned something at the Temple of Abydos. We don't know what it was, but whatever it was, they realized the leaker had struck again and if they continued with their plans they would most likely fail. I should add they may have realized they might lose more brothers, captured or killed."

He paused to take his breath and simply concluded:

"They may well be regrouping."

Ben smiled since Ayman was handing him a series of logical steps they had already discussed. Yet, he surely did not want to antagonize his contact and simply replied he could not find anything wrong with the analysis. He added, if he were in the Brotherhood's position, he might decide first to identify who was causing the leak and plug it. His conclusion shook Ayman back to his morosity as he just said:

"That's where the news for Gamal may not be very good."

Ben was somewhat surprised. In prior instances, whenever the issue of Gamal's health or safety had come up, Ben thought Ayman had almost become emotional. Ayman's reply to his last conclusion was almost clinical and did not show the emotion Ben had noticed earlier in the call. Suddenly, Ben realized he might have missed hints of what Ayman might be trying to communicate. He thought, *what if he is even more worried for himself than for Gamal?* He changed the topic, asking:

"Ayman, do you feel you need protection now?"

Ayman hesitated for a short while and then blurted out:

"Sayyid Ben, I don't really know. On the one hand, I feel it would be hard to get to me given how little Gamal knows about me. On the other, you never know."

"Well, remember, the offer is still on the table. We can have you, your wife, and your two sons visit Alexandria. I have a contact there who can get you a guest apartment on El Gaish Road. You would just need to cross the street to be on the beach."

Ben paused briefly to let Ayman think. Then, with Ayman staying silent, he added:

"You can still call me any time, with our special phone. Nobody can find out where you are, no geolocation possible."

"But what about my other phone? What if one of my contacts calls me?"

Ben was surprised and his first instinct was to ask a question he had already asked in earlier meetings, "how many phones do you have?" But he decided he would not gain much and could destabilize Ayman. So, he simply told Ayman that he, Ben, had access to someone who could take a look and make sure any geolocation feature that might be on Ayman's phone was de-activated. He paused and added: "By the way, you should also bring your wife's cell phone as well.

How about your sons?"

"They are too young. They don't have their own cell phones."

"Well, I would suggest you meet me at Beano's Café, right behind the Israel Embassy. Call me when you get there but come alone. Bring your cell phones as well as any laptop or tablet you may have.

My friend Eli Goldberg, whom you know, will be with me. He will disappear with the electronic stuff and bring it back quickly."

Wanting to make absolutely sure that Eli's cover was in no way breeched, Ben added:

"By the way, you should know that Eli is not the person who can look into your phone. But he can jump into a car and get it done quite quickly."

Ayman seemed to smile but was still not convinced. He asked:

"How about my shop?"

Ben was getting impatient and working as hard as he could not to allow his voice to show it. He asked Ayman about the staffing at the shop, to which Ayman replied they had a couple of people working there. Ben asked whether they could manage things for a short while. Ayman conceded it was a viable short-term solution, though he added his wife was always there to supervise. He expressed his worry about what would happen if she were not there. Ben quickly decided the dialog had gone long enough. He still did not want to rush Ayman, but he could not keep running around in circles. He asked him point blank:

"Rather than leaving with your wife and sons on a short holiday, would it be easier if you were to go to Alexandria by yourself for a while? Tell your wife it's a business trip."

∎ ∎ ∎ ∎ ∎

After hanging up from his call with Ayman, Ben decided he needed to have one more telephone conversation. He directly dialed the cell phone number of Raymond Baker, his opposite number at the U.S. Embassy:

"Ray, sorry to bother you. Ben Kaplan here."

"Ben, you never bother me. Is there something I can do for you?"

"This phone line is scrambled, right?"

"Correct."

"I don't need your help right now as we speak, but I may well need it in the near future."

"What's the problem?"

"One of my contacts is having safety issues."

"You want us to hide him?"

"No. Not him. He tells us that one of his own contacts may be in the same pickle."

"I see. You want us to help the other contact. What is going on?"

Ben explained to Ray the role Ayman had played in helping him bring the Egyptian government in the loop concerning a terrorist bombing attempt.

"Wouldn't be the Luxor bombing, by any chance?"

"It is. Congratulations on your sources of information. The Egyptians had told us they would keep the whole thing under wraps."

"Well, you know how it goes."

Ben switched to explaining the role played by Gamal, going as far as giving his first name to Ray. He said there were a number of inconsistencies in the developments of the last several weeks, but he felt he needed to be ready to protect Gamal if he requested it. He added:

"For all the obvious reasons, I cannot offer him protection since he does not know that Ayman works with us, and I would rather it stayed that way."

"Ben don't worry. Call me when the time comes. I'm sure there are things we can do, even if it simply means keeping him on embassy grounds temporarily."

He paused and jokingly added:

"That's what friends are for, right?"

Ben simply said:

"I'll owe you one."

CHAPTER.24

TEL AVIV, ISRAEL AND OFFSHORE HUDAYDAH, YEMEN

With the *Charm of the Seas* now well-lit, inclusive of all its underwater lights, and the other two Israeli vessels hidden, one underwater and the other with all lights off less than two miles away, the three Israeli captains were following very attentively the progress of the six Yemeni zodiacs, each of which seemed to carry up to six people. Barack Decker had been informed that the zodiacs had first slowed down to a crawl when the underwater lights of the *Charm of the Seas* came on. The initial reaction of the Houthis had been to slow down to bring their boats closer together. Barack assumed, correctly as it turned out, they needed to confer among themselves as to any required tactical change. People who act as pirates and attempt surprise takeovers of unsuspecting commercial ships would have been startled by a boat whose lights suddenly lit up after having only navigational lights on. They would realize they had been detected. Barack had initially thought that the rebel zodiacs would simply turn around and return to port once his boat had been lit above and below the waterline. He had thought: *what was there that could be valuable on a simple supply boat? More to the point, why attack such an insignificant target particularly as there would be no surprise effect?*

Barack was therefore surprised when the leader of the Yemeni "expedition" did not appear to change his plan. The conversations among the Yemeni pirates was brief and judging by their subsequent actions and resumption of the attack, whatever discussion that took place had to be quite short; ostensibly, there had not been time to convey any significant change. The six enemy boats rapidly resumed their fast progress toward the *Charm of the Seas*. About 15 minutes later, the six boats and their contingents of pirates had become quite visible with the high-power, night vision binoculars onboard Barack's ship. Hershel Simon, the Officer of the Watch, called out to Barack:

"Captain, I can see at least one machine gun on each zodiac."

Barack was not particularly surprised by the announcement. He calmly ordered the three gun turrets to be manned and prepared to fire. That meant the three guns were rotated around their horizontal axes, with the guns now clearly exposed above deck and the small turret with the protective shield right behind each gun. Barrack added:

"Do not shoot until my command. Remain protected behind your shields. Light up all projectors on the port side."

He paused for a second and ordered:

"M320 grenadiers to your stations."

The two sailors armed with the M320 grenade launchers quickly ran with their weapons and ammunitions to stand respectively by the gunner at the bow and by the stern gun station on the port side of the boat. The system they were using was not new, though the Navy had only recently switched from its U.S.-made M203 to the new M320 system. Besides the grenade launcher, it offered technological enhancements such as day/night sights and hand-held laser range finders.

Captain Decker ordered:

"Grenadiers, load illumination grenades into your launchers. I want to see the enemy as if we were in plain daylight. Shoot on my count: 1, 2, shoot."

The insurgents slowed dramatically as the first round of grenades burst in their direction and transformed the night into day between them and the *Charm of the Seas*. They had not expected what they thought was a small supply boat to carry the kind of arms it seemed to carry. For the second time, Barack was surprised they did not abandon their attack. He asked himself: *what do they know about our ship which we don't think they do*? He took this a step further, sharing his sentiment on Sonar with Captain Ayel and Captain Aaron, seeking their advice. They both replied they were as surprised as he, though they still thought the Israel contingent had all the firepower they needed.

The Houthis separated into two groups of three boats each, one veering to their port to navigate in the direction of the bow of the *Charm of the Seas*, while the other kept going straight, working to attack from the port side of the stern. Surprisingly, since they had seen the kind of weapons Barrack's ship carried, they started firing machine guns before they were close enough to hit a target. Barack noted their action was a waste of ammunition but discounted its importance considering they meant to frighten his sailors. Calmly, he ordered:

"Grenadiers, fire two pike missiles from your grenade launchers. Aim 100 feet to the front of the lead boat in each group. Immediately reload and be ready for the next round."

■ ■ ■ ■ ■

Pike missiles are precision-guided mini missiles which measure not more than a foot and a half in length and weigh less than two pounds. Though principally used by infantry, Yael Orbach had decided to provide them as defensive weapons to the two spy-ships, as they could do quite a bit of damage and had a range of more than a mile and a half. Barack and Moshe had agreed, thinking that they were more powerful and impressive than traditional grenades and should serve as a strong dissuasion.

■ ■ ■ ■ ■

While the insurgents were even more surprised when the two mini missiles splashed so close in front of them, they kept coming toward the *Charm of the Seas*, at a reduced speed, yelling incomprehensible slogans at the top of their voices. Barack really did not understand what could be motivating them, as their attack seemed so obviously doomed to fail. He wondered: *what could they possibly be after*? He could not believe there would have been any leak within the Israeli chain of command. So, any intelligence the rebels might have had, and which might have motivated them to risk their lives to take over the ship, had to have come from a shore station which nobody had noticed. Again, he asked himself: *could it be Al Jazirah? Did our earlier inspection miss one or several defensive outposts*? At that point, he was wondering whether the peninsula that had seemed completely deserted higher north in the Red Sea might have been manned? Then he even added an iconoclastic thought: *Could they be in hysterics on drugs?*

Captain Decker reminded himself he, Captain Aaron and Captain Ayel, had a plan of action. Now was not the time to doubt or to change the plans. That is when he elected to bring on his newest and most serious defensive weapon. He ordered:

"Power up the electric safety belt."

■ ■ ■ ■ ■

It was Marvin who had one day realized the two spy boats only had one major weapon to ensure their survival in most circumstances: their ability to shift to hydrofoil mode and outrun any other ship.

Yet, as he had heard of the risk of encountering pirates in either the Indian Ocean or the Red Sea, he concluded there was one weakness which needed addressing and could in fact be addressed easily and cheaply. His reasoning assumed any pirate who could find a way to climb onto the boat surreptitiously could, if armed, surprise the crew. That scenario was not good since it involved risks to the crew and it would reveal to the pirates a number of still secret features and armaments on the boats.

He came up with the idea of the electric safety belt, which could be used both in a semi-passive as well as an active mode. Semi-passively, the belt could create a mild electrical field in the water around the boat so anyone coming into it would trigger an alarm. The alarm would signal an impending invasion, and the crew would have time to get ready and either fend off any enemy or use the speed of the ship to escape unscathed. The active use of the belt required a couple of additional features, the most important of them being two high-voltage backup batteries which had to be kept fully always charged.

The protection was called a belt because it made use of a series of needles, about a half-inch in diameter and nine inches long, located all the way around the ship at three- to four-foot intervals and about one foot under the ship's floatation line, within the black part of the hull. These needles when not in use would retract into individual tubes protruding on the inside of the hull. There, they would not be connected to any electrical source to minimize any risk of electrical mishap. When activated, the needles would first extend outside of the hull, with rubber isolation at their base to ensure that any electrical current remains within the system and did not leak into the boat. Once powered up, the electrical tension would increase, though set quite a bit short of full voltage. The two batteries connecting to the system would be charged by two alternators, each powered by one of the boat's two engines. Once the needles were extended and powered up, they would send powerful electrical shocks. The lightning current from these shocks would then spread out in all desired directions within twenty feet of the boat.

When used in active mode, the belt is divided into four zones, covering the four quadrants of the ship. The quadrants can be switched on individually or collectively. This allows the captain of the boat to direct the electrical shock he eventually commands in as narrow a field as possible, thus avoiding the unnecessary use of battery power. Additionally, it helps mitigate one unfortunate side-effect of the system: any fish swimming close to the surface within the electrical field would usually be electrocuted. This side effect is impossible to eliminate as the goal is to electrocute attackers swimming at or near the surface, although it can also hit boats that are nearby.

■ ■ ■ ■ ■

The rebels on the incoming boats kept indiscriminately shooting in the direction of the *Charm of the Seas*, though everyone on board was calmly at their posts shielded as needed against any incoming bullets. Barack had originally elected not to shoot directly at any of the individuals, hoping that the incident could resolve itself when the rebels realized the enemy was stronger than they expected. Unfortunately, this peaceful strategy did not seem to work. Barack then ordered his troops to shoot at the boats, hoping that one or several bullets would hit their air-filled rubber ballasts and stop the attack. With the first of the rebel boats now closing in on the *Charm of the Seas*, Barack ordered:

"Stop all shooting. Launch the first electric shock on the two units on the port side. Only use 50% maximum power."

Though the electric shock was weak when it reached the first boat trying to get to the stern of the *Charm of the Seas*, the flash surprised the rebels who slowed to a crawl. A couple of sailors jumped into the sea and started swimming toward the back of Barack's boat. That was when he asked for a second shock with 75% maximum power which, this time, was sufficient to be clearly felt by the sailors who were in the water. They yelled incomprehensible words and swam back toward their own zodiacs as rapidly as they could. Barack smiled to himself at the thought that the strength of the jolt had not been sufficient to kill anyone, but he resolved the next one would be if they kept moving forward. The other group of rebels who had aimed for the bow and, getting uncomfortably close, received the same treatment as their comrades, though no one had jumped into the water. Yet, the odd hand or foot that was dragging overboard the zodiac delivered the same message: don't mess with these guys.

Barack could see rebels talking on their radios. He assumed they were going to move away and leave him alone. He told the two operators of the Emerald Whale, which was on her return voyage after having dropped the third of her three marine mines, not to have her come to his boat, the *Charm of the Seas*, but rather to send the drone further south. He surely did not want to take the drone out of the water and bring her back inboard anywhere near the current spot. In fact, he sent a Sonar message to Captain Ayel on *INS Storm*:

"Am sending the Emerald Whale further south. I think it's better for you to load her onto your submarine a bit further from the current activity."

The captain replied:

"Visibility not much of an issue as we would go through the airlock. Yet agree with your plan as I'd rather take her on when things are quieter."

Captain Ayel immediately sent a second message:

"What about the controllers?"

Barak replied:

"We'll need to find a quiet place for their transfer as planned, probably at night, further south."

"Sounds fine. Where is the Whale drone now?"

Barack asked the one controller who was near him. He told him the Emerald Whale was six nautical miles south of the current location of the *Charm of the Seas*, resting on the bottom of the Red Sea in 52 feet of water. Barack communicated the data to Captain Ayel. He replied he was going to have the *INS Storm* shadow the *Charm of the Seas* to make sure they could make the full transfer as soon as possible.

Meanwhile, the rebels had turned around and retraced their steps back to the harbor. Barack had decided to remain vigilant, though he was still hoping this was the end of the incident. However, about 10 minutes later, the distant sound of a helicopter motor became clearly audible. Barack called Moshe and asked whether he had the aircraft on his radar. Moshe replied he did and added:

"Glad that Mark thought of equipping the *Sailing Princess* with these two missile launching units hidden in our hold. I prefer to use them rather than our uprated bow machine gun. The orders are clear: respond with a missile if we are attacked. I don't want my special cargo for Iran to be damaged!"

Barack agreed, though he suggested a small variation, inviting Moshe to hold his fire for a couple of minutes. He sent out a distress radio call saying that his boat, a supply ship named *Charm of the Seas* and flying a Malta flag, was under attack. He said that he had repelled pirates trying to board his ship but now could see a helicopter that was heading in his direction. Seconds later, a radio response came:

"Captain Edward Smith here, U.S. Navy, *U.S.S. Laboon*. *Charm of the Seas*, we have you on our radar. Do not worry. We have you covered."

Barack then heard the message Captain Smith broadcast on the local general offshore radio frequency and clearly intended for the rebel helicopter:

"Incoming helicopter. This is *U.S.S. Laboon*, maintaining freedom of navigation in the international waters of the Red Sea. Cease and desist. If you do not turn around in the next one minute, we'll shoot you down. On my count, 1, 2, 3 . . ."

The next Sonar message between the three Israeli vessels expressed relief and joy. The helicopter did not turn back and a laser-guided missile from the *U.S.S. Laboon* destroyer brought it straight down. Everyone hoped the aircraft would still be close enough to the coastline allowing any survivors to be rescued, but the force of the explosion made it unlikely there would be many survivors.

Barack informed his colleagues he was not waiting around for the next wave of rebel attacks, adding:

"We know they have missiles onshore and have shot at ships earlier. Let's not hang around here."

He said he was turning all navigation lights off, as well as all lights onboard the ship. He would then change the white-hulled *Charm of the Seas* into the red-hulled *Sailing Joy* with her Gibraltar flag and would switch to hydrofoil mode as soon as he was convinced nobody could see his boat well enough to notice the change. Moshe replied he would eventually follow a similar protocol, as he would change to the red-hulled *Sea Riches* with her Panama flag, adding:

"But first things first. I must sail as close to *INS Storm* as I can. When we're in formation, I'll fire a couple of missiles at the harbor infrastructure as planned. *INS Storm* will launch up to four more powerful rockets."

He paused and concluded:

"Nobody will stay around to assess the damage. We have satellites which can do that very well."

He paused and added:

"I'll then start the hydrofoil move with all lights off as well and eventually change the boat's identity as we've just discussed.

Interestingly, Barack, both your and my vessel will look quite similar again, except that our hulls will no longer be white, but red."

Barack jokingly replied:

"We'll still be flying different pavilions."

"Quite true. Anyway, even in the event the red hulls should become suspect, we'll still have one more hull color up our sleeves."

Barack replied, still the practical mind:

"Great. I would suggest the three of our Israeli vessels set a heading toward the west side of the Hanish Islands. They're about 60 nautical miles south of where we just were."

He paused and added:

"It's an area disputed between Yemen and Eritrea, though it's controlled by Yemen now, except for a couple of small rocks here and there. There does not seem to be any significant military outpost. Let's get the tanker there as well so we can fill up on fuel and execute our last hull change before going through the Bab Al-Mandab Strait. That may well be a more serious hurdle. I'm going to talk to Mark in Tel Aviv and hope he can get us American protection."

CHAPTER.25

CAIRO, EGYPT, TEL AVIV, ISRAEL, AND SINGAPORE

Mark called Ben to ask how Ayman's relocation had been working. Ben replied that Ayman had decided to go to Alexandria by himself and that he had moved in without any problem. The person who met him at the address Ben had given him was a bona fide consulate employee who did not have any link to *Mossad* and did not know that Ben was anything other than the Vice Consul in Cairo. He accepted the idea that Ayman needed a place to find peace and quiet after a difficult adventure. Ben, however, told Mark that Ayman did not want to stay more than a few days. He added:

"I'm not sure I understand everything though. There's one thing that still doesn't make much sense. Ayman seems less and less worried about Gamal. It is as if he did not care anymore."

"Maybe there's a message in there. Any idea?"

Ben could only reply he did not know. He added that the question he was pondering was why Ayman did not want to be protected in Alexandria for more than a few days. Mark readily conceded that Ayman's reaction on that point looked strange to him, too. He inquired:

"Again, did you ask him why?"

"I sure did. His reply was totally confused. First, he argued that he did not need long-term protection because whoever was after him would act quickly and presumably be eliminated. I pointed out to him that it did not make sense: how could we be sure that whoever was after him would move quickly? Why would he not wait for the right moment? So, he turned around on a dime and proceeded to argue the almost exact opposite point. Frankly, I'm not sure he knows himself."

Ben added he had told Ayman there really was only one important question: either Ayman's life was in danger, or it was not. Ben reported to Mark that Ayman appeared to follow his logic up to that point. Ben went on arguing to Ayman that if his life was in danger, there was no reason the danger would disappear in a few days, adding for Mark's benefit:

"I said to him that, after all, whether the danger came from Gamal or more likely from someone else given what we've heard about Gamal having seemingly disappeared, the risk would persist until the people were identified and neutralized."

Ben paused and then told Mark he had mentioned to Ayman that if he felt, on the other hand, his life would soon no longer be in danger, then there seemed to be no reason there would be danger today, saying he had added:

"No danger today would have to mean there is no one to threaten you today."

Ben said that Ayman at that point had apparently nodded. He continued recalling the conversation with Ayman arguing:

"However, if there is some danger today but you expect that danger to be gone very soon, why would whomever you suspect would threaten you today no longer be a threat later? Are you counting on someone to eliminate that person? I've got to tell you that you shouldn't count on me or any of my contacts . . ."

Mark was nodding, telling Ben he seemed to have covered most bases. Ben smiled and added:

"My suspicion at this point is that he is totally irrational. I think he is scared and cannot function logically. I hope a few days in a calmer atmosphere will get him back on track. In truth, that's the only danger which could disappear with some rest."

Seeing that Mark appeared surprised, Ben explained the danger he was referring to was that people who cannot function logically can easily make mistakes, adding:

"Something like that can be lethal in the spying business."

Mark could not disagree, but he asked:

"What about his family? Why doesn't he seem to worry about them as well? You've said to me that Ayman has told you Gamal doesn't know who he is, although I know you are aware of his real identity. How could he be in danger and his family not be?"

"That's a very fair point, Mark, though there is always the simple explanation: Gamal knows his "trade name" but not his real identity. If he doesn't know his real identity, he doesn't know of his family either. Yet, I decided not to go there. As I said, he appears irrational and the last thing I want is for him to say he was coming right back."

Mark nodded and asked:

"Ben, a stupid question: can you keep track of where he is?"

"You bet. The phone he has does not allow others to geolocate him, but it does allow us to follow him quite closely. Another thing. When he came near the embassy to hand us his phones for checking, Eli Goldberg determined what car he drove and placed a bug on it. So, in fact, we have two ways of tracking him."

"He had used a car despite Cairo traffic?"

"Yes. My guess is he was going to go directly from there to Alexandria."

Mark noted an inconsistency:

"Couldn't be going straight to Alexandria unless he was to meet his wife nearby your office. He must have had to go back home if only to hand to his wife the phone you checked . . . Anyway, this is unimportant. He had a car and was getting ready to drive to Alexandria."

Ben nodded and then said to Mark there was another change in Ayman's behavior which looked surprising and not in character. He argued that Ayman was beginning to blame Gamal for some of what was happening, asking how and why he could have given him a fake tip."

He paused as if he were digging further into his mind to clarify the confusion he was feeling and just concluded:

"It's almost as if Gamal has gone from informer and friend to enemy."

Mark decided to let Ben proceed at his own pace to be sure not to disturb his thought process. Ben surprised himself as he then added: "Ayman's last comment seemed destined to make me fear that Gamal might be after me or, if not me, at least *Mossad*."

"Did you ask why?"

"Sure did. He didn't come up with a straight answer. He even downplayed what he had been saying somewhat. He said his words had gone further than they should have. Yet, I did hear warning signs."

"And?"

Ben calmly replied:

"Well, as you'll remember, there was a time a few weeks ago when I asked myself if the target was not different from what we thought. The Taliban link up with the Muslim Brotherhood might simply be a story to draw me into some sort of a trap."

"I do remember that. So, where do you stand now?"

Ben replied that he had envisaged a scenario where someone he didn't know was after *Mossad* in general or him in particular.

He took the point further arguing the current conflict between Israel and Hamas could not make Israel look good in the eyes of most Egyptians. The look on Mark's face was telling Ben he had to explain more, since Mark simply did not follow with any questions or comments. Ben kept going, arguing it might make the Brotherhood more popular if it somehow managed to have one or several Israeli "spies" killed or at least officially expelled from Egypt. Mark conceded the scenario was plausible, adding he had not personally thought of it before. Yet, he injected a solid note of caution:

"Remember they've already had two attempted bombings; one worked, the other didn't. We don't know what the story is with respect to the third."

Ben interrupted:

"Which still hasn't happened by the way."

"Right, but it could still happen."

Mark paused and argued the Brotherhood might be paying quite a lot to achieve what might only be a small public relations success. He pointed first to the damage that could still be inflicted on monuments which most Egyptians revered, adding:

"I'm not sure what is more powerful: destroying an old temple or getting a couple of Israeli spies caught and expelled."

Looking at Ben on the screen with a smile, he added:

"Unless they got the spies killed."

Returning to his main rationale, he pointed to the potential cost in terms of personnel who have already been caught by the Egyptian secret services, concluding:

"And there could be others. In short, my friend, I'm not ready to buy your conclusion. At the same time, you should remain very cautious. But there, I know I'm preaching to the choir!"

Ben smiled back and thanked Mark for the piece of advice.

Mark innocuously added:

"The more I think of this counterespionage theme, the more I'm convinced that though it's remotely possible, it's not realistic. Now, if you tell me danger comes to you from Iran, China, or Russia, though I don't know how Ayman would be involved, I would be quite a bit more worried."

Ben, suddenly looking quite a bit more serious, said:

"Right on. I had not gone there, but the door you opened is quite serious. In fact, I think I'm going to ask my wife and children to fly back to Israel ASAP and suggest to the ambassador we take maximum precautions at the Embassy. I'll stay around here, though I'd love to be able to seek help and protection from the Americans if that's at all possible. Do you agree?"

Mark did not allow any room for misinterpretation:

"Leave it with me. I'm on it. Assume that your family's protection is the top priority. You may get a call from David if he needs more detail, but, in the meantime, make sure you manage the local environment with care."

Mark paused and mentioned almost as an afterthought:

"The Yemen expedition was successful, and our guys are on their way to the Persian Gulf. I would suspect no action will take place for at least three or four days but be ready to hide in a hurry if anything misfires.

■ ■ ■ ■ ■

Wong Hai Chock had just called Mark to let him know that what he called the cyber side of the Iranian expedition, was ready. He told him that being able to go through several entry points into the computer systems of the National Iranian Oil Company had turned out to be quite useful. He explained he had found out they have a relatively well-protected environment. In particular, he found partitions within the various divisions of the group:

"Think of mini-Chinese walls. They are not hard blocks. You can go through them. But to do that, you need special permissions, effectively passwords. I suspect these permissions are granted to senior people who can have a look across the whole operation, while employees lower down on the totem pole are more constrained."

Hai Chock paused to take a breath and then gave further details to Mark. He suggested the one individual located at the group's headquarters in Tehran certainly looked quite a bit more senior than the others, adding:

"He seems to have all permissions required."

Mark asked:

"So, what were you able to do?"

Mark could clearly see Hai Chock smiling when he simply replied:

"Not much, really. They will simply discover that all their systems ignore any form of fire alarm if there is one."

Hai Chock paused as Mark chuckled. He then disarmingly argued his solution seemed to be the most practical answer to the problem Mark had posed. Mark agreed, though he joked:

"Let's hope they don't have an accidental fire before we strike. They would be bound to find out that their alarm system was not functioning properly and might discover the problem and fix it too early."

Hai Chock conceded the point, though he corrected his earlier statement which he said was too broad. He argued he had only attacked the fire alarm protection provided to production sites as well as distribution networks. He concluded:

"Any issue at headquarters or in any commercial office would not be affected."

Mark smiled and shifted to quite a different topic, asking about the status of the four people Hai Chock used to penetrate the Iranian oil company computer systems. Hai Chock was categorical, arguing they were totally in the clear. He explained they all seemed dutifully to have opened the attachment as requested and then responded to the email as prompted. He reminded Mark that this last step erased every trace of the incoming email as well as of the attachment. Mark still asked:

"Can anything go wrong there?"

Hai Chock looked surprised and questioned:

"Where?"

Mark rephrased the question asking whether there could be sub-systems within the overall setup that would anticipate the kind of worm Hai Chock and Nathan had developed, concluding:

"Could there be different sets of audit files?"

Hai Chock smiled broadly. He told Mark that once he was inside the oil company systems he had been able to look at all the various functions. He said he satisfied himself that the individuals were safe. He could not hide his self-satisfaction when he explained his system safety was, in fact, double-barreled. He briefly mentioned the safeguard he had just discussed which erased any trace of his own email. Turning to the second, he listed a couple of what he called "cute" features, using a word which he really seemed to enjoy. The address from which his own emails to the four recipients appeared to come was disguised. More to the point, each of the four people seemed to have received the first email from four different senders, adding:

"So that even if all four emails were discovered, no one would be able to establish any link among the recipients. Second, and even better, the reply each individual sent back to me appeared to have been sent to the one person with whom they had the most frequent communication."

Hai Chock paused, realizing Mark seemed a bit confused. He explained to him the secondary virus he had introduced had gone through the inbox of each recipient and looked for the internal address that came up most often. It was easy to find the person from whom they'd received or to whom they had sent the most emails in the prior week. Each recipient of Hai Chock's email would then appear to send a reply to that one person. Smiling broadly, he added:

"That email, however, was blank and did not show any trace of the incoming one I had sent. At worst, each of these individuals will receive a surprised response from the colleague with whom they most frequently correspond."

Mark came straight back:

"So, there will be some trace left?"

"Depends on what you mean. There will be a trace of one blank communication to some internal colleague, with no message and even no header for the email. But there will not be any trace of my email, the worm, or the viruses."

He paused, and smiling even more broadly, he added:

"And, by the way, I retain entry into their systems. So, I could play a few more tricks in the future if we ever need to. I'll keep monitoring the system for the next several days. I'll let you know if anything untoward manifests itself."

CHAPTER.26

TEL AVIV, ISRAEL; THE RED SEA; AND THE PERSIAN GULF

The four Israeli ships, the two supply boats captained by Moshe Aaron and Barack Decker, the *INS Storm* submarine, and *Central Support*, the small tanker based in Eilat found themselves in the channel to the west of Hanish Islands near the southern end of the Red Sea. Everyone had been delighted when they read the message they received from Mark:

"Damage to Hudaydah harbor significant. The missiles hit their targets. A first wave of mines exploded as ships were moving around the harbor. Assume there are still more active mines. Congratulations."

The Hanish Archipelago primarily consists of three main islands forming an inverted "L," at the center of many smaller islets and protruding rocks. The three main islands are the northern Zugar Island and the southern Great Anish, with the Little Anish nothing more than a dot between the larger two.

The Israeli convoy had elected to rendezvous to the west and abeam the middle of Zugar Island. They agreed that this would be the area most likely to allow the Israeli Navy to execute two important maneuvers.

The first point of the rendezvous was to transfer the two officers operating the Emerald Whale from the *Sailing Joy* to the *INS Storm*. The Emerald Whale herself had already been recovered and brought onboard the submarine through the airlock, with both submarine and drone safely under water at the time. The team had decided they preferred to carry out the transfer of the drone operators with the submarine on the surface of the sea. Its sail could be partially hidden from view on one side by having *Sailing Joy* navigate alongside. *Sea Riches* could provide partial line of sight cover from the other side. The two operators would move from the ship to the sub using a small dingy, while their equipment would be moved directly from *Sailing Joy* to the submarine using the ship's crane. Emerald Whale's batteries could be fully charged while on the submarine which had a high voltage battery charger onboard. Eventually, after the drone's next mission, the operators would be able to program her for autonomous operation and send her back to Haifa on her own.

The second goal of the rendezvous was more relevant to the rest of the mission. *Sailing Joy* and *Sea Riches* needed to top up their fuel tanks. The 40 miles which both ships covered in hydrofoil mode had depleted their fuel reserves and they preferred to take an early opportunity to refuel. They knew they could buy fuel at any of several harbors on the western side of the Gulf, where countries ranging from Bahrain, Qatar, Kuwait to Saudi Arabia would surely welcome the opportunity to sell diesel fuel to commercial ships. Yet, discretion being the order of the day, they felt most comfortable refueling in open waters. With *Central Support* still having more diesel fuel available, they decided to keep her navigating in the vicinity of the other ships without being part of a formal convoy.

■ ■ ■ ■ ■

Captain Decker had asked Mark to look into some protection for his and Moshe's supply boats as they traveled through the Bab Al-

Mandab Strait. He did not want to have to fight the Yemeni Navy should it decide to attack one or both of the two supply ships. With a name which means "the Gate of Grief" in Arabic, the Bab Al-Mandab Strait is located between Yemen on the far southeast side of the Arabian Peninsula, and Djibouti and Eritrea on the other side, both of which are on the Horn of Africa. Djibouti is a French- and Arabic-speaking multi-cultural country, home to one of the saltiest bodies of water in the world, Lake Assal. The strait connects the Red Sea to the Gulf of Aden and is a strategic link between the Mediterranean Sea to the north and the Indian Ocean to the southeast. It is only 16 miles wide, with the island of Perim dividing navigation into two parallel channels. Two U.S. destroyers were awaiting the two-boat convoy as they went through the western channel, known as *Dact-El-Mayun*. It has a width of about 13 miles and a depth just above 1,000 feet. The US destroyer captains requested using this wider channel since the narrower eastern passage brought them closer to the Yemeni shores and the US did not want to penetrate Yemeni territorial waters.

Both Moshe and Barack were very thankful for the U.S. escort which made their transit uneventful. Truth be known, they were even more thankful they did not have to change the identity of their boats. They had both preferred to wait and change the appearance of the boats after they had left the Gulf of Aden and turned to port into the Strait of Hormuz. Whether it was a real danger or not, they had decided shifting from the red hulls to the dark-green hulled *Sea Dragon* and *Flying Dolphin* would ensure the Iranian Navy on the east side of the Strait of Hormuz would not be alerted. The plan was for the two boats to revert to their white hulls as they sailed through the end of the Strait of Hormuz on their way out of the Persian Gulf. The U.S. destroyers turned to port toward the Strait of Hormuz.

They were lined up, one behind the other about 1,000 feet apart, sailing slowly as they passed abeam Muscat on the port side. They were still over 200 nautical miles from the strait proper, as they followed a 320-degree heading. *INS Storm* was also in the vicinity, although it sailed as close to the center of the channel as possible, maintaining a depth of 350 feet. The *Sea Dragon* was right behind the first U.S. destroyer. Because traffic in that area is relatively heavy, both boats were keeping to the right side of the channel leaving room for ships exiting the Persian Gulf. Moshe's *Flying Dolphin* was at least one to two nautical miles behind, only a few thousand feet ahead of the second U.S. destroyer. The convoy had managed to catch up to a number of other vessels, so that the line they created looked perfectly normal, since smaller crafts normally involved in fishing or the oil service industry mixed with larger boats, while a few tankers of varying sizes were clearly navigating empty, with most of their hulls above the water.

The next morning, the head of the convoy would get to the actual strait and make a sharp, 90 degree turn to port as the vessels had reached the narrowest point of their current voyage. Between the Omani Musandam Peninsula and Iran, the strait is only 30 miles wide, with shipping lanes just two miles wide in either direction. Besides the usual challenges created by narrow shipping lanes in a crowded area, this was the spot where the convoy was in the most danger. It sailed abeam Bandar Abas and along the coastline of Qeshm, an arrow-shaped island separated from the Iranian mainland by the Clarence Strait. Qeshm is the largest island in Iran and in the Persian Gulf as well. More importantly for the convoy, the island was known to have Iranian Revolutionary Guard installations, which together with those found on the next three smaller islands—Greater Tunb, Abumusa and Siri—constituted the backbone of Iran's maritime forces in the Persian Gulf, excluding the ships at anchor in Bandar Abas. Together, that 120-mile stretch of water was the area where the convoy would most likely be attacked, if it were the target of Iranian ire, whether triggered by Yemeni requests or by just being aroused against commercial ships plying the region's waters.

CHAPTER.27

As the two Israeli spy vessels navigated abeam Siri Island on port and Farur Island on starboard, they found themselves sailing alongside the tiny Faroor Koochak Island, a barren desert amounting to less than 0.6 square miles. They were careful since a few Iranian missile batteries were supposedly located near the highest point of the island, barely 60 feet above sea level. Throughout the voyage in the Iranian waters, both Israeli captains had been particularly vigilant, relying somewhat on their country's submarine and the two U.S. destroyers which remained in the general vicinity. They knew their first target, the South Pars field, would be barely 180 nautical miles further ahead. At that point, the two spy ships would slow down and move outside of the shipping channel. They would drop anchor and wait for a signal from Captain Ayel on *INS Storm* to resume their journey northwards. While still in the hold of *INS Storm*, the Emerald Whale was being loaded with seven powerful marine mines.

■ ■ ■ ■ ■

The South Pars field covered a 1,400 square miles area located in Iranian waters, with an area almost twice as large claimed by Qatar in its own territorial waters. It rested nearly 10,000 feet below the seabed, in waters averaging about 200 feet in depth. Iran already held the third place in the world rankings of natural gas producers, and it was estimated South Pars contained approximately 50% of Iran's gas reserves.

■ ■ ■ ■ ■

While controlled remotely from inside *INS Storm*, the Emerald Whale when first released into the Red Sea plunged all the way to a few feet above the seabed. Its cameras, helped along by two powerful projectors at the front of the drone, allowed the operators to see the environment around them and thus to navigate in an area where the seabed was not flat. Mini underwater hills, ranging from a few feet to as much as 50 feet or more, described the landscape which was also home to a multitude of tropical fish and other aquatic creatures. The landscape included numerous obstacles built over time, with several of them serving as hosts to small coral reefs. Though nothing in comparison to the Red Sea reef ecosystem, which is one of the longest continuous living reefs in the world going all the way up the Gulf of Aqaba, these multi-colored corals offered a beautiful spectacle to the operators of the Emerald Whale. That they could not see many tropical fish in various sizes and colors was the only negative, but they were fully aware that the mission did not include any form of underwater touristic experience.

Mark and his team in Tel Aviv had used both public and not-so-public information to draw a map of the location of the more than 100 wells already drilled in South Pars. Though a few were connected to offshore platforms built in the more recent phases of the development of the field, all processing (the separation of oil, gas, and water) still took place onshore. Thus, there were either "Christmas Tree wellhead" or subsea completions, each of which played a different role in the exploratory drilling to the production phase. The primary purpose of a Christmas Tree was to control the flow of oil or gas during production. In practice, it was comprised of a series of valves which could alter flow rates. A subsea completion was a remotely controlled wellhead structure located on top of a producing well. It was connected through flowlines on the ocean floor to a central surface processing unit. The map which Mark had provided suggested the order in which the various mines should be dropped, though everyone knew that any unexpected difficulty would lead the operators to bypass that particular wellhead and move to the next one.

As they approached the first well designated by Mark and the Tel Aviv team, they slowed the progress of the Emerald Whale to a crawl. They opened the drone's air lock on its starboard side and toggled a button pushing the first mine out. They had positioned the drone so that the first mine dropped right by the wellhead they were targeting. After dutifully verifying that the mine came to rest where it was supposed to, they immediately moved onto their next target, conscious of the fact the Iranians might have equipped the field with sensors to detect any form of attack. As they had dropped the second mine and not seen any enemy reaction, they started to relax. With the holding capacity of the Emerald Whale limited to seven of the powerful marine mines they would be using, Mark and his team had focused on what he called the "main wellheads" where several flowlines came together. The main surprise the operators encountered was the significant depth difference between one target and the next; the deepest was 235 feet below sea level, while the least in depth was barely more than 170 feet.

The Iranians provided one surprise to the team as the Sea Dragon's radar operator, Joachim Meister, called Captain Barack Decker:

"Captain, a couple of Iranian boats are sailing in our general direction."

"How far are they?"

Joachim replied:

"More than 12 miles."

Captain Decker asked:

"Can they see *INS Storm*?"

Joachim came right back:

"Don't know about them, but I can see her."

Captain Decker ordered:

"If we can see her, the Iranians can as well. Send sonar message to Captain Ayel. Turn off all active sonar equipment. Enemy in sight; two small ships."

Captain Ayel thanked Barack and did as suggested. He knew the operators of the Emerald Whale also used sonar signals to guide the drone. He ordered:

"Are we outside Iranian territorial waters?"

"Yes, sir. We're a nautical mile outside."

"Good. Stay the course."

At the same time, Captain Ayel informed the operators of the Emerald Whale of the possible problem. They quickly switched to autonomous guidance, maintaining maximum depth to be on the safe side. The *INS Storm* also dove to the deepest level allowed by local underwater geographic conditions. As they had switched to autonomous mode, the Whale operators had programmed her to navigate gently back toward the airlock of *INS Storm*.

Quickly, finding nothing untoward in the vicinity of the gas deposit, the two Iranian boats disappeared from the immediate area. Everyone assumed that they were probably on a regular patrol route. This allowed the Whale operators to shift back to manual remote control so she could be brought next to and loaded into *INS Storm*. There, her battery would be recharged before the drone was called to action for the next part of the mission. The Emerald Whale and the rest of the Israeli Navy contingent would be very far away when the mines exploded, six days hence, to correspond to the explosions planned for the other two expeditions.

I I ■ I I

With *Central Support*, the Israeli tanker having by then continued northwards and thus away from the others, the three-ship convoy resumed its northward journey in the Persian Gulf, with their next target being offshore the southern end of Kharg Island. About 15 nautical miles south and west of Kharg Island, the *Flying Dolphin* veered to port toward a point where it could safely rendezvous with a U.S. Marine helicopter. The aircraft would be flying Joshua Reiner and Jacob Weinberg from Camp Arifjan, near Sabad al Ahman, the U.S. military base in Kuwait located about 30 miles due south of Kuwait City. The *Sea Dragon* and *INS Storm* would sail northward about 15 nautical miles further and veer to starboard when they came abeam Kharg Island.

The rendezvous point between the helicopter and the *Flying Dolphin* had been selected reflecting the fact that the mission would be using a small helicopter. The U.S. Navy had chosen the smallest available helicopter because of the size of the rear deck of the *Flying Dolphin*. With a length just short of 33 feet, the helicopter was short enough that it had ample space with the 80-odd feet available behind the bridge of Moshe's spy boat. The Boeing AH-6 was initially made by McDonnell Douglas and then aptly named MH-6 Little Bird, at the time Boeing and McDonnell Douglass merged. A small aircraft with a six-bladed front rotor, the Little Bird was typically unarmed and outfitted with outboard "benches" designed to ferry up to three commandos on each side. The plan called for it to hover about two feet above the deck to allow the two men to jump. It could land if needed, but the maneuver might be unnecessarily complex if only because of the sea swell aggravated by the helicopter rotor. Navy pilots had brought hovering to an art form. The Little Bird, with a usual range of about 230 nautical miles, would likely have a shorter actual range in this mission. It would need to fly lower than its normal cruising altitude of 5,000 feet to avoid detection, even though the *Katsa* transfer would take place at night.

Meanwhile, the two operators of the heli-drone and the heli-drone itself had been transferred from Moshe's to Barack's ship, the *Sea Dragon*, to allow them to conduct a detailed reconnaissance flight both around and, to a much lesser extent, over Kharg Island. Mark had provided the team with a map of the entire island. It showed precisely where the three modified sponge bombs were to be positioned. It also sketched at least two or three reasonable routes the men could take from the shore to their targets. However, Mark and David, always cautious and concerned with the safety of their field operators, had decided that the heli-drone was small enough and equipped with enough stealth-features that it could take a closer look to make sure both that the map was still totally correct and that the coast was clear at the time. A local source had mentioned patrols would frequently proceed randomly along a variety of pathways to deter and, if necessary, intercept anyone attempting an unauthorized entry.

The survey which the heli-drone conducted suggested only a minor change to plans. It pointed to a shorter and safer route, though it involved a larger change in altitude the men would have to climb on limestone rock polished by time and saltwater spray. Kharg Island had a broadly triangular shape slightly longer north to south than east to west. It had a couple of offshore docking areas both parallel to the axis of the island and located roughly one nautical mile from shore, one to the east and the other to the west. This allowed larger oil tankers to anchor and depart when full. The northeast end of the island had an airport, which motivated the team to choose the other end, even though it was the most populated; all the oil handling facilities were located near the south end of the island. More than 50

244 | ANDREW B. LOUIS

tanks of different sizes had been built on the longitudinal spine of the island. Though the two offshore jetties made wonderful targets in theory, the team had quickly concluded they were both too heavily guarded and less prone to the damage caused by sponge bombs. As is almost always the case in oil and oil product tank farms, the team had identified at least four major "connection centers" which would make good targets. The various tanks connected in a sort of grid allowing the delivery of the specific kind of crude oil distillate ordered by each customer. Correspondingly, the distillates flowed to the appropriate tank using other pipelines within that grid.

■ ■ ■ ■ ■

Following the conversation which Mark had with Marvin, a small modification had been conducted in the sponge bombs' design. After Marvin had confirmed the *aqua regia* would not interfere with the polymer chemical reaction, a precise amount of the corrosive liquid had been placed in a box attached to the grenade. An aluminum sphere had been inserted in the middle of the partition between the two plastic containers holding the polymers. The spheric shape was preferred to a simple box because of the geometric properties of a sphere: its center was equidistant to all points on its surface. A remote-control timer triggered by the agents placing the bombs would open a valve allowing the corrosive liquid to flow into the aluminum sphere. The amount of liquid had been determined to be sufficient to allow the dissolution of the aluminum container two days after triggered. At that point, the polymers would meet each other, foam up, expand, and harden, obstructing the passage of the oil or oil products in the pipelines.

■ ■ ■ ■ ■

Meanwhile, Mike Robert and Heim Meister had landed in Kuwait City having flown in from Istanbul, Turkey. There was no commercial flight between Israel and Kuwait City. So, their arrival into Kuwait City from Istanbul would be as innocuous as possible. They had no difficulty going through customs and immigration with the Kuwaiti passports which *Mossad* had created for them. They easily found the minibus, Shuttle Express, which they had pre-booked, and which would take them to Al Abdali. There, they knew from their earlier research, only one car rental agency was in operation from which they could pick up a rented vehicle. They found a Nissan Kicks, a subcompact SUV. It was grey, leading Mike to joke would be almost ideal in terms of hiding sand and dust.

The 50 miles separating Al Abdali from Basrah were uneventful, including the crossing from Kuwait into Iraq. Their general explanation of just passing through, since they were looking to return home to Iran to look for an oil industry-related job there, seemed reasonable. They had no difficulty convincing the authorities that as Iranians, it was logical for them to return home as soon as they had been told they would most likely find the oil service jobs they wanted. The crossing from Basrah into Iran, just before they reached Khorramshahr, was quite a bit more challenging. Though the immigration officers had no difficulty with the men's papers, they kept asking questions about the purpose of their trip. The men had to show their passports. The officer was surprised that their Iranian passports were new. Mike explained that their old Iranian passports had expired, and that they had gone to the Iranian embassy in Kuwait City to get the new ones they were presenting, adding:

"That's why there is no stamp other than the visa for Iraq which we needed to come in from Kuwait."

The immigration officer asked several questions about their stay in Kuwait, at which point the men were delighted that *Mossad* had prepared a number of pieces they could show: a recent electricity bill, a rental receipt for the flat they were both renting, and a few other additional items. The officer then shifted his line of questioning to

246 ANDREW B. LOUIS

the car they were driving. He asked: "Why a rental car if you are really returning home? "Mike politely replied that there was no bus going from Kuwait City to Khorramshahr. They had to rent a car to get there. He added: "Once we have found a job, we'll buy a car in Iran and return this one to Abdali."

The immigration officer was not through. He asked why they had so little luggage if they were returning home. Mike again calmly replied they wanted first to find a job before they moved their personal goods. He even added with a smile:

"We'll zero out our bank accounts and bring everything to Iran. Though it's not a fortune by any means, we were able to save some money there."

The officer had seemingly run out of questions and granted them permission to enter Iran. As he was returning their passports, he still had a final query:

"How long will you be in Iran?"

Heim replied they did not precisely know but hoped to get a job quickly. They said they had read newspapers which proved there were many jobs which they would be happy to accept. They returned to the car left in the parking lot in front of the immigration building and drove to the center of Khorramshahr, along the Karun River. They booked themselves into the Negin Hotel, a modest place in keeping with the kind of people Mike and Heim claimed to be. One could have argued that returning Iranians who had made some money in Kuwait would want to show off a bit, but the men had preferred discretion on the grounds that neither of their characters were supposed to know anyone in Khorramshahr. Thus, why would they try to show off? Who would they want to impress?

They went straight to the room they had booked and decided to sleep until they received the signal from the heli-drone pilots on the *Sea Dragon*. Prior to falling asleep, they had sent a message to the pilots saying they were about 20 miles from Arvand Kenar, suggesting it would take them about 40 minutes to get up and drive to the rendezvous point.

CHAPTER.28

CAIRO, EGYPT; AND THE KHUZESTAN REGION OF IRAN

Ben was genuinely surprised when his cell phone rang. The number was not one he used frequently, though he knew he had used it recently. He picked up the phone:

"Benjamin Kaplan here."

"Hey, Ben. Ray Baker here. We need to have a talk, preferably face-to-face."

"Can you tell me more?"

"Not on the phone, even if it is scrambled. I have important news for you. Have no idea what it means, but I'm quite sure you'll figure it out. Let me simply say it relates to our last conversation."

Ben immediately recalled their last phone conversation had to do with Ayman and Gamal. He asked:

"Where and when?"

"Don't mean any offense, but the U.S. Embassy compound is as you know quite a bit larger than the grounds around your own embassy. Why don't you meet me at the main entrance, 5 Tawfik Diab Street, in Garden City."

■ ■ ■ ■ ■

The U.S. embassy grounds covered almost 10 acres and formed a rough triangle in one of the nicest areas of Cairo. The grounds are comprised of three major buildings, including a 12-story tower in the center and two smaller structures to the southeast and the east of the main tower. Except for a garden near the official residence in the smallest building, the whole compound contained no real grassy area. The periphery of the compound was walled. Covered parking and miscellaneous offices backed up to the walls of the complex. Their roofs were strong enough to serve as landing spots for helicopters and firing stations if the Marine force dedicated to the security of the grounds found it necessary to reply to any shots from the outside. The complex boasted two pools, including one for the private use of the ambassador, while the other was available to all employees, several of whom actually lived on the premises.

■ ■ ■ ■ ■

A couple of days earlier, a man had approached the entrance gate of the U.S. Embassy in Cairo. The U.S. Marine on duty asked whether he had an appointment, to which the man replied he did not. As he kept pressing, the U.S. Marine asked whom he wanted to see. The man replied he had crucial information on certain terrorist activities and would only talk to someone "who was high enough to be able to act on it." The Marine-on-duty had experienced several such encounters in his career in Cairo and elsewhere. He knew what the orders were in these circumstances: gently help the man leave the gate area, without any fuss. Yet, something in the man's eyes told him this situation might be different from others. He asked his colleague to take over for him briefly and called the one number he had for the representative of the Central Intelligence Agency in the embassy.

Raymond Baker coincidentally was alone in his office at that time and picked up the phone seeing that it was an internal call:

"Ray Baker here."

"Marine Sergeant Jack Schreier, front gate, sir.

Ray smiled as he heard the emphasis which the perfectly trained Marine placed on the word "sir" even on the telephone. He simply replied:

"What can I do for you, Sergeant?"

Sgt. Schreier gave a quick explanation and added he had taken it upon himself to call because the man's eyes were "speaking to him."

Ray Baker asked a couple of clarifying questions and, respectful of the sergeant's intuition, replied he did not want to be the first person to meet the man but would have him see a junior officer in his office. Sgt. Schreier thanked Baker and said he would send the man with an escort, after having checked him for any weapons.

The visitor smiled broadly when Sgt. Schreier told him someone would see him. He was less enthused when asked to submit to a virtual strip search but said he understood when the sergeant told him the reason for the search. Schreier felt the man's response was a further indication he might be for real.

Once in the unmarked suite of offices occupied by Ray Baker and his team, the man was escorted to a small conference room where he waited for the individual who was going to listen to his message.

■ ■ ■ ■ ■

Floyd Azram was the man Baker sent to meet the visitor. Azram was born in northern Minnesota and was fluent in the Egyptian form of Arabic. His father had emigrated from Egypt in the mid-1970s when Anwar Sadat was President, succeeding Gamal Abdel Nasser Hussein who had served as the second president of Egypt, from 1954 until his death in 1970. Floyd's father had initially been impressed by the goals of the Egyptian revolution of 1952. King Farouk, effectively the last king of Egypt to rule, faded into obscurity after the bloodless coup when Nasser and his Free Officers seized control of the state and transformed it into a fully-fledged republic. Nasser's fall from grace remained legendary, though he probably had a decent streak behind the corruptness and wastefulness of his regime. In fact, Floyd's father highly approved of the far-reaching land reforms which the revolution introduced. He would surely not have called himself an opponent of the regime, but he gradually became disgruntled under Anwar Sadat, and in 1974 sought the greater opportunities he believed available in the U.S. He said the three-week October 1973 Yom Kippur War was the catalyst. Though no fan of the Jewish state, he bemoaned Egypt was meddling in Israel's affairs. He believed Egypt had enough work raising the population's poor standards of living and was unhappy the regime used some of his tax money to lead the attack against Israel.

■ ■ ■ ■ ■

While smiling, Floyd calmly but firmly explained to the man he was willing to listen to his story but was not prepared to spend hours going around in circles. He added he would only allow the interview to continue for as long as the information was forthcoming. He went as far as telling the man he was quite lucky he got this far, adding:

"I can't tell you how many supposed informers don't make it past the front gate."

His first question unsettled the man somewhat, though it was perfectly natural:

"What is your name?"

The man seemed to hesitate until Floyd made a move that suggested he was getting up and leaving the room. The man blurted out:

"Gamal Al-Sahid."

"See? Was it so hard?"

"I'm not used to revealing it to people I just met."

Floyd smiled and seemed to flip the man around when he said:

"I understand. Let me assure you nothing said here will go outside of this embassy provided you do not confess to a crime."

"I'm no criminal. I can assure you."

Gamal proceeded to discuss his recent past, including the fact that he had helped someone he called Ammon. He said he told Ammon of two impending bombings by the Muslim Brotherhood, which was supposedly working with the Taliban of Afghanistan. Floyd recoiled a bit when he heard of the connection between the Taliban and the Muslim Brotherhood, but remembering his mission was to find out more about the man and to decide whether Ray should see him simply asked:

"Why would you tell him?"

"I knew he had journalist friends in Cairo, and I was not comfortable with what looked like an attack on our country's archaeological heritage."

"OK. I buy that. What happened?"

"Well, the first bombing took place, at the Djoser Pyramid, but damage was not terribly important. I believe the bombing was intended as a message."

"Message to whom?"

"I don't know, but I suspect it was meant to signal to the government that the Muslim Brotherhood was back and capable of acting."

"Why did they need to send a message?"

"The Brotherhood has been banned since September 2013. The following December, the military-backed interim government declared the movement a terrorist group following the bombing of a security directorate building in Mansoura. Don't you remember?"

"Hate to tell you this, but that's before I arrived in Cairo."

Floyd did not give the man any chance to discuss any more of Egypt's distant history. He followed up with his next question:

"What about the second bombing?"

"I don't know what happened, but the Egyptian government got ahold of the Brotherhood's intention to bomb the Colossi of Memnon near Luxor. The terrorists were apparently caught."

"You should not be surprised. Didn't you tell your friend, Ammon?"

"I did. That's right."

"What did he do?"

"He told me he passed on the information to his usual newspaper reporter, but that was it."

Floyd paused for a few seconds and then asked: "Why do you need us?"

"Are you in the position to offer me protection?"

"I would have to talk to my boss."

"Then, I'm sorry, but I cannot reveal anything more."

Floyd looked surprised by Gamal's change in behavior, yet he remembered the quick introduction Ray had given him prior to interviewing the man. He also remembered the earlier comment of the possible link between the Muslim Brotherhood and the Taliban. He simply said:

"I understand. Please, wait here. I need to find my boss and brief him. He will then let me know if and when he is available to meet you."

■ ■ ■ ■ ■

The quiet and restful time which Mike Robert and Heim Meister had expected to take at the Negin Hotel in Khorramshahr was less than they had hoped for or even needed. The time included the afternoon, late evening, and early night when the calls to prayers were the closest together and the hotel was very close to a mosque. Nevertheless, as they had planned, they got up in time for the last prayer in Islam, *Isha*, around 2:00 a.m. They started driving toward

Arvand Kenar. The route was not complicated, though it included driving through several cities, for the streets were well-marked and generally deserted. Initially, as the hotel was on the north bank of the Karun River, they stayed on that side of the river until they intersected with Highway 96. It offered one of the few bridges they could use to move from the north to the south bank. Probably more importantly, Highway 96 was the highway they would follow for a while.

As they reached the north end of the Abadan International Airport, Highway 96 took a sharp left turn. They remained on it until they arrived at Ahmadabad Ahvaz, a small city snuck in between the Karun and the Shatt Al-Arab Rivers. While inside the city, they carefully followed their GPS map until they reached Sardaran Boulevard. As Highway 96 crossed over to the east bank of the Karun River, they left the highway and followed Sardaran Boulevard due south until the Shatt Al-Arab River veered to its right, about 20 miles into their 25-mile journey. As they entered the Arvand Kenar city limits, Mike, who was driving, pointed to his right and noted:

"Glad that the Iranians chose to build this military base here rather than five miles further south!"

Heim replied:

"You can say that again. But it shouldn't surprise us that our people in Tel Aviv knew about that. By the way, looking at the message we received from the heli-drone pilots, it seems we should find a road to our left in about two miles, before we get to the center of Arvand Kenar. You should take it. Drive 1,000 feet until you reach the Karun River. The area is totally deserted and there is no bridge across the river within a couple of miles in either direction."

"And then?"

"Switch off your headlights and blink them three times, two short and one long burst in between, in other words: a short, a long, and a short. The heli-drone will be hovering above, all lights off, and land as quickly as it can after turning on a landing light to let us know our signal was received and everything is OK. If the landing light is turned off immediately, it means that we should leave as fast as we can and await further instructions."

Mike followed Heim's directions to the letter and was delighted when he saw the heli-drone softly and relatively silently land less than 20 feet away from the car. Mike jokingly exclaimed:

"Hello, old friend. Haven't seen you in quite some time!"

He did not need to explain the joke to Heim to whom he had told the story earlier. The men quickly opened the cargo hold of the drone and transferred both the three sponge bombs and the small arms which they felt they needed but had not wanted to carry until then.

Less than five minutes later, the motor of the heli-drone revved up and the aircraft took off, first due east in the direction of the salt marches, and then in the general direction to return to the *Flying Dolphin*. Mike and Heim took the blanket which had come with the bombs and placed it over them in the car's trunk to hide them.

They drove straight back to Abadan where Iran once had one of the world's largest refineries. Mike could not resist a joke:

"I know it's quite dark, but I can still see something with those headlights. Well, the landscape is just as desolate on the way back as it was on the way out."

As they reached Abadan, the men remembered their briefing. They had learned the Abadan refinery complex had been destroyed in the Iran-Iraq war. The first phase had been rebuilt while the second phase of the project was halted in 2020 because of the worldwide COVID pandemic. The men looked for Door 18, which their map indicated was close to the three holding tanks where they were to drop their three sponge bombs. A smaller, incendiary bomb was placed near each of the sponge bombs, with a timer to coincide with the detonator of the sponge bombs. When they exploded, the bombs would force open the walls of the holding tanks and thus trigger a massive leak of gasoline, naphtha, and diesel fuel. The combination of the two explosions should create an important fire, while the hardening of the sponge bomb chemicals should require the construction of new holding tanks, idling that section of the refinery for some time.

The men quickly retraced their steps and found Highway 96, which at that spot was also called the Abadan-Mahshahr Road. They were delighted to see it become an autoroute five miles away from Abadan. Yet, whether they looked right or left the landscape was both boring and not particularly attractive. Heim noted:

"At least when you drive through the Negev desert in Israel, you could argue the landscape offers points of interest: small canyons, nice sandy-colored hills, valleys, and still quite a few trees and bushes. Here, there are hardly any trees anywhere we look. Can't even see more than the odd bush not higher than three feet, if that. Add to that marshy land with many small "lakes" which probably were more the remnants of some mining activity rather than some divine intention and you almost have the full picture."

Mike surely agreed and even added:

"The usual orange-yellow desert sand has long ago given way to wet, muddy greenish earth. I love your comparison with old mining operations except that the lakes were not very deep. Plus, these lakes seem all quite black, though I'll give them the benefit of the doubt. They might be lighter later in the morning when the sun shines on them."

They drove about 50 miles until they arrived at the secondary road which would take them around the north end of the small local airport. Once they had made a sharp turn to the right, they found the spot which the heli-drone pilots had selected for the next rendezvous: an area to the side of the road extending at least two miles in each direction. There was a minimum risk they could be surprised by an incoming car. The heli-drone responded to the same headlight signal and landed as close as possible to the car. The men found four sponge bombs and four incendiary bombs in the cargo hold. They transferred the bombs to the trunk of their car, and quickly closed the cargo hold, so the heli-drone could take off as soon as possible.

They carefully checked that everything placed in the trunk was as well hidden as they could, using the same blanket as earlier. They then returned from the parking spot they had found less than 30 feet from the road and took it until they returned to Highway 96 at the north end of Bandar e-Mahshahr.

Mike noted:

"We will return here after our last refinery trip. For now, we must first turn right and drive to the south of Bandar e-Mahshahr."

They first found themselves winding through town, although they had remained on Highway 96 and noted this road was always wider than any side street they crossed. After crossing Highway 5 to their right, they drove two and a half miles to the roundabout with the well-lit gas station. They turned south, in the opposite direction from Bandar Imam Khomeini. There, they started looking for the next two refinery targets. The road they took made that search quite easy as it clearly indicated it led to what they called "the petrochemical complex." Though the men knew there were several chemical plants, they were still impressed at finding no fewer than four different plants, each with a different ownership structure, based on quite different names: Karun, Takhte-Jamshid, Marun, and Arvand. Nobody was surprised that two refineries were needed to provide the required hydrocarbon feedstock for the chemical plants. Heim observed:

"The really good thing here is these two refineries probably also produce as much naphtha as they can."

Mike looked puzzled. Heim deadpanned:

"It's the preferred petrochemical feedstock."

"Understood. But we need to make sure we pick the right tanks. Diesel fuel does not ignite nearly as fast or as well as naphtha or gasoline."

The two refineries were both within one mile respectively north and south of the complex. Mike and Heim repeated the procedure they followed in Abadan, except they only targeted the two largest naphtha tanks in each of them, simply because naphtha is the lightest, most volatile oil distillate. It should be easiest to ignite, and the operation would bring to a temporary halt a major industrial area.

Once their last bomb drop-off was complete, the men retraced their steps on Highway 96 back to the north of Bandar e-Mahshahr. They stopped to buy a couple of snacks since it was quite a bit past their lunch time. They then kept driving east and mostly south on Highway 96. They would take the highway to Cham Kalgeh and Hendijan on the way to Bandar e-Deylam, about 100 miles away. Bandar e-Deylam was on the shore of the Persian Gulf where they were to transfer to the *Flying Dolphin*. They would wait until they got to Hendijan to send a message to their colleagues. Mike joked:

"Mark said that we would have three options. I hope at least one of them works."

CHAPTER.29

CAIRO, EGYPT; AND KHARG ISLAND, IRAN

Meanwhile, the following night, Joshua Reiner and Jacob Weinberg were ready for their mission on Kharg Island. They knew all the other bombs had been placed and their timers set for 24 hours hence. On the one hand, they were confident their mission should not last more than a couple hours, three at the most. They should, therefore, have plenty of time. On the other hand, they clearly understood there was no going back after tonight. They had to get it right the first time. If not, it would affect both their ability to hit their target and their personal safety. The Iranian guards would be on high alert if something had happened elsewhere affecting the oil industry, broadly defined to include petrochemical operations.

Captain Moshe Aaron, from whose boat the attack would be launched, had contacted Mark in Tel Aviv with an idea that could add to the safety of the mission. In his words:

"What if we had the heli-drone fly high enough to minimize the risk of detection, and yet close enough of the activities on the ground to offer sufficient advance notice if anything might go wrong."

Mark immediately agreed the idea made a lot of sense, though he remarked:

"What is funny is that Kharg Island did not seem to me the riskiest of the three operations."

He did not volunteer which of the other three activities had the highest risk in his view, but Moshe felt it was the attack on the Houthi harbor at Hudaydah. If pushed, Moshe would have easily argued the two riskiest points in the whole expedition were not a point where the team was on the attack, but the moments when it was on the defensive and vastly outgunned as it passed through the Bab Al-Mandab or the Hormuz straits. There, the Israeli team had relied both on the implicit defenses provided by the U.S. Navy and the stealthy nature of the two spy ships.

Josh and Jacob donned their wet suits while still on the *Flying Dolphin*. Noah Feldman, the third man, was already onboard *INS Storm*. He was one of the usual crewmembers and the one with the most training in underwater activities. Before jumping into the water 13 nautical miles west of Kharg Island, Josh and Jacob verified for the last time their scuba equipment was in perfect working order and the small plastic bag containing their guns, an extra magazine, and walking shoes was perfectly sealed and attached to their respective backs to not impede them in any way. Moshe for his part checked the beacons the men were wearing on their suits and the beacon detector which was incorporated into their dive computers. All had to be in perfect order. The men also carried a dive lamp, although they would use it only as needed to minimize the risk of being detected.

Once in the water, the two men dove in the direction of *INS Storm* which was idling 30 feet below Moshe's boat. They found it easily, and having located the airlock, climbed aboard. They found themselves in a room where they could see the Emerald Whale and a few people milling around it. They removed their diving masks and spent a few minutes rehearsing orally with Noah all the various phases of the dive to be fully prepared for as many contingencies as they could imagine. The divemaster aboard the submarine provided Josh and Jacob with a buoyancy control device which served the important purpose of achieving and maintaining neutral buoyancy during the dive. Josh and Jacob checked that the integrated weight pockets had the right weights for the dive they had planned. Having slid in a diving knife and a scuba octopus to serve as a backup breathing apparatus in case of emergency, they were almost ready to go.

The three men went on to inspect the compartment in which they would travel while onboard the Emerald Whale. Jacob, who was known to his mate as the most likely to use humor to defuse a tense situation, noted the irony of having people currently in a full-fledged submarine traveling in a drone submarine which was meant to be used remotely and thus without a crew.

The guys noted the sufficient reserves of oxygen tanks inside the drone. They knew they would need their oxygen equipment to breathe during the time they were in the drone, time which they estimated could be just short of an hour. Noah did a final inspection of the underwater scooter, asking both Josh and Jacob to hand him the equipment they would unload on the island. He checked the hooks provided were solid and yet would not harm the oxygen tanks or the breathing tubes.

The final preparation step involved verifying that all the communication equipment worked. The men would not be able to use sonar out of the water, so they needed waterproof radios to communicate with the *Flying Dolphin,* while the people onboard the *Flying Dolphin* needed sonar communication to reach the Emerald Whale and, thus, Noah. They all agreed that the weakest link in their setup was this dual need in communication methods. Sometimes messages needed to go through air, thus using radio waves, and sometimes messages had to go through water, thus using sonar.

The three men climbed aboard the Emerald Whale and heard her airlock door being closed. They checked, as planned, that they could trigger the air lock if needed in an emergency. Everyone was happy to see the door open. It closed again, and the men could feel the Whale being moved into the airlock and let out of the submarine. They could not discuss anything among themselves as they had their breathing apparatus on, but they later agreed the one surprise in the exercise had been how silent the electric engine powering the Emerald Whale was.

■ ■ ■ ■ ■

Ben Kaplan had arrived at the U.S. Embassy and was delighted to note that he was expected. The Marine sergeant at the gate only needed to verify his identity before he made a telephone call. He led Ben through the entrance hall, complete with the x-ray test as in most airports, and waited with him until Ray Baker arrived:

"Thank you, Sergeant. Ben, my friend. I'm happy to see you. My story is going to prove that coincidences do happen to all of us, including members of the intelligence community."

Ben grinned as he returned the greeting, though Ray could clearly see his eyes betrayed some form of reservation.

"You don't believe me, do you?"

"How could I not believe something I have not heard?"

Ray smiled and suggested that the two of them walk in the large triangular courtyard of the compound, arguing the heat was quite tolerable as the day had morphed into late afternoon. Ben agreed, though he automatically loosened his shirt collar and tie he was wearing. Ray declared:

"Let me give you the punch line first. We can always dive into details later."

He paused and noted Ben had nodded his agreement. Ray continued:

"Someone walked into the embassy the other day and I think he could well be the informer we discussed a short while ago."

Ben did a double take and replied:

"Gamal Al-Sahid?"

"Precisely. Or rather, yes, that's the name someone gave us."

"Very interesting. Did he say anything about my contact, Ayman Al-Khafaji?"

"Yes and no."

"What do you mean?"

"Well, he did not give that name. He called the fellow Ammon."

Ray paused for a second and went straight to his conclusion:

"However, the story he told us fits almost to a "T" what you shared with me. In fact, I think I know a bit more now than I did before. So, I am willing to bet that your contact used a different name with his own informer than he used with you."

"Totally possible. In fact, we know our contact's real name is Khaled Al-Moghrabi."

"Won't ask you how you got that. But be it as it may, you may have a real problem if what Gamal says is correct."

"Let's hear it. I have come across so many stories involving these two characters and seen so many inconsistencies that I am ready for just about anything. Yet, I've got to tell you that so far, I've been tempted to believe that Ayman was the good guy and Gamal the bad one. Are you going to change my mind?"

Ray smiled but did not directly answer Ben's question. Rather he went on to explain that Gamal had revealed something about Ammon which, if true, could mean that Ammon was the bad guy.

■ ■ ■ ■ ■

Gamal seemed hesitant as he shifted on his chair in the nondescript conference room where he had first met Floyd and was now meeting Ray Baker.

"Well, Gamal, my colleague, Floyd Azram, tells me you have something you will only share with me. Let's hear it."

"Sir, first I need to hear you tell me you can protect me."

"I can promise you we should be able to protect you, first, if your information is truly new and important and, second, if it is relevant. I can't say more until I hear what you have to say."

Gamal felt Baker's words were not strong enough for him, but he decided to proceed, saying out loud:

"I guess someone has to trust someone and I guess I'm not the one in the driver's seat."

Ray deadpanned:

"Glad you see it that way."

Gamal explained that five days earlier he had been meeting with a tourist client who was staying at the Sheraton Hotel and Casino in Giza, on Corniche El Nile. He reminded Ray his main activity was being a tourist guide and said it was normal for him to get his clients back to their hotel after a day visiting the sites. He added:

"I can't afford a taxi to take me back home, so I was walking toward El Tahir Bridge. I was planning to turn left on El Tahir and get on the subway at Dokki Metro Station."

He added he was leisurely strolling around Al Galaa Square when he saw Ammon in the distance. He was with a Caucasian gentleman, and they were walking on Charles de Gaulle Avenue, a block in from Corniche El Nile. He said he decided to follow them from a distance, as he put it:

"Just out of curiosity."

Gamal concluded the big surprise was when he saw Ammon and the gentleman walk onto the grounds of the Embassy of the Russian Federation.

"You saw them get in the embassy?"

"I saw them walk into the grounds. By the time I arrived in front of the main gate, I could not see them anymore."

He paused and added:

"I have to assume the gentleman was known and they did not need to go through any security checking."

"Are you saying that Ammon might be a Russian spy?"

Gamal did not want to come straight out and accuse Ayman, though he surely had serious doubts about him:

"I don't know. After all, I don't know much about him. He just told me he gave the odd information I was passing on to him to a journalist friend in Cairo."

Ray's next question did not surprise Gamal:

"You mean, could it be that the information you passed onto him went straight to the Russians?"

■ ■ ■ ■ ■

Facing Ben straight on, Ray concluded:

"That's when I thought of you. By the way, I didn't know you had a journalist cover."

Somewhat agitated, Ben replied:

"Let's not joke. This is quite serious. I know that Ammon and Ayman are one and the same person. He once played back for me a dialog involving Gamal. In effect, he told me then that Gamal called him Ammon. There is no doubt he has given us valuable information. He has so far surely not disappointed us. How could that be if he was working for someone else? Something is missing . . ."

"Could whatever he gave you have been even more valuable to his other master?"

Ray paused for a few seconds and then came the zinger:

"Could they have found a way of using you to do their dirty work?"

CHAPTER.30

Meanwhile just offshore Kharg Island, the Emerald Whale had come to a stop as close to the shore as it could while remaining at least about 30 feet deep. She had approached the southwestern end of the island and had thus avoided the two pumping piers located to the east and the west. Josh and Jacob rolled out of the airlock first, followed very closely by Noah and his underwater scooter. They proceeded together and were about 350 feet away from the shore and less than 20 feet below the surface when Josh heard a sound, which his training had emphasized had to be taken seriously: a sort of metallic thud, which scuba divers are taught to use underwater to call the attention of other divers. He immediately understood Jacob was sending him a signal, using the metallic part of his diving knife which he was tapping against his oxygen bottle.

Jacob had seen ahead of him a light moving along the shore, possibly a guard patrolling the shoreline. The two men along with Noah swam back to slightly deeper water, careful not to offer any surface reflection that could be seen by the suspected patrol. A couple of minutes later, as the light seemed no longer around, Noah moved closer to the shore on his scooter. He could escape the fastest if the guards picked up any sight of him. If he saw anyone, he would use the scooter to move in the opposite direction from Josh and Jacob, to draw the enemy's attention away from them. The two men had the smallest possible sonar signal receptor so they could receive any communication signal from Noah.

A few hundred yards further, Noah came closer to the surface and, seeing nothing, decided to stay above water. This allowed him to send a radio message to the *Flying Dolphin*. Moshe asked the heli-drone operators to focus their cameras on the area where the men now were. The drone operators quickly confirmed a patrol of two guards seemed to be walking along the shore but heading away from where the men were supposed to come onshore, adding for Noah's benefit:

"Must have people who make routine patrols. We'll keep looking at them and for anyone who might follow them at some distance."

Noah signaled to Josh and Jacob that the coast was clear. He swam back to where they were standing in about four feet of water. They removed their breathing apparatus and their flippers, together with their buoyancy control device and handed them to Noah who used the underwater scooter to bring the load back to the Emerald Whale. Josh and Jacob climbed onshore, donned walking shoes, and started a fast walk in the direction of their targets, whose coordinates had been entered into the small GPS system included in their watches. Both had their guns in their right hand, just to be able to take care of any emergency. The magazine in the gun contained only hypodermic needles to tranquilize their targets. The other magazine, which could be exchanged in a couple of seconds, contained the bullets. Suddenly, Josh who was walking in front stopped. He moved quickly to his right where Jacob could see a sizable limestone rock. He immediately thought that his partner must have seen or heard something that told him to seek cover. Jacob found another suitable rock to his left and hid behind it, gun at the ready.

Using the ear pods they used to communicate above water, Josh said under his breath:

"Just saw movement straight ahead. I'm confused. First, the patrol which we had no reason to expect. Second, another possible guard here: Could we have been betrayed by one of Mark's sources?"

Josh knew every word he said to Jacob, and vice versa, would be heard by Moshe or one of his sailors. Moshe assumed Josh's statement was meant to go further and immediately called Mark in Tel Aviv. Though he was sound asleep when the phone vibrated, Mark got up quickly to avoid waking his wife Minoo and took the call in his office, next to the bedroom. He was disturbed by the news and quickly replied that the men should use the alternate target and the alternate path to it. Moshe hung up and called Josh and Jacob with Mark's message.

They walked back a few steps and went for the alternate target which was another set of holding tanks. The men walked to the north and then resumed the mild climb to reach the top of the hill. They passed by a small triangular pond and then reached the top of the island a full 250 feet above sea level. They had been careful to avoid walking too much to the east as they could see a small building, which they thought might be a barrack. They strolled in between a group of five tanks on their right and another three in front of them. They went left until they reached three parallel pipelines which led them to the small holding tanks where they would deploy their sponge and incendiary bombs.

As they were walking back along the same path, they were warned by the heli-drone that they should use a different route: a few more guards were on patrol. They walked in the direction of the diving school around the corner, opposite from where the patrol was coming, and then went straight down the hill, heading due west.

They had to be careful walking down as the slope was steeper and seemed to comprise both sand and limestone rock which could be slippery, on its own or with some sand on its surface. They radioed the new rendezvous point to Noah, about one mile north of where he had dropped the two men off. As they arrived at the seashore, they removed their shoes and kept them in their hands as planned until they walked into the water where they were to find Noah.

They were surprised that Noah was not where he was supposed to be. They waited a few seconds and then decided to use their well-rehearsed escape scenario muttering under their breath that it was the wrong time for something like this to happen. They stuck their shoes in their hoods, placed the hoods over their heads, and started swimming in the direction indicated by their beacon. They knew they would find the Emerald Whale about a mile offshore, at most 30 feet down. A hundred meters farther they saw a light coming at them. Was it Noah or a trap? They both had the same thought: *Where does one hide underwater?*

■ ■ ■ ■ ■

Ben called Mark to report what he had learned from his colleague at the American embassy, Ray Baker. Mark's first comment suggested some rising frustration, though he immediately regained his self-control and asked:

"Has Ayman ever accused Gamal of being a double agent?"

Ben smiled and replied with a simple no. However, he immediately noted he himself had had suspicions about both Ayman and Gamal. He reminded Mark about the inconsistencies associated with the placement and the damage caused by the first bomb that had made so little sense that they had started to wonder whether the real target of the Muslim Brotherhood was not the Israeli secret services in Egypt. He added:

"That's when we questioned Ayman's loyalty."

"I remember that. I know where you're going next. We then suspected Gamal of being a double agent."

"Exactly. I discussed that with Ayman when he reported the phone call from Gamal telling him about the death, or more precisely, the murder of Mohamed, Gamal's informer."

Ben paused briefly and then continued arguing Ayman himself had never directly accused Gamal, adding that, if anything, Ayman kept supporting Gamal. Mark replied that between the two Egyptians, only Gamal had accused Ayman of being a double agent. Ben remained silent for a few seconds and then said:

"I just had a thought. Quite convoluted I might add, but a thought, nevertheless. What if Ayman's game had been to defend Gamal to lead us to infer that Gamal might be a double agent? Wanting as he did to hide in Alexandria for a short while, Ayman was telling us that his life might be in danger. What if, unsaid, the danger to him in his mind was Gamal who might be looking for him and not the Muslim Brotherhood?"

Ben paused and then seemed to reject his own hypothesis:

"No. I'm taking this too far. The most he ever said was Gamal might have been killed by the Muslim Brotherhood. So, he surely was not after Gamal."

Mark conceded the point, but came right back:

"But now Gamal is openly telling you Ayman is a double agent. The only difference I can spot is the other party would be Russia."

"I know. What would Russia want of him?"

"That's what you need to find out."

■ ■ ■ ■ ■

Jacob was the first to notice the light coming at them now. He was doubly surprised when events unfolded in a few seconds. First, he saw the scooter coming at them abandoning its course and diving deeper. Another light was right behind the first scooter and appeared to follow the same pattern, except that, as it was then closer to Jacob, Jacob could see why the first scooter changed course. The man driving the scooter had been hit by a harpoon which was coming from his right, in effect from the left of Jacob. It took him a second to understand. Noah had probably been delayed as he was coming to the rendezvous. As he had arrived, he could see the two Iranian scooters coming at his colleagues. He accelerated as fast as he could and attacked the scooters before they could do anything to Josh or Jacob. Josh and Jacob gave him a thumbs up when they recognized Noah. He gave his teammates their scuba gear which they put on as well as they could in the circumstances.

In fact, with his scuba mask on, Josh went down to check on the two Iranians and saw they were no longer alive. He noted they did not seem to have any stronger weapon than a speargun each. He concluded their mission was to capture the intruders not to kill them. The trio returned to the Emerald Whale as fast as they could so she could make her way back to the *Flying Dolphin* safely. All three men believed someone had told the Iranians about the upcoming project, leading them to add two patrols and a few underwater guards to catch the agents as they left. The quicker they were safely on the spy boat, the lesser the risks they incurred.

Back on the *Flying Dragon*, Josh asked permission to call Mark to report. Mark needed to know one or several of his local contacts was no longer dependable.

272 | ANDREW B. LOUIS

CHAPTER.31

CAIRO, EGYPT; AND NORTH SHORE
OF THE PERSIAN GULF, IRAN

Mike and Heim had, by then, reached Bandar e-Deylam. From the early reconnaissance work, they knew they had to avoid the northwestern quadrant of the town, which, coincidentally, appeared to have been laid on a grid, within a general squarish outline. Though the fishing port might have offered a great location for a pickup, two major elements argued against it. The first was though the *Sea Dragon* could be disguised as a fishing boat with no difficulty, it would have easily been twice as large as the next largest vessel, and possibly more. This was bound to attract unwanted attention. More importantly, the second element was the location of the naval base just north of the harbor. While entry into the port might have been possible and even easy, if only on the grounds the ship needed to purchase some fuel, concern over its size might trigger a response from one of the fast navy boats at the base. The *Sea Dragon* would, therefore, have risked being stuck in the harbor, with its crew captured and its secrets eventually discovered.

Mark and the team had identified a spot which appeared both more secure and quite discreet though a bit further out. Mike and

Heim drove into Bandar e-Deylam following Highway 96 and less than 3,000 feet later came upon a roundabout, with a nicely designed circular park measuring almost 150 feet in diameter. They veered sharply to their left, still following Highway 96, now named Gavaneh-Deylam Road. Less than a mile on, a sharp right turn and they were out of town. The Iran Khodro car dealership which they passed on their left looked like they were near closing time. About two miles later, they came to the north end of a massive shrimp breeding complex, which their car's odometers told them was a full four miles long. The pictures from the satellite had shown them that the complex comprised more than six hundred individual rectangular ponds neatly arranged on a grid. Heim joked:

"Probably not the best time to open the window, right?"

Mike smiled and did not reply. He was concentrating on his driving as he knew that about eight miles further down Highway 96, he would need to find a small road on his right. It would lead to what the locals called a "tourist spot" on the shore. That it only looked like a pass from the Persian Gulf into a shallow bay, with nice beaches all around, was secondary. It was a tourist spot which meant there had to be a parking lot. Though Captain Decker had anchored a full 12 miles from the shore, he had sent one of his crewmembers with a semi-rigid dingy to collect Mike and Heim. They were going to park their car in the lot reserved for tourists and walk calmly toward the entrance of the bay where the dingy was supposed to collect them.

As they got out of their car, they were surprised to meet a gentleman in uniform who told them the tourist spot was closed for the evening and the night. Mike took over, asking the gentleman politely to let them through as he wanted to take pictures of the sunset. The spot was ideal as it was facing due west, and the view was completely unobstructed. The guard refused his entreaties, declaring the rules were set and there were no exceptions.

Meanwhile, Heim could begin to see the dingy approaching in the distance and started to worry the guard would see it and raise an alarm. He quickly decided to use his handgun, the one with the hypodermic needle magazine. He discreetly removed it from his pocket and shot from the hip at the lower half of the man's body. The effect of the sedative was immediate. The man fell down and started what would be at least a 30-minute sleep. They threw the keys on the driver's seat of their car, closed the door, and ran to the beachhead where the crewman and the dingy were waiting. Less than 30 minutes later, as the guard was beginning to wake up, they were by the side of the *Sea Dragon*, with the dingy ready to be hoisted on the back deck.

■ ■ ■ ■ ■

Back at the Israeli Embassy in Cairo, Ben had decided he could not meet Gamal Al-Shadi in person, since he had no proof Gamal was genuine. In fact, Ben had drawn up a couple of lists for himself. He wanted to summarize everything which he knew on both Gamal and Ayman and thus try to figure out what the missing elements were and, more importantly, to judge which of the two men was playing games.

Focusing first on Ayman, he initially concluded Ayman had done his job. He had identified a couple of operations which Ben and his team had been able to use to defeat enemies. He had signaled three possible bombings, two of which had come about exactly as expected. The first bad mark against him was that the third never occurred. However, was it his fault or Gamal's? Ayman had said Gamal was the source of the information on all three incipient bombings. He also had never directly accused Gamal of anything wrong and even looked surprised when Ben suggested Gamal might be a double agent. However, refusing to reject Gamal's information out of hand, Ben kept asking himself why would Ayman meet with a Russian operative?

As Ben turned his attention to Gamal, there were a number of uncertainties, but no smoking gun. The first bombing looked clumsy, and the actions attributed to Gamal's contact, Mohamed El-Shenawi, seemed odd at best. His being murdered seemed feasible, though it was surprising Gamal did not seem to panic when he found out. After all, if Mohamed was killed for having betrayed the Brotherhood, Gamal had to be next in line; why did he not appear worried? What if Mohamed never existed and if so, what did that mean? Also, why did Gamal seemingly disappear from the picture, making it impossible for Ayman to contact him? Why would he suddenly reappear?

Weighing these thoughts, Ben felt he had made little progress. He decided to shift his line of logic to scenario analysis. What scenarios could he create that might make sense? Ben started with the assumption Gamal was a double agent. It seemed the simplest and rapidly led him to an inevitable conclusion that Gamal needed help to get rid of Ayman. But why? Nobody needed any help to get rid of Mohamed. What could Ayman know that would threaten Gamal? Ben kept turning the question in his head and could only conclude that Ayman was the person who had leaked the information which Gamal had leaked to him. So why would it worry Gamal that Ayman did that? One obvious first avenue was that Gamal had second thoughts about revealing future Brotherhood actions. Maybe, he had convinced himself the cause justified the means. Maybe, he realized he was not martyr material. So, the one way to remove himself from the list of suspects in his Brotherhood cell was to eliminate Ayman. Nobody would be left to point a finger at him. Coincidentally, Ben noted this might explain why Mohamed had been killed, though the murderer would have been Gamal and not someone within the leadership of the Brotherhood. Ben grew satisfied with his logic until a new question jumped to his mind: why would Gamal have stopped taking Ayman's calls?

Ben then turned the problem around and started with the assumption Ayman was the double agent. The obvious first question was why did he do what he did? Why did he point to imminent bombings? That led to an important fork in the road. Was Gamal in the picture at the beginning or not? Assuming that Gamal was out of the loop simplified the problem. If Ayman were a member of the Muslim Brotherhood, one could believe his motivation might be a desire to move the cell away from the extreme actions of damaging Egypt's national artistic patrimony. While that made some sense, why did the menace of the third bomb never occur? Ben turned his thoughts in a new direction. What if the reason for Ayman's leaks was not to prevent the Brotherhood from becoming too extreme? And what if Ayman's link to the Russian Embassy was the real reason, he set up a relationship with Ben in the first place? Answering his own question, he said the logic did not hold up unless one assumed a very long-term game. Ayman had approached the Israeli Embassy three years earlier. Why would the Russians be thinking so far ahead? Yet, he had to admit this was not totally out of character. The only subsidiary question left was whether the Brotherhood was complicit or not? Ben had difficulties with saying yes because the Brotherhood members would face being killed or captured in a counter-terrorist operation.

If Gamal was in the loop from the beginning, Ayman's behavior was even less understandable. The anti-Brotherhood motivation for the leak about the forthcoming bombings would start with him and not with Ayman. Ben realized he might be dealing with an even larger conspiracy. The Russians' goal would hypothetically have been to infiltrate and somehow neutralize *Mossad* in Egypt. They would use a "sleeper agent." Ayman would thus contact Ben and begin their relationship. One day, Gamal, maybe worried about the drifting of the Muslim Brotherhood, offered Ayman the opportunity in his work with the Russians to get *Mossad* involved in some prevention of the bombings and eventually be caught in some trap. Ben leaned toward that thought but then realized a missing piece: why did the third bombing fail to materialize?

Reaching a roadblock, he decided he needed more information to answer the question Mark had asked. Someone had to talk to Gamal and that could not be him. At the same time, he had to talk to Ayman and try to get more out of him. He knew he could not reveal what he knew from Gamal, but he could surely mention someone had told him Gamal was alive and well.

278 | ANDREW B. LOUIS

CHAPTER.32

CAIRO, EGYPT; AND PERSIAN GULF

With Mike and Heim onboard the *Sea Dragon* and Josh and Jacob aboard the *Flying Dolphin*, the maritime part of Mark's campaign was nearing its end. The two spy ships and the Israeli submarine were navigating in a southern direction when the sponge bombs exploded. The fires triggered by the blasts were visible for miles and miles since the bombs were spread out over a long front. The Iranian press could not hide the problem since the fires were visible and photographed by spy satellites belonging to all parties of the global geopolitical chess game.

After they had allowed the Emerald Whale the time to fully recharge her batteries, her operators, still on Captain Ayel's *INS Storm*, programmed her for an autonomous voyage back to Eilat at the top of the Gulf of Aqaba, the eastern extension of the Red Sea in the direction of the Mediterranean Sea. The drone's passage through the Straits of Bab Al Mandab and Hormuz should be uneventful since she was fully submerged. The challenge for the operators was her transit from the Red Sea to the Mediterranean Sea. The traditional option would be to use the Suez Canal, allowing the Emerald Whale, once through, to sail directly to Haifa, her home port. They decided, however, the risks were too big in the Suez Canal because the drone had to slide in between other boats. Though equipped with significant artificial intelligence, the Emerald Whale could face a serious risk from unexpected behavior by another boat. The operators chose the safest approach by sending the drone to Eilat and having her transferred to Haifa by cargo plane.

Captains Decker and Aaron calculated they might be the ones facing a challenge passing through the two straits. By the time they began passage through the Strait of Hormuz, they knew the sponge bombs had exploded. They, too, had seen some of the fires. How would the Iranians react? They knew Iran had threatened in the past to close the Strait of Hormuz if its own ability to export oil was threatened. Though they never went ahead with a complete blockade, the risk remained. With what Iran could now describe as a series of attacks on its oil industry, it might challenge navigation through Hormuz. Moshe and Barack therefore, decided to change the identity of their vessels, returning to the white-hulled *Charm of the Sea* and *Sea Princess* since they believed the Iranians had not seen the white hulls yet. They would then switch back to the red hulls to go through Bab Al Mandab.

They still agreed, and Tel Aviv supported them, that they should request a discrete escort by one or two U.S. Navy ships currently cruising in the Gulf of Oman. With about 600 nautical miles to navigate until they got to the danger area, their request provided time for the Americans to respond.

I I ■ I I

"Multiple explosions hit three oil industry sites." The headline, repeated with small modifications in Iran and the Middle East and then broadcasted throughout the rest of the world, certainly caused a major shock. Though the immediate reaction in Iran was to blame Israel, the claim by the Paris office of the National Front of Iran upset the apple cart. The press release made two points. First, it claimed responsibility for all the bombings, citing with some precision the location of each of the explosions. Second, it thanked Israel for having agreed to provide it with the sponge bombs that were used.

Mark smiled when he saw the puzzled reaction both in Iran and elsewhere in the world. He knew very well the press release everyone was quoting was disinformation by *Mossad*. Simultaneously, an article placed in the Israeli Press and then spread abroad questioned the second point made in the purported National Front press release. The main doubt it raised was how could there be delayed triggering of the bombs? It quoted an unnamed military source confirming the sponge bombs used by Israel explode immediately after they are placed. Thus, how could these bombs all have exploded simultaneously in so many different locations? Was there an army of terrorists? That brought up the explosion of the mines at South Pars. Finally, the Israeli article noted the total failure of the fire prevention and fighting capabilities of the national oil company had magnified the destruction of the sites by fire.

Though the article might return suspicions to Israel, there was no evidence pointing to that country. The accusations were really a rehashing of everything said in the past. Mark and David smiled as they saw the dialog in the press become totally confused. Simon had warned the War Cabinet missile attacks on Israel were possible in retaliation, though he expressed full confidence nothing short of an all-out attack would penetrate the Iron Dome. He was referring to Israel's all-weather, air defense system, which was designed with the help of the U.S. to protect the country against incoming rockets or artillery shells.

A small volley of rockets which were sent in the direction of Israel by both Hezbollah and the Houthis rebels in Yemen were successfully intercepted by Israel's three-layer, anti-missile, defense system.

Hezbollah's rockets were all intercepted by the Iron Dome which was designed to deal with short-range incoming fire. Houthi Rebels had to rely on ballistic missiles because of the distance between their country and their Israeli targets. The Arrow-2 system was implemented using ballistic missile interception either in the upper atmosphere or even just beyond it. The relatively small size of the attack, despite the unusual coordination between Hezbollah and Houthi forces was read by many observers as a sign that Iran had decided to react through its proxies and to do it in more of a reflex action than some planned counteroffensive. That fit perfectly with the reality that no one could determine who was really behind the multiple explosions within the Iranian oil industry.

■ ■ ■ ■ ■

Eli Goldberg had invited Gamal Al-Sahid to meet him for a coffee at the Villa Belle Epoque, a villa dating to the 1920s, in the same general neighborhood as the Israeli Embassy and several others. The boutique hotel was a 12-minute walk from the Maadi metro station and less than seven miles from the ancient Roman Babylon Fortress and the third century Hanging Church, two prized attractions in Cairo. Eli Goldberg had set up the meeting there to see if Gamal confirmed he followed Ayman and the gentleman from the Dokki metro station to the one near the Russian Embassy, the Maadi station. At the same time, the Villa Belle Epoque was less than 500 feet from the Israeli Embassy. This had allowed Eli to organize a discreet tail to follow Gamal and find out where he lived, and, if possible, what his real name was, if the name he had given was a pseudonym. Gamal had been told to look for someone seated at a table on which a small bronze pyramid was placed in full view. Eli hoped he could be seen as a tourist which would fit with Gamal's official activities. He knew whom to look for since he had seen the pictures of Gamal taken surreptitiously at the American Embassy.

A gentleman wearing elegant local clothing approached the table and asked:

"Mr. Goldberg?"

"Gamal Al-Sahid, I assume?"

The man nodded. Eli continued:

"Forget the 'Mr.' and call me Eli, please. Happy to meet you."

"Thank you for making the time. The gentleman I saw at the American embassy did not tell me what your role was."

"Nothing nefarious, I can assure you. I work as a private investigator. I've got to concede I probably have more clients in the diplomatic community, but that's probably because all of them come into Egypt for a few years and leave four or five years later, if not sooner. They like to meet someone who knows the lay of the land as well as its culture and its language. I should add that I am undercover. You should feel free to assume that Eli Goldberg is not my real name."

"I see. How long have you been here?"

Eli lied:

"Here in Cairo only three years, but in Egypt more than 10."

"Where were you before?"

"Alexandria."

Eli did not want the time he had with Gamal wasted on his own background, so he shifted the flow of the conversation:

"Anyway, Gamal, what can I do for you?"

He paused for a second and added:"

"Before we get there, can I offer you a cup of tea, or something else?"

"A cup of tea would be great. You know it's the national drink in Egypt, right?'

"That and beer for those who do not abide by Islam's restrictions. Now about your problem?"

Gamal realized Eli had decisively and quite deftly brought the conversation back to business. He went through the story he had told both Floyd and Ray at the U.S. Embassy. Eli decided to push on a couple of details. He chose to focus on the bombings which he knew had taken place and that were supposed to have been flagged to Ayman by Gamal. He asked Gamal to take him through the events as they happened. Gamal replied with a smile:

"I see you are very well-informed. Well, there were two of them, one at the Djoser Pyramid and the other at the Colossi of Memnon."

Eli followed up with the obvious next question:

"Can you tell me how you found out about them?"

"Yes, but I cannot give you a name."

Eli asked why and Gamal gave him two reasons. The first one he mentioned was that the man who told him of the Djoser bomb had been murdered, adding:

"Most likely after having been tortured. So, you can imagine that I don't want to be found out. But I also want to protect his family. They have suffered enough."

"Who knows about that murder?"

"Strictly the man's family. And me."

"Did the man know you?"

"He knew of me, but neither knew my real name nor where I lived if that's what you're asking."

Turning to the second reason, he noted the tip for the second bombing came from someone else, adding with some dark humor:

"My first contact could not talk to me. He was dead." Eli played dumb and asked:

"I think we've been through that one. And you passed the information on to someone in Cairo?"

Gamal told him he passed on the information to someone who went by the name of Ammon. Eli asked why he did that. Gamal replied Ammon said he had contacts in the Egyptian press. Eli seemed not to follow, so Gamal added:

"I wanted to use the press to drive our cell of the Muslim Brotherhood away from the idea of bombing historical sites."

"I see. And did that work?"

Gamal's face told Eli success was not overwhelming. Asked to explain further, Gamal explained the first bomb did go off and did very little damage. Eli mischievously remarked this could be defined as a success from the point of view of Gamal. He smiled, but said he was not sure he could take any credit, adding:

"I don't know why the damage was so minor. Was it planned that way? Did the bomber have to change location at the last minute?"

Eli jumped on Gamal's last statement, arguing something did not compute. Seeing Gamal looking surprised and even incredulous, Eli explained his train of thought. He said:

"You said you belonged to the Brotherhood cell, and you did not know the detail of the plan?"

"I see the confusion. First, I am only loosely connected to the cell. I used to belong but have dropped away, although I have never been seen as an enemy. Second, I heard about the Djoser bombing from this informer."

"The one that was murdered?"

"Yes."

"Do you know if he was also the one who placed the bomb?"

"I'm not sure."

Eli concluded he was not going to find out anything more about Djoser and thus asked about the second bomb. Gamal explained that the bomb was not planned for the Giza area, but for a site near Luxor, more than 400 miles south along the Nile. Eli followed up asking how Gamal found out about it. He matter-of-factly replied he had another informer, this time in Luxor. For the second time, Eli pointed out an inconsistency:

"You tell me that you are based in the Cairo area and maintain a low profile, at least within the Brotherhood . . ."

"Not a low profile. I don't really attend any of the meetings of what used to be my cell."

"OK. I'll grant you that. Then why would someone in Luxor know to contact you?"

Gamal's face changed a bit, but he did not look embarrassed. His features became a bit sharper as he explained:

"I'm not the only one opposed to the destruction of our cultural heritage."

"Doesn't that make you an enemy of the Muslim Brotherhood?"

"Surely not of the whole Brotherhood. The group is not monolithic, you know. There are many different tendencies, some quite extreme, some so moderate that they could, and in my view should, be a part of the current political process. I'm navigating in the middle. The overall leadership has no reason to suspect me, but I've recruited individuals here or there. As far as my cell goes, I've simply stopped behaving as a brother. But I make sure I am not a visible enemy."

"Would you describe yourself as a leader of some sort of opposition?"

"Don't know I am a leader, but the Brotherhood knows I am a moderate. And other brothers do think of me as a useful mentor."

"Let's move on, but you'll have to admit there's confusion here. So, what happened at the Colossi?"

"I assumed Ammon had been successful. There were policemen waiting for the bombers. The two terrorists were captured or killed."

"Any news from Ammon?"

"He's been trying to reach me, but I haven't called back."

"Why?"

Gamal breathed a long sigh and said sadly the big change in his own behavior occurred after he had seen Ammon get into the Russian embassy. He added he lost confidence in him at that point.

More ominously, he said his worries about the connection Ammon might have with the Djoser pyramid and even the Colossi went up. He asked himself whether Ammon was playing him. Eli felt this might be an opening. He came a bit closer to Gamal and, speaking in a softer voice, said he would not know whether Ammon was playing Gamal. Yet he asked:

"I heard there was a third bombing menace, but the bombs have not gone off yet."

"A third bombing menace? Are you sure? News to me. When? Where?"

The adamant nature of Gamal's reaction was a surprise because Eli had never considered that Gamal might not be the source of Ayman's third warning. He parked that thought in a corner of his mind to discuss it with Ben later. Not wanting his surprise to show, he simply replied:

"Don't know the details, but I think I heard the terrorists were seeking to bomb Abydos, a week ago, maybe a bit earlier."

Gamal asked:

"Abydos?"

"Yes."

"Again. Never heard of it. By the way, Abydos is quite vague. Something smells!"

CHAPTER.33

CAIRO AND ALEXANDRIA, EGYPT

To say Ben was surprised by Eli's report concerning his visit with Gamal was an understatement. Gamal's affirmation he had nothing to do with the prediction of a third bombing at Abydos was a potential game changer. At the same time, Ben realized it could be a massive lie intended to sink "his friend" Ayman. He called Ayman officially to see how he was doing. Ayman sounded happy, though he said he missed his family. Ben asked whether he was ready to come back to Cairo. Ayman was hesitating when Ben added what he thought might be an incentive:

"By the way, your friend, Gamal, has surfaced."

"Sayyid Ben. I have told you already. He is not my friend. He is an informer."

"Sorry, I had forgotten. Anyway, I was using the word friend loosely."

"What do you mean by 'surfaced'? Did he call you?"

"How would he do that? I thought you told me he did not know about me?"

Ayman was not flustered by Ben's question. He simply replied he had indeed never mentioned Ben to Gamal. Yet he asked:

"How would anyone know of Gamal among the people around you?"

Ben conceded the question was valid. He knew he could use the truth and still avoid revealing a few key details to get to the bottom of the mystery. He suggested:

"Why don't I drive to Alexandria. I can meet you and we can discuss this face-to-face. I don't like using the phone for a conversation such as this one."

"That's a lot of bother for you, Sayyid Ben."

"Don't worry. It's barely more than 130 miles using the Cairo to Alexandria Freeway. Should take no more than a couple of hours given the 62 miles an hour speed limit, despite stopping at the various tolls. Plus, remember: Meir will be driving me. So, I can use the time to read or work on my computer tablet."

Ayman seemed to agree, albeit somewhat grudgingly. So, Ben said he would meet him right before lunch time at Costa Coffee Shop, on El-Gaich Road, not more than a couple hundred feet from the guest apartment offered to Ayman.

Three hours later, Ben walked into Costa, a counter-service coffee shop, a part of a chain serving hot drinks, iced coolers, sweet snacks, and sandwiches. He was surprised not to see Ayman waiting for him, though he was not concerned. He was a good 10 minutes early because Meir had taken advantage of the car's diplomatic plates to exceed the speed limit by a comfortable 10 miles an hour. Ben ordered a coffee and an egg sandwich. He indicated to the clerk at the counter he was expecting a friend to join him and chose a table near the back of the shop, in a corner with a couple of colorful posters hanging from the wall. Fifteen minutes later, with no sign of Ayman yet, Ben picked up his phone and called him. Ayman answered at the third ring, apologizing for the delay. He said he was no more than 100 feet away and would join Ben in a minute or so.

Indeed, shortly thereafter, Ben saw the door of the coffee shop open. Ayman entered and, seeing Ben from the corner of his eyes, waved at him. Ben got up to signal to Ayman he should come to him before ordering anything. Ben remarked to himself Ayman looked a bit tense but did not think twice about it. They said hello and Ben asked:

"What can I get for you, my friend?"

He added:

"For my part, I ordered a coffee and a sandwich because I am hungry. Can I get you tea and something to eat? I believe they also have sweet things, like baklava, rice pudding, basbousa, knafeh, and even sesame seed bars. The choice is yours."

Ayman chose tea and rice pudding. Once served, he placed his cell phone on the table and looked Ben in the eyes as if asking, *what do you have to tell me?* Ben understood he would need to control the flow of the conversation and returned to the question of Gamal. He said:

"This morning on the phone you asked me how anyone around me would know of Gamal. Remember?"

"Certainly do, Sayyid Ben."

Ben smiled and proceeded to take Ayman back to the time he was worried about his safety and that of Gamal. He reminded him, at that time, he had said he could not do anything for Gamal as he did not want the Israeli Embassy to come into the picture. He mentioned he had suggested he could turn for help from the U.S. embassy. He asked:

"Remember?"

"Sure. But the part I did not know is you would ask for help before I had heard Gamal needed assistance."

"Well, you know, I simply wanted to be ready. I may have misread you then, but you seemed very worried, and I did not want to disappoint you."

Ayman smiled a forced smile and said:

"I still don't understand how that call to the U.S. Embassy got someone to call you about Gamal?"

"You're right. The link is circuitous. For a start, I had nothing to do with Gamal going to the U.S. Embassy. He apparently went there on his own asking for help."

"He did? He must have been worried. But why didn't he pick up the phone when I called him? I could have helped him . . ."

Ben chose to ignore this last question since he had other items on his list before getting to the real answer. He explained Gamal's description of his predicament reminded the person he spoke with at the U.S. Embassy of the preliminary conversation this person had had with Ben. It must have led him to realize Gamal might have been the person Ben had described. He concluded:

"Simple as that. My American friend called me. Unbelievably, Gamal was using the same name with them as with you."

"Really? Surprising."

He immediately changed tack and asked:

"Have you met him?"

"Absolutely not. Several weeks ago, I did not want there to be a connection and I had no reason to change my mind. He met someone I know, and I got the large bulk of his story through that person."

"Eli, your colleague at the embassy?"

Ben lied:

"No. A friend who works as a private investigator. Didn't want the embassy involved in any way."

He continued:

"Most of what my friend reported fits with what you told me. A couple of points differ, and that's why I wanted to talk to you. The last thing I want is to fall into a trap."

Ayman did not look all that comfortable, yet he kept trying to project calm as he said:

"Very wise, Sayyid Ben. Very wise."

Ben noted Ayman was not doing anything to extend the conversation. He was not even doing much more than messing around with his food. Ben thought, *he's going to make me earn whatever I find out.* Turning to face Ayman as directly as he could, Ben asked:

"Before I go any further, one question has been bugging me. Whatever happened to the third bombing menace?"

Ayman smiled and replied with a straight face:

"I'm not surprised. I made it up."

Ben's voice rose a few decibels as he repeated:

"You made it up? Why in the world would you do that?"

Ayman told Ben it was a bit of a long story. He started by emphasizing everything he had said about Gamal was true. He was an informer. Gamal had a firmer relationship with the Muslim Brotherhood than he himself did, adding:

"I think the Brotherhood see me as neutral. They know I am no enemy, but they also know I do not support their violent tendencies. Gamal is more one of them, but I believe he does not support violence either. That was why I started trusting him."

"So far so good, my friend. But why the lie about the third bomb?"

"I'm getting there. I became worried when I heard Mohamed El-Shenawi had been murdered. That did not make sense. I know you and I discussed it, and I went as far as asking myself whether Mohamed had even really existed. Could Gamal be setting me up? That's when I was at my most worried."

"I remember that."

"He still gave me the tip about Luxor and told me he had another informer in that area. That got me thinking. A mere member of a local Brotherhood cell does not have that reach. I made discrete inquiries and discovered Gamal might be more than I thought. I still did not know what, but I started having doubts. Then I saw whomever you contacted to head off the bombing in Luxor was quite powerful given how the attempt at the Colossi of Memnon failed miserably."

Ben noted so far, the story made sense, but he said he still could not see why Ayman would pull off the trick that he did, lying about the third bombing. Ayman suddenly appeared very contrite and said:

"I might as well tell you the whole thing. I worried I had become dispensable. If Gamal was more powerful than me, I wondered whether I should not be the one who should be eliminated. That's when I took two stupid steps."

"Two steps?"

"Yes, Sayyid Ben. The first was my inventing another bomb threat. The second was worse. I approached the Russian Embassy."

"You what?"

"I approached the Russian Embassy. I was looking for protection."

"Wait a minute. Weren't we giving that to you? After all, who got you here?"

"I know. I know. I've regretted it ever since, but I was caught in a loop and have been working scenarios in my head to get out of the mess I created."

"Let's go back a few steps. What would warning us of a nonexistent bomb threat do for you?"

"For me, nothing. But it might get you not to trust Gamal?"

"Why would that matter? We didn't have any contact with him?"

"You didn't then, but he might approach you and cut me off."

"Believable, but crazy, nevertheless. Not our style but continue."

Ayman remained silent. Ben probed further:

"Why the Russians?"

"Same."

"What could you offer to them?"

"I haven't given anything yet, but I said I had contacts with a few secret services in Cairo."

Ben's blood was getting close to the boiling point. He replied:

"You know this terminates our relationship?"

Ayman replied with a surprised look on his face, which Ben thought looked genuine:

"Why? I've come clean, Sayyid Ben."

Ben's eyes became ice-cold as he told Ayman with a calm, firm voice:

"My dear Ayman. You're not cut out to be a spy. You're too emotional. I cannot take the risk that at some point you will again start to worry and blurt out my name to get yourself some short-term help. You're either with us all the way or against us. I'm sorry."

Ben could see Ayman was disintegrating before his eyes. Ayman now realized his error was even bigger than he thought. Though he had a heavy heart, Ben next took one of his pens from his inside coat pocket and appeared surprised when he dropped it between his chair and Ayman's. He bent down to retrieve it and jabbed Ayman's leg.

Ayman suddenly said:

"Hey, what was that?"

"Oh, just a needle, my poor fellow."

Ben casually picked up Ayman's cell phone on the table, verified it had his own number and he was not leaving any trace behind, and stood up. He walked to the counter, telling the waiter the fellow who had joined him seemed to have fainted, adding:

"I can't stay around; I must run. I hope he will be OK."

Then, Ben left the café.

EPILOGUE

TEL AVIV, ISRAEL

Though I never directly participated in the day-to-day operations in this adventure, I can vouch for the fact I was intimately involved. Nevertheless, I must thank all the main protagonists for having so kindly given me the details I needed to tell the story.

I feel terrible for the fate that befell Benjamin Kaplan's contact Ayman Al-Khafaji. He had uncovered what could have been a major development in Egypt and on the broad geopolitical map. He had allowed us to deal with a couple of potentially problematic troubles and, with the help of Gamal Al-Sahid—as we did find out was his real name—made it possible for us to uncover the suspected alliance between the Taliban and the Muslim Brotherhood. This was not a pan-Egyptian plan but instead related to two local Brotherhood commanders, one in Giza and the other in Luxor, who were attempting to raise their own profiles in the broader nationwide movement. They wanted to become the new leaders of the Brotherhood. The alliance of Brotherhood and Taliban could have progressed further had it not been for Ayman bringing Benjamin Kaplan into the picture.

At the same time, his inherent psychological weakness led him to two errors destroying his credibility, not only with Ben, but also with Gamal. More than that, Ayman had become an outright threat. Ben shared with me the hesitation he felt once Ayman had confessed. Though on the human level he wished he could have helped Ayman out of his bad choices, Ben realized that someone who was capable of the two massive errors Ayman committed could not possibly be entrusted with any information that might mean the difference between life and death for agents. At that very moment in the cafe, he already knew too much. The risk he might reveal Ben's real activities in Egypt, out of spite or because it would help him achieve some other goal, was simply not acceptable. His death was ruled a heart attack. The drug Ben administered was designed to trigger just that outcome. A modest but still significant sum of money was anonymously wired to his widow to help her deal with the accident. Gamal eventually confirmed that he found out that Mohamed had been tortured by the head of his own Brotherhood family because he was held responsible for the failure of the Djoser bombing. In fact, Gamal disclosed to Eli and thus to Ben that he had finally met with the *naqib* of his *usra*, in what he called a neutral place. He explained that though he was told that Mohamed had mentioned his name, the *naqib* could not pin anything on Gamal: the attack has failed not because of any external circumstance, but because of either poor planning or a last-minute change of mind on Mohamed's part.

Looking ahead Gamal is continuing his efforts to oppose the extreme violence in a fringe of the Muslim Brotherhood. He has started to serve as a direct source to *Mossad*, though he still does not know anyone in Cairo other than Eli Goldberg. He still believes Eli is a private investigator with tight connections in the diplomatic community. He knows Eli has contacts with the U.S. Embassy but has not been told Eli has anything to do with *Mossad*. We hope the contact we have made with Gamal, who shares some of our values, even though starting from different religious bases, will help push the Muslim Brotherhood from moving toward a terrorist nature and toward a genuine and respectable political party.

The various skirmishes I organized against both the Houthis in Hudaydah and against Iran's oil industry certainly carried useful messages. However, the damage caused to the Hudaydah harbor infrastructure was never going to be a game changer. Labor is cheap and cement plentiful there. If there was a loser in Hudaydah, it unfortunately was the couple of foreign boats captured by the pirates. While they were not damaged per se, they could not be rescued at least as of this writing. I can't help but feel sorry for their crews being kept away from home.

The damage to Iran's oil infrastructure was more significant. The idea of using modified sponge bombs in tandem with incendiary devices proved to cause substantial disruption. Since it came when the global economy was slowing down, it did not produce as large a loss of market opportunity as we wanted. Wong Hai Chock's virus which is still present in the computer system of the Iranian National Oil Company should allow us to keep sowing trouble from time to time. Interestingly, the Iranians did not notice the issue with their fire prevention system. They simply believed the calls placed on it by multiple, unconnected, alarms had simply overwhelmed it.

The main long-term benefit may be in the South Pars area. On the one hand, although the damage to the wells targeted was material, the size of the field and the number of drilled wells would allow production to be easily rerouted. On the other hand, Iran has probably realized their failure to engineer a special protection against an underwater endeavor had to be corrected. At a minimum, this will delay the 12 other phases of construction that have not yet begun. More importantly, it will increase the cost Iran will have to pay for the natural gas it is extracting.

The actual impact of our campaign on Iran's use of proxies to attack the West in general and Israel in particular is still unclear. Our own experience shows Iran dealt with the severe blow we inflicted to its nuclear enrichment industry years ago by simply rebuilding what was destroyed. What it may mean is, once again, the damage inflicted to the oil industry siphons off resources from the Iranian people and places more commitment to military goals. We are saddened by that. The only truly positive feeling I, for one, took away from this adventure is that navigation in the dangerous waters of the Red Sea, Persian Gulf, Gulf of Oman, and the Indian Ocean are still well protected by the U.S. Fifth Fleet. Our ships being able to navigate both straits and return to their Haifa base is proof the U.S. deterrence works. Now how long will that hold? Only time will tell.

Signed: M.L.